Big Sky Blues □ □ □

Big Sky Blues

ROBERT SIMS REID

Dedication

This is for Andrea, who caught

her first trout, a rainbow, on May 5, 1983,

at the confluence of the Blackfoot

and Clearwater rivers,

Missoula County, Montana, using a #14 Adams.

Reasonable Doubt . . .   □ □ □

Eight days after the shooting, Lieutenant Woodruff called Culp and Bartell into his office. He finally had the FBI report on the drifter who called himself George Rather. Rather turned out to be a guy named Sam Armstrong, who was extremely wanted in Arkansas for cutting his wife and her boyfriend into lunchmeat.

"That closes the book," Woodruff said. "The whole thing makes sense, just like Rather/Armstrong told Roy that night. He just got trapped here by the cold. Too cold to hitch a ride or hop a freight out. Then he stabbed that woman in the warehouse. He must've been on the dodge long enough to know he could risk a few days on a misdemeanor, before the ID on the prints come back. A felony pinch, though, like for the woman, and he'd have got his ticket punched clear back to Dixie."

That put a whole new wrinkle on things, since any dirtbag looking over his shoulder at the electric chair would surely never surrender. Unless the guy was just plain tired of running, which seemed entirely plausible to Bartell. In any case, he decided more emphatically that he should apologize to Culp. Bartell didn't know why he didn't just do it, but he didn't . . .

Prologue

When things turn to shit, there is a place where Ray Bartell likes to go, a place with lakes. Three of them. Graver, Tamarack, and Little Sleeping Child. These are Montana lakes, way the hell and gone in the mountains on the other side of Bride's Canyon northeast of Rozette, which is the town where Bartell lives. It should be easy to get to these lakes, except that it isn't, since they lay high in the lap between four peaks, miles from the nearest road. But when you are just about asleep, or just about awake, you can almost feel the sharp breeze blowing off the water, roll in the scent that is just the right blend of coniferous trees, trout, and pure air.

You can see the lakes from a gnarled, igneous outcropping above the Bride's Canyon and Burnt Milk divide. Sit there and let your feet dangle below the rock in sheer air while you catch your breath after the long climb up Bride's, so long it's usually night when you get back home to Helen and Jess. Helen is Bartell's wife. Jess is their twelve-year-old daughter. Helen and Jess never go along when he hikes the canyon. That's because they fight a lot and all the shouting gets on Bartell's nerves. Well, they did go with him once a few years ago, and he threatened to throw the both of them off a cliff. The three of them make a joke of it now. The time Dad lost his marbles. But Helen and Jess haven't asked to come along since.

The divide itself is a sparse saddle off to your left as you look down into the Burnt Milk country. The saddle is always thick with elk sign, tracks and turds both cold and fresh. Sometimes you get so close to the elk you can smell them, that damp fecund musky smell that's not like anything else. You can smell it even above the sting of sage and juniper. Bartell hunted the saddle once, raised the crosshairs of his 7mm. Sauer right square on the neck of a spike bull as the bull, really whipped, stumbled across into Burnt Milk on the run from a volley of shots down in Bride's. A perfect shot and he passed it up. When he had told his partner,

Paul Culp, about passing up a clean shot on an elk, Culp had looked at him like he, too, thought Bartell had lost his marbles.

Bartell was dreaming about that passed shot one morning after working a routine night shift with Culp. Helen and Jess had just slammed the back door of the house on their usual breakfast battle, and he was trying to get his blood pressure back down within the confines of survivability.

Burnt Milk is a huge country, dropping away for miles around the Joseph River, and up at the top, near ten thousand feet, is where it all starts, with the three lakes, three glassy steps just down from the saddle. The geologic term for the three bodies of water is *pater noster* lakes. Our Father. The origin of the term resides in somebody's observation that such lakes resemble the beads on a rosary. *Pater noster* lakes start when glaciers gouge the sides of mountains, then melt away and leave behind depressions, like footprints, which gather water. Graver, Tamarack, and Little Sleeping Child are all strung along the thin chain of Burnt Milk Creek, which joins the Joseph River miles below, out of sight.

It wasn't any use. Bartell held his breath and tried to hear wind, but all he could hear was the echo of Helen and Jess snarling, like a pair of cats kicking at each other's bellies.

Bartell tossed onto his side. He glanced at the clock and counted on his fingers. Four hours is not enough sleep. He was doomed to be exhausted for the rest of his life. He drug his legs over the edge of the bed, pulled on his robe, and padded down the carpeted stairs into the bright new room he and Helen added on a couple of years ago. He poured coffee, gathered up the remains of the newspaper, and went back upstairs and groaned his way into the reclining chair across the room from the bed.

Bartell liked the bedroom. When they bought the house, that room existed only as a bare, unheated attic, with a roughed-in floor. On impulse he decided they should turn that dead space into a bedroom, a bedroom with skylights. He began with the stairway, then he cut holes in the roof (Christ, you haven't been nervous till you've chopped a hole in your goddamned roof) and installed two plastic skylights, which leaked. That first winter he and Helen slept under mounds of blankets, without insulation or heat, and in the morning the exposed points of the roofing nails over the bed would be covered with big globes of frost, like stars. It had reminded him of when he was a kid, wintering in all those line cabins with his old man, Cash Bartell, who was a wrangler and a drunk in the ranch country east of the mountains.

Bartell set his coffee on the floor, careful not to spill a drop, since Helen had a mother's eagle eye for new stains. He folded the newspaper on his lap and reclined in the chair. It was snowing outside, huge wet flakes settling onto the dark boughs of the cedar near the window.

Bartell shut his eyes and listened to the silence.

That's the goddamned trouble. You're always coming home to a houseful of sleeping people, or waking up into a room where everybody's just left. Then after a while you get used to the solitude, the peace and quiet of being alone, where nobody is drunk, where there aren't impossible demands made by people who won't remember the next day, when they sober up, what you told them. Or what they told you.

And then one day you realize that sometimes the people you love make you feel like you're still at work. Because they aren't perfect. *Perfect like your solitude is perfect.*

So it's easy to give up on people, all of them, even yourself, strip them down in your mind and dump them in a padded cell. Sometimes Bartell wondered if that's what went sour with Culp's marriage. Who the hell knew? Among cops, a man's private life is his own business, which was a pretty bizarre code when you considered that his professional life is community property, fair game to all in the form of gossip. Gossip and rumor. Rumor is the supreme distillate of gossip, gossip given life. Who's being reassigned, who said what about whom. Who's chippying on the job. *It's none of my business and I like the guy, but* . . . and then the needle, jabbed into a man's affairs like social acupuncture. Leave a secret alone and all it does is fester.

Bartell heard a scraping noise outside. He went to the other end of the room and leaned over the rumpled bed and looked out the window. Across the street a frail old man was already out shoveling snow from his sidewalk, even though there was barely enough snow to cover, and what snow there was seemed to melt on the leading edge of his shovel.

There you are, Ray, Bartell said to himself. The authentic and essential Ray Bartell. Living alone, renting out the basement room to help take up the slack in the pension, scraping away the sky's residue from a slab of cement.

Bartell went back to the recliner and looked out at the cedar tree. Green. By the time he went to work later in the day, it would be dark again, the town vastly changed, as though night were a different locale, a land of infinitely moving shadows and color that somehow could be absorbed but not actually seen, a blue jungle.

But today the world is green. That's the dominant color of Burnt Milk. Green, where the spike bull ran after Bartell let him go.

Bartell leaned back in the chair and shut his eyes. A moment later he kicked his heels against the rock and shifted his weight on his hips. Then he reached to his right and dragged the knapsack closer, wanting something to eat. As he reached, the wooden stocks of the revolver on his belt gouged his ribs. He straightened up and looked down at the gun, a reminder of his most surprising invention of all, Bartell the Policeman. Pretend you're something long enough and it comes true. He changed his mind about eating. He looked behind him, where far off through the summer haze, Rozette unfolded like a map along the Holt River from the mouth of Bride's Canyon.

Then he looked back into Burnt Milk, where there was no city, no story, where there was green, the green of a thousand million trees, and the brown of rocks and of late summer grass and hidden elk, and the smart blue and white of sky. And silver. The silver of lakes.

Chapter 1

□ □ □

The four of them were all members of Mitchell's Maggots, and that night they were breaking one of Lieutenant Tobe Mitchell's golden rules, which was that only two of Tobe's cops should be at coffee at the same time in the same joint on the same side of the Holt River in the same city of Rozette, Montana. For dispatching purposes, Rozette is divided into two districts, North and South, and if you are assigned North and you are called out from coffee to handle a call, any call, and you happen to have been in a South restaurant, why, then it's a regular screaming, code-three-red-lights-and-siren crisis. We're talking serious.

"Screw him," Ike Skinner said. Skinner was a big tall guy, a lank guy with buck teeth and heavy black glasses, the kind like Buddy Holly used to wear, only with a peeling Band-Aid over the bridge to keep his nose from getting raw. Ike always looked like a fellow who had just thought of something important, except that he never had. His brows grew in high, peaked *V*s. The overall effect was of looking back at an amazed and intelligent cow.

"You wait," said Collie Proell, who had once played backup defensive tackle for the Denver Broncos. Collie can carry a medium-sized cow elk by himself, and he's cheaper to use than a horse, since he doesn't need a saddle. But then a horse eats less, and he doesn't tell all his drinking buddies where you hunt. "The old fart'll drive by and count all them police cars outside there and tomorrow we'll be having a meeting and Tobe'll step into the pulpit and away we go." Proell stopped talking to belch, then looked at Bartell. "Right, Ray?" He belched again.

Before Bartell could answer, Skinner said, "Let him." He dumped a fourth teaspoon of sugar in his coffee and clanged his spoon against the inside of the mug. "A guy in this department spends half his time walking around bent over anyhow. The brass always say we're screwin' 'em, but it's always me pulling up my drawers. Let him bitch. I wrote a traffic ticket tonight. Money ticket, too, speeding, not one of them phoney broken headlight warnings that don't cost anything. Tobe wants to hard-ass me, I could give up arresting people altogether, and then . . ." Skinner's voice trailed off eloquently and he licked his spoon. "Then where would this city be? On its knees, that's where."

"In the toilet," Proell agreed.

"Yer goddamn rights," said Skinner.

In the weeks after the holiday rush of suicides, domestic disasters, last-minute armed robberies, and other demonstrations of holiday spirit and familial love, Rozette had gone dead. It was a cold night in January, so cold the snow squeaked under your boots and made the hair stand up on your neck and you could feel the ice crystallize inside your nose when you took a deep breath.

The four cops had been inside Roosa's for about five minutes. It was just after midnight, and the place was empty, except for Bullah Watkins, the night cook, and a forty-year-old bum wearing a hardhat and at least three generations of bad luck. About ten seconds after the cops came in, the bum disappeared into the men's can.

Roosa's is a long, narrow tunnel of a place, lit by a hooded band of neon around the pressed-tin ceiling. The kitchen is blocked off by a long counter, which extends the length of the place, like a pier. Bullah fixes real food back there, the kind that comes off a griddle or out of deep fat. She uses the kind of oven that works with real heat instead of mysterious electronic tricks that make your pacemaker go tilt. Three booths squat like fat pink life rafts behind the kitchen. Culp and Bartell sat on the far side of the rear booth, with their back to a big white upright freezer. Proell and Skinner faced them across the table.

"You guys done anything exciting tonight?" Skinner was asking Bartell because he knew better than to ask Culp, knew Culp wouldn't say anything, just nod his head yes or no, which doesn't do squat to pep up the conversation.

"Not so you could tell." Sometimes Bartell wasn't much of a raconteur himself.

Culp slumped deeper in the corner and stared over Proell's shoulder at the front door, not saying anything. Just watching the door, like he always did. By now Bartell knew Culp's habits almost as well as he knew his own. By mutual agreement they were partnered on the three nights of the week that they shared. Their other two, each worked alone. The Culp-Bartell partnership had survived over three years, longer than most.

"You?" Bartell took a sip of water and looked over the rim of the glass at Proell and Skinner, who both worked alone all the time. He knew from the radio traffic that their night had been as slow as his and Culp's.

"Moved out of the house on the way to work," Skinner said.

Culp's eyes shifted to Skinner, then settled back on the door.

"Got me a room over the Cloverleaf. Rented it cheap off old Nails Hogan."

The Cloverleaf is an all-night cafe and card parlor right across the alley from the police station, which makes it a kind of transient barracks for divorcing cops. You can get a drink there until two a.m., and after that, you can get brains and eggs for breakfast, if you've got a sewer for a gut. Nails Hogan, the proprietor, will hear your confession until all hours, or give you last rites in the ultimate bind. Hogan's flop used to be a whorehouse. That was back in the days when Rozette was a real busting-loose town, before World War II, when the population was over a hundred thousand, not the sixty or seventy thousand like today. All the mills and the railroad were going strong then, and there were plenty of whores, all of them being tamed in cribs over joints like the Cloverleaf. They say in the old days the cops would walk through the cribs and the gals would roll up twenty dollar bills, roll them real tight like a cigarette, then reach down to the end of a guy's holster and stick that bill up the barrel of his gun: .38 caliber paydays, the old-timers called it.

"I didn't know you and your old lady were in a jam," Bartell said. "Sorry." Bartell always had an attack of nerves whenever another cop got served for divorce.

"Hell, son, don't be sorry." Skinner slurped his coffee. "My old lady, shit, she belongs in a kennel. We got no kids. I'm better off this way. Long as I don't get scabies before I move out of Hogan's. Gonna get me a place in that singles outfit up in Aztec Heights. The one where Thomas Cassidy lives." Cassidy, a detective, is the Department's role model for single men. Cassidy is so good at being single, he's trying it now for the fifth time.

Bartell glanced over at his partner. Reading Culp was like trying to understand a foreign language when you've never heard the accent. His sandy hair was always longer than regulation, but he hated guys with anything close to a hippie hairstyle. A brushy mustache fell like a dark glacier over his long upper lip, covering his mouth in such a way that his speech often seemed the product of ventriloquism. He had a long waist, powerful legs, and quick hands, like a wrestler. Getting a fix on Culp was made even harder by his eyes, which tended to wander in different directions, so you never knew if he was looking at you or around you, looking instead at some unspecified object of interest that has escaped your attention. After his divorce, Culp's ex-wife took their two kids, boys, and moved to Kalispell, where she married some guy who worked at a radio station. Waiting for Culp to talk to somebody like Skinner about something like divorce was like putting a stopwatch on the second coming of Christ.

"I tell you," Skinner went on, "a couple of weeks ago, there was this headline in the paper. personality may cause cancer. So I read this, see, and I cut it out and show it to my ball and chain and I tell her she's as good as dead."

"You're all class, Ike," Proell said, tugging at his mustache. "Ain't he got class?"

"Well, next thing I know she's got a lock on the bedroom door and I'm eating all my meals in this dump."

"Watch where you're calling a dump!" Bullah shouted from the kitchen.

"It ain't polite to eavesdrop." Skinner didn't even bother to turn around and look at her.

"You must have me confused with somebody," Bullah said.

"Yeah, I better learn to be nice to women, I'm gonna be single. I'm sorry, Bullah. You look pretty good tonight. . . . What happened?"

Bartell couldn't help laughing at Skinner. He always laughed at Skinner, ever since he was hired. Bartell could hardly believe it had been six years now since he'd walked into a bar for the first time wearing black leather and a gun, so long now he could barely remember that special sense of apartness you feel. Now, on those rare occasions when he went in a bar in civilian clothes, he felt naked. Six years of paychecks and contract fights with the city, threatened layoffs, cutbacks, grumbling about new police cars that are too slow and don't fit your body right, dirty police cars, drunks who puke in the back seat of your police car, cops who forget to put gas in your police car when they get off shift, dogs that piss on the seat of your police car and then eat your lunch. Squeaks and rattles. Film on the inside of the windows from cops who smoke tobacco, and spit streaked down the doors from those who chew it. Police cars were almost like home now, a flophouse where too many men have sat in the same chair and left behind peanut shells that stick to your hundred-dollar wool pants that have to be dry-cleaned, for Chrissake.

"What's so goddamned funny?" Skinner always sounded like he wanted to barbecue your knuckles for lunch.

"Cops." Bartell felt Culp look over at him.

"What's so goddamn funny about cops?" Proell sounded almost as highly evolved as Skinner.

"I just like cops."

"You're sicker than the rest of us," Skinner said. "There ain't nothing about this job worth a shit. You know that?"

Proell nodded and daubed a damp napkin at a spot on his shirt.

"That's right. You know, I been doing some thinking." Skinner was a great one for thinking. "I watched this thing on TV the other night called *Shogun.* All about Japs. Samurai. With them big-assed swords, you know? Whap! Some asshole's an obituary just because you don't like the way he says he's sorry for using up your oxygen."

"Yeah, I think I heard about that," Proell said.

"Damn rights. Whap!" Skinner chopped the edge of his hand against the table, slopping coffee from all four cups. "Cut their necks right down to a goddamn stub. I tell you, I got a lot of choice insights into police work from that show."

Everybody except Culp laughed and Bullah wandered back with a rag and a coffeepot and repaired the damage. Bullah looked like she'd been fifty years old forever. Twice a year she gets a new pair of white canvas sneakers from K-Mart because the heels wear down and her feet begin to spill over as she walks, mile after mile, a continent crossed within the one-hundred-foot channel from the front to the back of that restaurant, coffeepot a part of her hand, like a mechanic's wrench, an old, unskilled mechanic who can fix your car just by talking to it right.

"Samurai shit would make my divorce a lot simpler, too," Skinner said. "Whap!" He flooded the table again with coffee. "Make your old lady's head community property."

"I know you guys are on vacation." This time Bullah tossed a rag in front of Skinner for him to clean up his own mess. "But I was wondering if you could fit it into your schedule to kindly remove that guy from my rest room and my restaurant."

"What guy?" Proell perked up. He wasn't the kind to make his decline into work any easier than he had to, but removing people wasn't work. It was recreation.

"The guy in the men's room. I think he's homesteading in there."

Proell and Skinner glanced at each other, like coaches exchanging signals, then slid out from their side of the booth. Culp and Bartell followed them to the men's room, which was next to the back door, no more than half a dozen steps from their booth.

The door was unlocked and when Skinner pushed it open, Bartell saw the end of the bum's brown sleeping bag under the urinal. Proell reached around Skinner, took the bag in both hands and dragged the bag and its occupant outside. The hardhat clattered along behind, tied by a string to the head of the bag.

"Pull your hands out where I can see them," Paul Culp said.

"What the hell you want?" The bum's voice sounded like a rockslide. Half his face showed above the bag, like one of those old drawings of Kilroy.

"Get them hands out!" Culp said.

There was movement inside the bag and in a moment the bum's hands inched up beside his stubbled face, his gray eyes and short, pancaked nose.

"What's your name?" Culp said. "You got any ID?"

"George A. Rather. Got a card in my pocket."

"Get it," Culp ordered. "Don't bring out anything but that card."

"You wanna know what the *A* stands for?" Rather asked.

"Save your breath. It stands for *Asshole*," Proell said. He shared Ike Skinner's knack for philosophical observations.

The four cops stood around George Rather like a cut-rate crew of pallbearers as he fished for the card. Then he handed it out to Culp and Culp handed it to Bartell. It was a gold-colored card from the local food-stamp office. Bartell went to the phone up front by the cash register to check Rather for any outstanding warrants, using the name and Social Security number on the card, as well as the birthday that Rather had graciously supplied. Nobody wanted George A. Rather, not even to send him to jail, and when Bartell got back, Rather had the bedroll slung over his shoulder and his hardhat on his head.

"Too fucking cold out there," Rather was saying. He wore a shredded denim coat, fatigue pants, and mashed-down logging boots. He was about Bartell's height, about five ten or so, but thinner, much thinner, scarecrow thin.

"I don't make the weather, pard." Culp told him. "I catch you pulling this shit again and you'll go to jail."

"I'd rather be in jail," Rather said. His voice sounded southern, cracker, a voice full of humidity and dust.

"I ain't doing you no favors," Culp said, handing the card back to Rather. "Hit the bricks."

They watched as George Rather humped up his bedroll and started toward the back door. Then he stopped and squared his shoulders. He turned around and dropped his bedroll and screwed the hardhat down tighter on his head.

"Ain't gonna go out in no goddamn weather like that." His vocal cords sounded flayed from drinking anything he could swallow, inhaling anything that burned.

Back in the old days, when Bartell was a liberal, he would have believed that George Rather was summoning up something resembling pride. But hell, that didn't make a bit of sense. Men who sleep curled like a pretzel around public toilets have outgrown pride a long time ago. Besides, this grand display of fortitude was intended for nothing more honorable than to get George Asshole Rather, Esquire, bed and board for the night. Sure, Bartell used to be a liberal; now he was mostly just tired.

"Fuck you guys," Rather said. "Fuck all of you."

Culp shook his head and started to say something just as Collie Proell stepped around him with all the irresistibility of an avalanche.

"You want jail, buckshot, you got it." He took the front of Rather's coat and promptly jerked him out from under the hardhat. He twirled Rather in the air like he would have twirled a quarterback headed for the banquet circuit. Rather cut a dido and ended up facedown on the floor, the air wheezing out of him as Proell pinned him with a knee on the back of his neck. And even before Rather hit the ground, Skinner had his right wrist cuffed and Proell had the left ready and waiting. All of this had happened before Bartell could find an open spot on Rather to grab on to. Culp reached down and hauled Rather to his feet by lifting on the handcuff chain. Rather bellowed and accused the four of them of deviate sexual behavior with themselves, each other, and their mothers.

"Goddamn, Collie, you stole my show." Culp slapped Proell on his shoulder, which was broad and solid as a bridge piling.

"Needed a tune-up. Sorry." Proell pried the lid from a can of Copenhagen and offered it to Culp, who nodded and lifted a pinch.

"We'll take him in," Culp said.

"I can take him," Proell said. "It ain't no trouble."

"We'll take him," Culp said again. He was senior to Proell by more than four years. "There's two of us. You guys are alone. We'll take him. Besides, you better head back South before Tobe has the big one."

Bartell pulled on his leather gloves and gathered up George Rather's worldly goods. He wasn't about to handle the stuff bare-handed. Like they say, crabs jump six feet, and Bartell was still a relatively young man, too young to be contracting exotic diseases or providing a home to wayward parasites. He followed Culp and Rather toward the front door. Bullah stood by the cash register at the head of the coral-colored counter.

"Coffee's on me, boys," she said.

Culp shook his head and dropped a pair of bills on the counter as he walked by.

Outside, Culp and Bartell bent Rather over the trunk of their car, patted him down, and then stuffed him into the back seat. Bartell threw his outfit in beside him and they were on their way. Bartell drove. If Rather was going to stick with being a bum, he'd better learn not to give a bunch of bored cops something to do.

It had started out as a courtesy arrest, then gone sour when Proell decided he needed a little scrimmage. That's just the way life goes sometimes. Fuck around, fuck around. Bartell had learned a long time ago to ignore that dryness in the back of his throat, the kind you always get when things don't go quite like you think they should.

Culp lifted the radio mike and told dispatch that everybody was clear from Roosa's and that he and Bartell were on the way in with a customer. Tobe Mitchell called them right after that, but Culp ignored him.

"I'm going to arrest you," Culp said to George Rather, "for disorderly conduct. That's for blocking free access to a public rest room by sleeping on the floor. And I'm arresting you for obstructing a peace officer. That's for not clearing your butt out of there when I told you."

Bartell turned up the defroster and tried to see ahead through the fog, which had seeped out over the town off the Holt River a few blocks away and fell in dazzling flecks through the head-lights.

"The third one's for resisting arrest," Culp said. "That's for getting the shit beat out of you."

Rather snarled and kicked his feet on the floor behind Culp.

"Keep that up," Culp said, "you'll get a trip to the hospital, too. Knock it off."

Rather finally settled down and Bartell started to feel silly, worrying about the rights of a scrounge like that, who knew plain and simple that there are legal rules and there are street rules. Anyhow, Rather was only getting what he wanted, even if he was getting more of it than he'd bargained for. But that was what street rules were all about. Bartell asked Culp if he thought the resisting charge would hold up, but Culp didn't answer, and soon after that they were in the elevator up to the jail in the County Building.

Just before the elevator stopped, Culp put his hand on Rather's shoulder. "Plead guilty to all them charges. That ought to get you ten days. Maybe by then the weather'll break."

"Okay, Chief," Rather said. He bobbed his head and his eyes seemed to clear, and his stubbled beard took on a more dignified aura. He marched into the booking room, walked directly to the booking desk, and said, "George A. Rather, of the Planet Earth." Just like taking a suite in Vegas.

"I'm never sure about guys like that," Bartell said to Culp later as he drove. "You can never tell if a guy like Rather is a mad genius, or just a pretentious bum. Anyway, if he was a rainbow, he'd only have blue."

"They're all assholes," Culp said. "And I'm the rotten prick who'll arrest every one of them. I've arrested preachers on Easter, mothers on Mother's Day. Orphans. Retards. Babes in arms. Screw 'em. They can all fuckin' go to fuckin' jail."

That was maybe more words in a row than Bartell had ever heard Culp speak. It isn't always easy, working with a guy whose idea of an extensive conversation is telling somebody to kiss his ass. Bartell kept driving. Culp continued not talking.

When they'd emptied Rather's pockets at the jail, they'd found photographs, nearly a dozen of them. Portraits, mostly, the kind they take in supermarkets. Kids. Two boys, both of them under ten or eleven, wearing white short-sleeved shirts buttoned to the throat. And there was an older color snapshot with three kids, two boys different from the first two, and a girl. The girl stood between the boys. They stood next to a gray shingle house. Behind them, in the soft, infinite focus of a cheap camera, stretched cornfields. The three held out ice cream cones like trophies. They were smiling. Well, two of them smiled. The third, tallest face had more of a squint. Bartell recognized the tallest kid as George Rather, before his nose had been punched flat. The other two looked like his brother and sister. And in another snapshot, this one in black and white, the same three kids stood lined up along a tired Chevy station wagon. A woman, almost as slight in stature as her eldest son, stood with them, holding a fourth child, a baby.

"Let's get some gas in this hog hauler and get the fuck out of Dodge," Culp said finally.

"You think Rather'll plead guilty?"

"Who gives a shit," Culp said.

Street rules.

Chapter 2

After he got off work on the night they arrested George A. Rather, Paul Culp said good night to Bartell and walked home to the room he rented upstairs over Brisco's Second Hand, a storefront on Lawrenson less than two blocks from the station at the corner of Lawrenson and Ross. It wasn't really an apartment that he lived in, but a large, open storeroom that Lucky Brisco, a retired cop himself, let Culp have for whatever Culp could afford to pay at the end of each month, which was usually nothing. Ever since the divorce and his father's bad luck at the mill, Culp's financial picture had been about as bright as the Black Hole of Calcutta.

Not that money mattered much to Culp. Food and shelter. Fishing a couple of times a month. Hunting in the fall. That was his one extravagance, if you could call it that, hunting. But he always got meat, so it was more a matter of sustenance than recreation.

Culp's only other expense was ammunition. Lucky Brisco helped out here, too, selling him reloads at cost. Lucky was a good man. He'd learned the secondhand trade by popping burglars for twenty years. Lucky was also a gun freak, who always had an extraordinarily sensible gun deal on tap for Culp, which Culp always declined. Although he did a lot of shooting, Culp didn't own a lot of guns. Just his Model 70 Winchester for hunting, and two handguns, a pair of Smith and Wesson stainless steel .357 revolvers, with two-and-a-half and four-inch barrels. The four-inch was for working in uniform, the two-and-a-half for plain clothes. Some cops were walking arsenals, but for Culp's money, only two things really mattered in a firefight. The first was always carrying your gun in the same place, so you reached to that one place instantly out of habit. The second was being able to shoot the gun you put your hand on. And being *able* meant being *willing*. Gunfights are really very simple. Almost as simple as they are *fast*.

Before he went upstairs to his room, Culp checked the front

door to Brisco's shop, then walked around to the alley and checked the back. Then he unlocked the stairway door and headed up. Outside the door at the top of the stairs, he turned keys in two deadbolts, then nudged the door open with his toe. The door swung quietly on oiled hinges.

Culp listened, and heard only the faint *click . . . click . . . click* from the neon sign that Brisco kept on all night on the front of his store.

Before going in, he watched the shadows inside the room, shadows from Brisco's sign and from the streetlights that flanked the building.

None of the shadows moved.

Culp went inside and locked the door and turned on the light. He took off his leather jacket and hung it from the back of a straight chair at the table and looked around the room, looked at the double bed in a darkened corner, looked at the white stove with three out of four burners that worked, looked at the brown sofa with faded green and yellow flowers, the black and white TV, the matchwood table and chairs, the refrigerator, the battered chest of drawers with mirror, all of which were being "stored" in his place by Lucky Brisco, who threatened to sell the whole lot any day now. Culp took off his gunbelt and lay it on the bed, then stripped down to his thermal underwear and hung his uniform carefully in the small closet near the bed. His boots were wet from the snow, so he wiped them with a towel from the sink and left them under the table to dry.

He took the revolver from its holster and lay it on the shelf at the head of his bed, then rolled up the gunbelt and put it on a shelf inside the closet, next to the soft leather case where he kept the second gun.

From the closet he took a pair of sweatpants and a sweatshirt. Before peeling out of his underwear, he removed the survival knife that he carried taped on the inside of his right leg, just below the knee. The knife was the only backup weapon Culp ever carried. Nobody knew about it, not even Bartell.

Culp put on his sweats, then lay the knife on the shelf beside the gun, went to the refrigerator, and poured himself a glass of orange juice. There wasn't any beer in the refrigerator, no bottle of whiskey stashed in a drawer. Culp drank, but he couldn't afford to keep booze around the house. Not anymore. Not since the night he'd stuck a gun in Lucky Brisco's ear when Lucky used his own key and walked in unexpected, looking for a game of cribbage.

Even if he'd been sober, Culp would still have confronted Brisco. What scared him about that whole ugly business was not the near death of his pal Lucky Brisco, but the chance that he might have missed if Brisco hadn't been Brisco. It was a credit to Lucky Brisco's sensibility that he was apologetic for causing Culp to goddamn near put a bullet in his fucking brain.

It was starting to snow a little bit, the snow swirling in the cutaway off the alley between Brisco's building and the Bismarck, which was the name of the tavern next door to the west. Culp pulled the gray wool blanket from his bed, then turned out the light and dragged a chair over to the window, wrapped himself in the blanket, and sat down.

The snow made a bright kaleidoscope framed between the scarred brick walls of the empty cutaway. Sometimes during the summer, Culp would sit in his window and watch the drunks lay around down there among the broken glass and garbage, fighting and fouling themselves. Guys like that piece of dog shit Rather they'd bucketed that night. Vermin, all of them. Rats walking around till somebody stomped them good.

Culp shivered and wrapped the blanket closer around his shoulders.

Free or not, he was going to have to find someplace else to live before next summer. He couldn't take another summer overlooking that snake pit.

Culp thought about later in the week, when he'd get in his two shifts without Bartell. Their partnership was fine, but Culp still enjoyed those nights he had the car to himself. He glanced over at the gun, then turned his attention back to the window and shivered again.

He could never get warm in the winter. Never. At least not since he'd returned from his second tour in SEA and been discharged. Culp rarely thought much about Nam, or at least he never realized that he was thinking about it. It was more like a voice always muttering at him, not loud, just barely within earshot, like a whisper with teeth. It was a voice, though, he never let outside his own head, not like those guys who kept stirring up that shit. Professional veterans. All the time pissing and moaning about no welcome home, no thanks from a grateful nation. What the hell, maybe it was good that somebody kept reminding people about what happened, tried to keep the government honest about all those miserable fucks who'd come back in worse shape than Culp, who in the end considered it a bonus to come back at all. But making noise just wasn't Culp's cup of tea.

It was only the weather that bothered Culp since he came back. In the summer he could never get cool, and in the winter he was never warm.

And the rain.

Since those twenty-four months in the Delta, he always got claustrophobia in the rain.

"What the fuck." Culp got up and crossed the well-worn and oiled wood floor to the bed. He caught his reflection in the dark mirror as he passed the chest.

"You talkin' to me?" He laughed, remembering a movie about violence and sanity he'd seen one time. If he knew anything with certainty, it was that he was not crazy. Not hardly. He looked around the room, then back at the window that overlooked the alley, then back to the gun on the shelf above his bed. Crazy? If anything, he was excruciatingly sane.

Culp flipped off the light and lay down on the bed and closed his eyes.

"Welcome home my ass."

When they went to work the next night, both Bartell and Culp figured they'd seen and heard the last of George Rather. Bartell mentioned that he'd checked the court roster and learned that Rather had been given ten days on each of the three charges, which meant that he could be in the county jail for as long as thirty days, or as little as one, depending on the overcrowding situation in the jail and the mood of Judge Walter N. Clay. Judge Clay tended to divide crime and punishment into two categories: the Law and Justice. The Law was that set of rules which Judge Clay was bound to follow. Justice was what occurred once the Law was satisfied. So for George A. Rather, Justice was that station where the Walter Clay train would stop somewhere between one and thirty days from now.

Once, Bartell remembered George Rather's photographs. Why was it so many bums carried pictures? Like mirrors, that's what they were. A pissed-on wallet stuffed with wishful mirrors. There were those three kids with ice cream. Bartell could almost taste the ice cream. Vanilla.

As for Culp, he never gave Rather a second thought.

And then it was Tuesday of the next week and they were busy, so busy that they'd just cleared from bucketing a space cadet who was their third pinch of the night, and it was only just turning over twelve o'clock. There were wilder nights, but for a January Tuesday in Rozette, Montana, they were humming right along.

"I shoulda smacked the little bastard." Culp skidded the car through an icy turn and slowed for a string of potholes ahead. For all his ranting, Culp possessed astonishing patience with the authentically downtrodden. It was slime he didn't like. Sometimes he worried about that, and what worried him most was that the rules for being slime got a little looser every year. The rules really loosened up the year he got his divorce.

Bartell pulled his black leather gloves tighter around his knuckles and settled back into the seat as Culp raced the black and white over the snow pack. Wonderful things, black leather gloves. Help keep the good things, like heat and blood, inside your body, and the bad things, like cooties and cold, out.

"Just leaned back and stroked him," Culp went on. "I don't like it when people start poking their finger in your chest. Means they're willing to take a run at you. That really gets my motor running. Sons of bitches. Pricks. You know?"

"Creep-seeking missiles. That's what we need." If Bartell could just get a patent on those missiles, he figured to be set for life, Bill of Rights or no Bill of Rights. "You get the assholes in range, see, sight them in, then *whhoooshhhh!* They're on waivers in the Twilight Zone."

The moon was a day past full, flickering brightly, like Halloween, behind the bony canopy of trees along South Defoe. It felt like they were driving through the skeleton of a gigantic snake. Despite all the big talk about creep-seeking missiles, Bartell didn't especially like arresting people. But he didn't mind it too much, either. Generally, he tried to be civilized about it all, keep it in perspective. Life has to have more to offer than sticking people's butts in the crowbar hotel. It has to. Sometimes, though, a collar feels good, like dumping your guts when you've got a bellyache. The space cadet had felt good, but when you've got the old soul flu, that achy feeling always creeps over you again.

Of all Mitchell's Maggots, past and present, Chester Boyles made the most entertaining arrests. In fact, Boyles was almost dangerous to work around because watching him strut his stuff was addictive, like eating sugar, and before you knew it you had a toothache. But Chester was fun, a five-foot-seven, two-hundred-and-fifty-pound bowling ball, who did all the things you always wanted to do yourself, but knew you'd get your nuts crushed for if you did.

Chester did them.

Chester said them.

Like the night he told a distraught husband that the best solution to his marital problem was to kick down his old lady's door and beat on her a little bit. That might have been all right, except that she was a member of this outfit called Rozette Women's Action Coalition, RWAC, and her second cousin was a reporter for the Rozette *Free Independent*, and by the time all the hormones had settled, all the printer's ink dried, Chester was lucky still to be in possession of his vital parts.

"You remember when Chester Boyles told that guy to hammer his old lady?"

Culp laughed. "'Don't mark her up or nothing like that,'" Culp quoted. He could still see Chester rocking on his heels. Chester always rocked on his heels when he dispensed therapy.

"'Just knock the smartass out of her,'" Bartell finished the infamous phrase. Chester's words looked terrific in Maxine Fursten-Belt's column the next week.

Of course, Chester was not swayed from the true course of his destiny. Hardly a month later, on a night Culp had taken off, Bartell went on another domestic and Chester was there. A woman had called the cops because her husband had awakened her from a sound sleep and started browbeating her about the way she handled the kids, and she had to go to work the next day to support this schmuck, for Chrissake, and if the cops didn't haul her old man off so she could get some rest, by God, she was going to call her attorney right then and there, because she knew, *knew*, by God, her legal and constitutional rights, along with the legal duty of the cops to defend those rights, even if they were .. . *men*.

She was obviously a disciple of the gospel according to Fursten-Belt.

"He goes," the woman said to Chester Boyles, probably not knowing that he was *the* Chester Boyles, "or I'm suing you and the city both. In *federal* court."

Her old man rolled his eyes, sank lower into his chair, and opened another beer. "Now, baby," the man said.

"Don't you 'now, baby' me, you son of a bitch," the woman shrieked, adding that he was also a practitioner of several infamous crimes against nature. "Now, baby, my ass."

Chester Boyles was pensive. You could tell he was pensive because he folded his arms across his belly and nodded sympathetically and muttered, "I see . . . I see," many times through his pursed lips.

Finally, after carefully weighing the situation, Chester Boyle said, "Lady, for you I prescribe a frontal lobotomy. And for you, sir, next time let sleeping dogs lie."

And that was that. Case closed. Bartell almost went to the phone right then and there to call his attorney. For two weeks he was afraid to read the newspaper.

"Too bad about old Chester," Bartell said. They were driving under the south end of the Defoe Street Bridge. The city lights looked like flecks of ice on the slow water.

"He let his mouth override his ass," Culp said. As far as Culp was concerned, Chester's biggest problem was that he was infectious, like catching a disease, and before you knew it, you were tumbling through weeks at a time with complete abandon.

Chester's glory days with the P.D. ended last year, when the chief had his career for lunch. The whole miserable affair centered around a dog—or rather the corpse of a dog, which a woman on the south side claimed to have owned when it was a golden retriever. The dog—Champ, she called it in the civil suit—was a barker and the neighbors kept complaining and the woman was never home to get the good talking to that Chester Boyles knew she deserved. This went on for weeks.

The dispatchers could have shared the load by sending other officers from time to time. But they didn't. That was because just a few days before the dog problem began, Chester had decided that all dispatchers were pigs and started calling them Dispatch Durocs over the air, along with squealing and snorting all the time over the radio. This was terribly unfair to a group of women who did an impossible job well. But as with so many of life's mistakes, the name Duroc stuck.

The dispatchers were patient beyond belief, until finally they gave poor Chester this dog problem like it was a social disease. On his third visit of the fateful shift, Chester turned in the alley and called the dog to the fence. Then he pulled out his strictly unauthorized .44 magnum wheel gun with the eight-and-three-eights-inch barrel, his backup, hideaway piece, which he carried under his arm. This bullet launcher was so goddamn big even Dirty Harry wouldn't carry it. But *Chester Boyles* by God carried such a gun, and when he leaned out the window of that police car and proceeded to grind up a batch of golden retriever sausage, the last thing the poor beast probably heard was Chester Boyles moaning obscenities after he wrenched his back from hoisting his tremendous heater into combat position.

Nobody knew if Chester Boyles got the axe for smoking the dog, for smoking the dog half a dozen times with a renegade piece, or for holding the radio mike next to the gun through all six rounds, nearly knocking three Dispatch Durocs out of their chairs for having the bad manners to keep sending a senior officer like Boyles, *Chester* Boyles, back on a *goddamn dog call.*

By the time the great golden retriever fiasco was settled, the city was ten thousand dollars poorer, a tab that included two grand to settle the dog owner's outrage; medical and psychiatric bills incurred by the Durocs; repairs to damaged radio circuitry; and last but certainly not least, that portion of clerical salaries devoted to processing Chester's termination. Nobody attached much significance to the fact that the dog owner and the dispatchers were women, and Maxine Fursten-Belt never even hinted at male chauvinism when she covered the police commission hearings. But for Chester, it was all part of a grand conspiracy by the world's women to do him grievous harm.

So it was Chester Boyles, R.I.P., at least as far as the city police were concerned. Even Mitchell's Maggots had certain standards, and executing nonrabid house pets was definitely beyond the pale. Of course, the punch line was that a week later, Chester Boyles signed on as a senior deputy for Sheriff Riley Saulk over at the county, which proved that you can't keep a good man down. Bud Haller, the Uniform Patrol captain, said it was as inevitable as the fact that you can't teach a dead dog new tricks.

"I couldn't believe it!" Culp was raving again about the space cadet, whom they'd come across taking a leak in the center of Rankin Street, just in front of the door to Angel's Bar. "What are you gonna do?" Culp said. "You can't just drive by. Christ, people talk about you when you just drive by a thing like that."

Culp told the space cadet to put his business away and take it someplace else and the space cadet responded by poking a finger in Culp's chest and calling him a Nazi. From then on, it was not a pretty sight. Culp started by wrenching one of the space cadet's arms behind his back. Ten seconds later, Bartell managed to get a handful of hair and mash the space cadet's face into the hood of the patrol car while Culp cuffed him and patted him down.

It always bothered Bartell to realize that once in a while hurting people made him feel better. He liked to think he could talk to people, all kinds of people, get them to do things that maybe they didn't want to do. And most of the time he could. He was good enough at talking that the Department made him a hostage negotiator and sent him all the way back to Chicago to school. Sometimes, though, there's just no substitute for mashing a guy's face into the hood of a police car.

"They screwed up the moon," Bartell said.

"What?" It always made Culp edgy when Bartell started talking metaphysical.

"I said they fucked the moon up, walking all over it like that." Bartell found it hard to believe that placing humans on the moon had slid out of the news and into history.

"It's still up there, ain't it? What the fuck you want?" Culp slowed the car and let it idle over the snow. He turned out the lights, then hit the cutout switch for the brake lights. "I think you think too fuckin' much."

The moon flashed over snow and Bartell cranked his window down as Culp prowled quietly through the Defoe district, the section of rich old homes just south of the Holt River.

"You're off your nut." Culp snarled and turned up the heater. Colder than a meat cooler outside and there was Bartell, opening up the goddamn car like it was hotter than July.

"It makes me nervous, I can't hear outside," he said. "Somebody might scream or something." The radio had grown quiet in the last half hour since they'd come from the jail.

"My ass," Culp said. "Not in this neighborhood. These assholes got so much loot they don't know how much they've got. They don't even allow tooth decay in here. The only noise is between your ears."

Some of the houses in the district, large brick and stone buildings set deep behind trees and hedges, could serve as embassies for any number of Third World dictatorships. The tires crackled softly over the snow. Working nights, it was easy to forget that those houses held people, perhaps just two people, a man and a woman huddled in sleep in the farthest, deepest corner of twenty rooms, a man who catches his breath unconsciously, a woman stirring uneasily under the pressure of his hand cupped idly in her groin, both dreaming, setting free monsters to roam the night away inside the empty rooms. In the morning they will awaken with stiff muscles and bad breath, not knowing what has happened. Sometimes Bartell thought of his own house, of Helen asleep upstairs alone, of Jess dreaming about school in her small basement bedroom. It fascinated him to drive by very early in the morning and shine the spotlight through the windows and wonder what monsters were loose in his own home.

"Let's head over to Corso," Bartell said. "You mind?" Culp was the senior officer, so technically it was his choice where they went. But Bartell knew he wouldn't mind making a swing through the abandoned lumber mill.

Without answering, Culp pulled on the headlights and picked up speed.

The sky darkened in fits and starts as the moon played tricks behind a cloud bank. The cloud bank rose slowly over the mountains at the top of Yellow Pine, which is northwest of town, the next drainage west of Bride's. The car wallowed through twin channels of ruts down Defoe Street, then Culp jumped the ruts and turned west down an alley just before the Defoe Street Bridge and slipped quietly through Ragtown, a down-at-the-heels neighborhood just across the river from Corso.

Ragtown is Rozette's closest approximation to a ghetto. It's the oldest part of town, built by Corso at the turn of the century, when Rozette was a company town and Corso was the company. The company turned a handsome buck in those days by sawing dimension lumber and shipping it out by rail. Then, in the early fifties, millworkers began to earn enough money that they could afford to move out from under the company. In the years since, the trim, almost militaristic neighborhood had grown pocked with rusted-out cars and pickup trucks and vacant lots, where weeds overgrew the footings of burned-out shacks. Like a system seeking equilibrium, the houses that Corso built and abandoned on the south side of the Holt counterbalanced the mill that Corso closed on the north. Nowadays, if you were still eligible for unemployment, you could afford not to live in Ragtown. No matter what, though, you could never afford to live with those faceless, nameless people in Portland, who owned your job and put a lock on it.

"Think the old bridge is good for one more crossing?" Culp meant the California Street Bridge, a spindly old structure with a wooden deck that the engineering pooh-bahs from the State Highway Department had ruled safe only for pedestrian use.

"You're driving, you buy the car." Bartell was referring to memos from the chief, which warned that if any cop put a patrol car into the Holt off the California Street Bridge, he'd be docked for the car once he started drawing pay again after an unspeakable number of days off.

"What the fuck," Culp said. "We'll both be dead anyway." He edged the car around the cement barricade on the south end of the bridge and the tires thumped ominously on the shifting planks.

Bartell aimed his spotlight upriver along the edge of Lacy Island, through the tangle of cottonwood, alder, and willow. Lacy Island would be a great place to find a body. Late on a spring night, say, in the fog, with dogs howling and the river on the rise.

"Stiffs are like lightning," Culp said. "Never strike when you're looking." After working together two nights a week for over three years, Culp knew Bartell's quirks as well as he knew his own.

"You giving me shit again?"

"You deserve it."

Upriver from the bridge the old Corso Mill sat low and dark at the mouth of a large, barren yard, a field that once contained huge stacks of saw logs, mostly fir and larch, to be processed through the mill. In the good old days, they rafted the logs down the Holt out of Bride's Canyon. The last big float, though, had taken place before World War II, before they built the new bridge on Defoe Street, upriver from the mill, which jammed up the works, before people learned that rivers could be injured beyond healing. None of that mattered today, though, since most of the good first growth timber had been logged out of Bride's years ago. As Culp pulled around the northern barricade, Bartell watched the tall, boxy mill shift eerily against the shifting clouds, a giant child's cluster of giant tan blocks stacked helter-skelter in an empty field. There were no tire tracks in the crusted snow, which gave off a flat white glitter.

"Your dad worked here?" Bartell asked Culp as he drove through the open gate. He already knew the answer, but he asked anyway because he always asked when they drove through Corso.

"Twenty-three years," Culp said. "I was born back there." He nodded toward Ragtown. In the glow from the dash lights Bartell was surprised to see a flush of intensity on Culp's face as he spoke, an intensity that was like smooth asphalt rippling under an August sun.

"Twenty-three years," Culp said again. Not counting the layoffs and strikes, he thought. He could still remember when the house would be crammed with men and beer and threats. His old man had been steward for a time. "Worked here twenty-three goddamn fucking years, busted up his shoulder pulling green chain, then lost three fingers in a saw, then they shut the son of a bitch down, told everybody thanks a lot. Now, you tell me what a fifty-seven-year-old sawyer with seven fingers is supposed to do in times like these. Jesus Christ, half the mills in the country are laying people off."

"You still give him money?" Bartell knew that Culp's old man drew a small disability, but it stretched about as far as a police pension.

"Much as I can. Much as he'll let me. But hell, I'm already stretched to the limit, you know?" Culp shook his head. "I'm a day late with the child support and my ex's lawyer starts jerking me around. Jesus Christ, she don't even need the money . . . but they're my kids, my boys . . . what the hell."

Bartell thought about all the times his own father, Cash Bartell, had set him to packing the truck a day or so before they pulled up stakes and headed down the road for a new outfit, outfits like the Dogie out of White Sulphur, or Hodson's south of Cascade. Bartell's mother pulled up stakes, too, kept putting one foot in front of the other until she got to Nevada, the last he heard, Reno, where she was dealing cards. Winter, she blamed it on, that morning in the cafe at Townsend, smoking Winston cigarettes and drinking a 7-Up while she waited for the bus. She had bright blond hair in those days, bottle blond, bright as the snow. It had taken Cash three days to run her to ground, and when he heard that, heard her say, "Winter," he called it winter of the brain and stuck Ray back in the pickup and away, then went back out into the ranch country. Pickup trucks and dirt roads, wind and whiskey, cattle, horses, and sheep. That was the story of that.

"I wish to Christ I lived in Portland and had a mill I could sell off," Culp said.

"But they couldn't sell it. That's the trouble."

"Bullshit. It was taxes. They were better off taking the tax loss. I wish to Christ I had a tax loss." Culp looked over at Bartell in that funny walleyed way. "None of my losses are the taxable kind."

Corso still did plenty of logging around Rozette, on National Forest as well as huge tracts of company timberland. Over the years, though, the company had expanded into oil and electronics. At the time they closed the mill, it was still turning a profit, but when the board of directors sat back and studied the Big Picture, they realized that it wasn't turning enough profit to offset its value as a tax loss. Besides, they said, it was more economical to train the logs to the West Coast raw, ship them to Japan, where they were milled, and ship the lumber back. Now Corso was in the ship line business, too. The mill was up for sale, at least technically, but there weren't any takers. Not even that bunch of Arabs running around Montana last year with steamer trunks full of cash. Neither Bartell nor Culp knew much about the world of high finance, but both suspected that when you can't sell something big to a gilded Arab, you've got a real dog on your hands.

"You wouldn't like being an asshole," Bartell said, meaning that Culp would not enjoy the ethereal regions of multinational tax losses.

"I could teach myself." Culp doused the lights again and wove the car among the empty buildings, whose open overhead doors yawned silently in the cold.

Bartell dropped his window again and Culp moaned.

Bartell always enjoyed prowling, especially on the two nights a week when Culp was off and he worked alone. He liked to roam silently through the streets, playing with the radio, tuning in obscure AM stations around America, the ones you could only get late at night. Things seemed to be more coherent at night, at least as far as the job went. The town was smaller then, compressed by darkness, yet larger, since there was more, much more *out there* and you had to work harder, travel farther, to see it. Sometimes, after a night when nothing happened, he would lay at home in bed and suddenly find himself with a weird feeling, as though plenty of bad things had happened, only he had failed to find them. Helen never understood this unfocused anxiety. Bartell tried to tell her it was just a part of the job. More likely, he thought, it was a part of himself that the job brought out.

"You see that light in there?" Culp said very quietly. They were cruising past a row of windows along the front of a warehouse. Culp took the car out of gear and let gravity pull it to a stop in the snow. A noisy valve lifter inside the engine sounded like Fred Astaire tapping frantically across a huge empty stage.

Through a broken-out window, Bartell saw a faint orange glow painted against the wall at the distant end of the building.

"Fire," Bartell said.

"Goddamn bum." Culp drummed the heel of his hand on the steering wheel. Every cop in the city had bagged his limit of bums out of Corso. "Shitheads. Don't even have enough brains to go south for the winter. Roust the dirtballs and we trash their precious goddamn rights. Leave 'em alone to freeze and we're cruel and unusual. Shit," Culp said. "Lousy pukes." That was his indiscriminate label for anybody who was not a cop, and for a few who were. "Let's stick him in jail for the night. He ain't going to freeze to death or burn something down and screw up my shift."

Bartell got on the radio and checked them out, then Culp shut off the engine and they got out and walked through the crusty snow toward an open door about twenty feet ahead. Culp led the way.

At the door Culp suddenly stuck out his arm, holding Bartell back.

"You hear that?"

Bartell couldn't hear anything. The moon had slipped away, and despite the snow, it was darker than the inside of a crow.

"Sounded like somebody groaning. Sounded like a woman, maybe."

Bartell fine-tuned his ears and then he heard it, too, a sob that sounded animal.

"I'll go in first down the left side." Culp pulled his gun and held it close along the side of his leg. "You follow down the right. Be careful. And be quiet."

Bartell drew his gun, too, and followed Culp through the door.

The warehouse was starting to thicken with smoke and Bartell suppressed an impulse to cough. As he walked over the cement floor down the right wall, he could see by the muted light from the fire that the warehouse was empty except for a stack of packing crates, which walled off the scene of the fire. By the same light he could see Culp moving quickly but cautiously down the opposite side. The moaning was louder now, almost steady, and he heard Culp start to run and then he was running, too, running toward the fire.

The woman was laying in a fetal position in a pile of rags and wadded-up paper. She wore a brown wool coat. Her jeans were down around her ankles and she tried with one hand to pull them up, but she couldn't seem to hold them tight enough. Her bottom arm, the left, lay twisted behind her back and each time her grip broke, she rolled back on the bottom arm and gasped. When she looked up at Bartell, he saw that her mouth was ringed with blood, like a smile painted on a clown. The fire burned inside a cutaway oil drum.

When Culp holstered his revolver and knelt beside her, the

woman cringed and tried to burrow deeper into the nest of paper and rags. Bartell pulled off his leather jacket and spread it over the woman's bare thighs, which were bruised and scratched.

"It's all right now." Culp brushed a strand of hair from the smear of blood on her cheek.

"It's okay," Bartell said lamely, then coughed from the smoke.

The woman nodded. She licked at her swollen lips, then quickly gulped air and lay back on Culp's arm.

"Out there," she said, managing to point to a window behind Culp that was unbroken, but had been slid open. "Went out through there."

"How long ago?"

"Don't know. Couple of minutes, I guess. Don't know. My arm. I think he busted my arm."

They managed to get the woman turned onto her back so that her weight was off the injured arm. Then they helped her work her jeans up over her hips and Bartell put his jacket back on. As she moved, Bartell heard something metallic rasp hollowly against the cement. He dug through the trash and found a hardhat.

"George Rather." He held the hat out to Culp. It had been eight days since they deposited Rather in the county jail.

"Wonderful," Culp said. "Absolutely fucking wonderful."

"You hurt anyplace else?" Bartell asked the woman.

"Don't think so. Can't tell, my arm hurts so much." The woman coughed then and fresh blood spilled from the corner of her mouth. Bartell opened her coat and saw a small, wet stain on the maroon sweater under her left arm. He raised the sweater. The stab wound was still bleeding, sucking air each time she breathed.

"Paul?" He nodded toward the wound.

"Holy Christ," Paul Culp said. "Go call us a goddamn ambulance."

Chapter 3

The air inside the warehouse was cold and smoldering and by the time Bartell got to the car, he was hacking uncontrollably. He dug through his pants pocket for the spare key to the car, unlocked the door, and started up the engine. After a few seconds the radio was warmed up and he slipped the microphone from the console and took a deep breath. No more running and smoke than that and his throat was raw as a piece of steak.

"Any bullshit," came that loose, gravelly voice, "and I blow your brains all over the back seat."

Bartell looked up and saw George Rather standing beside the left front tire of the car. Rather held a handgun pointed steadily at Bartell's face, aiming between the door and the windshield post, aiming the gun straight at Bartell's goddamn face. You could have run a cow down the fucking barrel, it looked so big.

"There's the way now," Rather said. "Now put that thing back—"

"What thing?" Where had George Rather gotten the gun? He had no gun at Roosa's. Stolen? Or had he kept it stashed someplace all along?

"That mike, put it back where it goes, then put both your hands on the wheel. Don't need no eavesdroppers. There's the way now.

"Do like I say!"

Bartell replaced the microphone. As he did so, he touched on the brake light switch with his middle finger, then gripped the steering wheel at the top with both hands. He thought about Culp inside with the woman and he wondered how long it would take him to realize that something was wrong, how long before he came out hollering at Bartell to pick it up, the gal was dying, for God's—

"What do you want?" Bartell tapped his right toe on the brake. If Rather saw lights flashing, he'd shit razor blades . . . but Bartell had to do something to warn Culp.

"I just—"

"Shut up!"

"I just want to know what you want." Bartell tried to measure his words carefully, as though each phrase were an object landing on one end of a balance and George Rather stood on the other. Rather sounded drunk, his voice even more ragged and uncertain than the night at Roosa's. Christ only knew what a drunk criminal would do with a gun and a burned cop. The hostage negotiator's rule might be that the criminal always loses, but you still have to beat the son of a bitch.

"Ask the bitch inside. Ask her what I want. Hah!"

Bartell concentrated on the man, tried to grasp the moment, and beyond, when all this shit was over and he sat in the warm station, typing out his report while the dicks put a wrap on the charges and turned a key on Rather and that would be that, case closed, but the moon was gone behind clouds and Bartell's mind kept getting bogged down in shadows, shadows and the gun and Rather's voice telling him to get the fuck out of the car.

"I can't do that." He must have been nuts. This son of a bitch was going to fill him up with that gun, ventilate him but good, and there he was refusing to give the guy a lousy car that belonged to a city so ungrateful it wouldn't even give the cops a decent pay raise or install FM radios in the cars. Take the goddamn car, he should have said, take the car, his coat, uniform, gun, anything, bank account, take it all, chum, take it with Ray Bartell's best wishes and get the hell away.

"My ass," Rather said.

"No, honest to Christ, I can't do that. I mean, I want to help you get out of this thing, but you're gonna get me in a lot of deep shit if I give you this car. Trouble for you, too. Jesus, how far can you get in a police car? Now, if you want a car—"

"I could give you a coffin, that's what I could give you."

"That'd get you in trouble, too." Bartell wished that he could see Rather's eyes. He remembered the way Rather's eyes had relaxed and he had called Culp Chief when Culp put his hand on his shoulder. He wished he could reach Rather's shoulder. He'd put his hand on it, all right.

"Shit, I probably killed that woman in there, I stuck her, you know, stuck her, and she's probably dead anyhow and here you're giving me shit about trouble stealing a fucking car!"

"It's a lousy car."

"You think I'm some kind of dumbass?" Rather laughed, a short dry rumble.

"I'm just saying—"

"Ought to kill you just to teach you a lesson."

"—just trying to tell you the woman'll be okay, it looks like, and I can help you out of this beef—"

"You ain't helping shit, man! I seen all this—"

"—help you out of this beef if you'll just give me a chance."

"—seen all this bullshit on TV. This help-me bullshit, it's just a scam."

"I'm being straight with you, George."

"Nothing but a goddamn scam to eat time."

Bartell licked his lips and tried to force the gun away from the center of his attention. He wasn't having much luck; guns take up a lot of room. His palms were slick and began to slide down the steering wheel. He tightened his grip. It didn't help. "My name's Ray. Ray Bartell."

"Your name's Dead Meat, you don't give me this goddamned ride! Now!" The voice jerked ahead like a roller coaster. "You was one of the cops busted me. What the fuck I care what your name is?"

Bartell glanced down at the gear shift lever, figuring maybe he could jam the car into gear, barrel ahead, and the open door would bowl Rather over. But it was winter, the snow, slick . . . why the hell is it always winter in Montana? It wouldn't work. Flash and dazzle hardly ever works. Bartell kept on tapping the brake pedal slowly, rhythmically, like you milk a cow. Where the Christ was Culp?

"George, I think if you really wanted to get away, I think if that's what you wanted, you could've just run." Crazy as it sounded, sometimes people actually wanted to get caught, whether they understood that or not. At least, that's what the shrinks said. "You don't need a car," Bartell said. "Especially a police car."

Of course, there was always the chance that what Rather really wanted was to whack a policeman. If that was the case, though, nothing much Bartell might do would stop him.

"We never would've found you, I bet. Still wouldn't, if you just Bogarted out of here!"

Rather flexed his fingers on the butt of the revolver. "You still don't know who I am, huh . . . too cold to sleep out or travel . . . jail . . . I can't fuckin' believe it.

"Got no place to go. I'm all run out."

"Everybody's got a place, George!"

"No people."

"You could run. You could run all the way to Florida, you wanted."

"Never been to Florida."

"You'd like Florida. It's warm in Florida. No sleeping out in the winter."

"Too far."

"That's the point. You could spend the winter at the horse races." Bartell tried to laugh. He wondered if his laugh sounded as pathetic in Rather's ear as it did in his own.

"Hate fucking horses."

"The Keys, then. You like fishing? Fish for them big tarpon."

"Too far. I'd never make it."

"Arizona, then. That's closer, and it's warm there, too. Jump a train to Arizona. We'd never find you there." *Or California*, Bartell thought. *Go to California where people like you belong.*

"That'd be better," Rather said. "I got cousins in New Mexico. That's close to Arizona."

"See, everybody's got a place to go. They could hide you out."

"Hide me out, shit. They threw me out last time I was there."

"Yeah," Bartell said, nodding sympathetically, "yeah, George, that happens." His concentration wavered and he remembered a time years ago, when he'd slept on the seat of an old pickup after a night ride away from another of Cash's jobs, that one between Augusta and Choteau. "That happens."

"That woman," Rather said softly, "she's gonna be dead. Ain't she?"

"You hurt her. Hurt her bad. I won't lie to you about that. But she's a long way from dead. Especially if you let me get her some help."

"What about the other cop? I heard two of you talking. Where's the other cop?" Rather got excited again and turned toward the warehouse door and Bartell wondered if he had an opening, but in the instant it took him to think this, Rather turned back. "You're jerking me around, stalling. Get outta the car."

"Maybe you ought to give me the gun."

"Maybe I ought to blow your ass up!"

Bartell told himself over and over that if George Rather really wanted to kill him, he would be dead by now. That was the rational, measured answer, situation-wise. If the son of a bitch wanted him dead, he would be dead, but he wasn't dead. He was too goddamned scared to be dead. Dead men don't have chattering teeth and tossing bowels . . . they're just . . . dead. Goddamn, it was almost funny, almost hysterical. Bartell wanted to laugh and tell the guy, okay, you've done a great job of giving me the shakes, pal, now let's knock off the bullshit, it's time to go to jail.

"You get your pictures back, okay?" Bartell asked.

"What the fuck you talkin' 'bout?"

"Those pictures in your wallet. You get them back when they cut you out of jail?"

"You go through my stuff? You some kind of sick or something? What call you got to go through my stuff?"

"We gotta check for money," Bartell said. "They write down any money you got at the jail, so you get it all back. Those boys?" He was talking about the two in the supermarket portraits, the ones in white go-to-church shirts. "Look like good boys."

"Growed up now," Rather said. "Least I guess they're growed. Ain't seem 'em . . ."

"I got a daughter. Me and my old lady. Daughter that's twelve."

"Yeah . . . yeah." The gun hand began to lower. "Shit, though, you know, I never figured the one was mine . . . that bitch . . . I just . . ."

"Yeah. I never had that problem . . . but I know it's a real meat grinder."

"I never meant, you know . . ." The gun was at his side now and Rather was looking at the ground. "Fuck, I don't even know no more . . . "

"It's time to give this thing up, George." The words sounded strange as Bartell said them. Felt strange, too, like they'd come from somebody else, like the words had sliced through Rather's envelope of rage.

Maybe Bartell was wrong.

"I ain't going back!" Rather snapped. He looked back up at Bartell and his whole body seemed to flutter with tension.

"It's okay." Bartell forced the tremor out of his voice. "We'll work it out." He put a foot out onto the snow. The car seemed like it was a mile high. He watched Rather closely. The gun didn't raise.

"I'm gonna get out of the car, George. Why don't you put that gun down . . . just lay it on the hood of the car . . . "

The gun started up.

". . . that's it . . . just lay it—"

There were two shots within a split second and George Rather pitched forward against the car door, mashing Bartell's leg, then rolled over onto the snow, his belly reaching into the air as he arched his back, then he settled and he groaned once and was still. Bartell looked up and saw Paul Culp standing fifteen feet away in the warehouse door.

Chapter 4

□   □   □

Culp sat in the back seat of Tobe Mitchell's car and watched the exhaust fumes swirl forward into the headlights. He shifted his weight and noticed again that his gun was gone, taken as evidence by Mitchell. It felt funny, being in uniform and in a car and all without his piece.

He kept feeling as though Tobe or Bartell wanted to say something, but he didn't really care if they said anything or not. Bartell was probably close to a basket case by now. He carried around all that right and wrong bullshit, as if knowing right from wrong could keep you warm when you were cold, feed you when you were hungry, make you better when you are very, very sick. Blessed are the peacemakers, the Bible said. Culp could still hear his mother reading that stuff to him when he was a kid. In his experience, though, the peacemakers most often got shit on. That was what being a peacemaker got you, and Culp got shit on enough without going out of his way looking for it. Culp still knew exactly what right and wrong were, but by the end of the sixties, before he'd ever become a cop, he'd learned that wrong could keep you awake too many nights, and right could get you killed. Anyway, why the hell was he mulling over the subtleties of right and wrong tonight? He'd done a justifiable and necessary shooting. True, he'd never killed anybody as a cop, but he'd done it dozens of times before over *there*, so it wasn't like he'd just had his cherry popped. If Bartell couldn't live with that, then Bartell could take all his peacemaker crap and put it in a very dark place.

The woman had started to have trouble breathing and Culp couldn't figure out what was taking his partner so long to call a goddamned ambulance. If she was a lunger and she coded, they could have a homicide on their hands. And besides, from the look and smell of her, if CPR turned out to be their last and only chance, Culp had too much seniority to be doing the mouth part. He wasn't even that excited about putting his hands on her chest.

Either way, if Bartell didn't get his act together, the woman was in deep shit.

But Bartell kept on not showing up, so Culp settled the woman back on the stack of trash and told her to be still.

"He says I'm gonna die. The guy what done it, he said that."

"You ain't gonna die."

"I'm real cold . . . like I can't feel my toes no more. I'm dying, I can tell."

"Hell yes, you're cold. It's the middle of the winter. I'm cold too and I ain't dyin'."

"I tell you I'm dyin'. I tried to kill myself once and I know what it feels like. It feels like I feel right now."

"How'd you try to kill yourself?"

"Took a whole bottle of Tylenol."

"You must've got the wrong batch."

"I don't know, but I wanted to feel like I feel right now and for a little while I did. Felt like I was dyin', I mean."

"You ain't dyin'. Now knock that shit off."

He checked the chest wound, which still drew air. He didn't know what to do, then finally he wiped the lid from his Copenhagen on his pants and pressed it over the puncture to seal it. He told the woman to hold the lid in place, he was going to check on Bartell. She nodded once and let her head settle on back into the mess of papers. Culp coughed several times from the smoke of the campfire, then jogged through the dark warehouse toward the door where they'd left the car.

Culp still didn't know what it was that made him pull up at the door. Maybe it was just that he didn't want Bartell to see him running, see he was excited, something stupid like that. Whatever the reason, Culp had slowed to a walk by the time he got to the door and when he stepped out into the snow, he didn't know at first that he was looking at two men, one inside the car and one out, but then he saw Bartell's head outlined behind the wheel. The two men were talking.

Culp couldn't hear what they were saying but they kept talking in low voices and something about it all seemed out of whack.

The man outside the car had something in his hand. His right hand. And he held it down to his side.

Why did Bartell keep laying on the brake lights? The man looked familiar. Christ, what was anybody doing out there at that time of night unless he was a cop or an asshole?

The light kept shifting and Culp looked up at the sky and wished that the clouds would stay put for just a minute, the moon stay free of the clouds just long enough for him to see what it was that the guy outside the car had in his hand. He was still wishing this when he realized that he'd taken out his gun. He stepped back around the door and braced the back of his right hand, his gun hand, against the door jamb.

He kept his eyes on the man's right hand.

Bartell and the asshole were still talking.

Culp watched the hand.

The brake lights came on, then went out.

Then the clouds froze and Culp saw that the hand held a gun and he took a deep breath and a heartbeat later the hand started up and Culp shot.

In a half-assed way, it really did remind him of Vietnam. Not just the death part there in the snow outside the warehouse or the smoke and the babbling casualty and the shadows inside, but the attitude he knew some people would have toward it all, like it was more important than it really was. He could feel it there in Mitchell's car, a kind of urgent silence that meant Bartell and Mitchell didn't know how to handle a guy who'd just taken a guy off. You ran into that shit all the time in-country, from new journalists and admin types who kept trying to attach some kind of meaning or at least sanctity to all that death. It was just death, that's all, another column on some shithead's tally sheet. That's what you learned once your Stateside haircut grew out and you gave up shaving every day and saying *Sir* to every dude who looked like he expected it. And it didn't get much better when you came back, because the army, see, the army's had lots of experience with this sort of thing, so they sent everybody's next-of-kin this cute little form letter about not making any loud noises around your loved one or walking unexpectedly into a room where he's sleeping because he might jump up and murder your ass before he caught on you're just checking to be sure he's really back. So when he got home, everybody sat around him like Bartell and Mitchell were sitting around him now, like it all somehow mattered. Shit.

"Turn up the heat, would you, Tobe?" Culp's feet were getting numb from the cold. "How's come we can't just wait for Woodruff at the station?" Tobe had called for Frank Woodruff, a lieutenant in Detectives, to come down and investigate. He'd also notified the chief of police, but for now that illustrious person was leaving the matter up to his lieutenants. No doubt, though, the chief would show up before the night was over. Culp looked at his watch. Woodruff wasn't setting any speed records.

"He said he wanted the both of you here first, so he can get a firsthand idea of the layout."

For the first time in years Culp wanted a cigarette. He watched the car exhaust sweep through the lights and it reminded him of the way cigarette smoke looked in those old black and white Bogart movies when they backlit Bogart at night and the smoke was a bright veil that kept you safely out of reach. It took a real man to face cancer. Culp thought about asking Tobe for a smoke, then decided against it and reached into his jacket pocket for his Copenhagen. He'd forgotten about removing the lid. His pocket was full of loose tobacco. He scraped out a fresh chew, slumped down in the seat, and waited for the nicotine to take hold.

The first shot was near the center of the back, and the second about two inches higher. He knew that the low shot was the first fired because it was the recoil from that shot, along with Rather falling forward and down, which accounted for the elevation of the second. Either shot alone was enough to put George Rather underground.

Bartell didn't get out of the car right away. Culp remembered yelling at him to get some cover, even though he knew from the way the man had dropped like a bag of empty clothes that he was the same as dead. But Bartell didn't move and finally Culp moved out from his cover, holding his gun on the corpse until he was close enough to kick the gun away. That was when he saw that it was George Rather. Rather clawed with his hands at the snow, then lifted his head and looked down at the two ragged exit wounds in his chest.

"I was . . . I never . . . who done this?"

"I did," Culp said. The wounds were steaming in the cold.

"Am I gonna die?"

"Yeah," Culp said. "You're gonna die."

Rather's head fell back on the snow. "Tell Jolene . . . in Arkansas . . ."

Culp rolled Rather onto his belly and cuffed him, then felt his throat for a pulse. There wasn't any. He looked up. Bartell was still in the car.

"What the fuck happened, Ray?"

When Bartell didn't say anything, Culp reached in front of him for the radio mike. Bartell seemed to come around then. He brushed Culp's arm away and started talking on the radio himself. After he'd made all the necessary calls, Culp sent him back inside to wait with the woman.

About the only thing that disturbed Culp about having killed George Rather was that everybody seemed to expect him to be disturbed. Maybe that was something else he'd learned in Vietnam, something all kinds of guys learned in all kinds of wars. Who the fuck knew. The one thing he knew was that it wasn't the kind of thing he could talk about, because it made people very uncomfortable to learn that you aren't particularly bothered by having killed people. Maybe he was bothered once, back at the start, but if he was, he couldn't remember it now, and thinking about it only made him feel like one of those professional veterans, guys who've spent their entire life after the military looking to blame somebody or something for their maladjustment. Other people probably felt differently about it than he did. That was their business. He was just himself. Besides, who the fuck wasn't maladjusted? Maladjusted people make the world go round. The dead asshole in the snow had been maladjusted when he was alive. Bartell was maladjusted with all that worry about right and wrong. Tobe Mitchell was maladjusted from the core of his crooked old heart to the tips of his nicotine-stained fingers. The whole world is *fucked up* and trying to assess blame for that is a solid-gold waste of time.

"He say anything to you, Ray?"

"No."

Bartell sounded even more distracted than Culp had expected.

"I told you guys not to talk about it," Tobe Mitchell said, turning sideways in the seat so he could look at Culp.

"You talked to him for a long time," Culp said.

"He said—"

"I told the both of yous not to talk about it." Tobe sucked on a cigarette that was burned nearly to his fingertips.

"Tobe, I got nothing—"

"I don't give a fuck! I told you from the start even if the thing looks straight down the line, I ain't gonna have you talking yourselves into a jam by saying something around me. You got something to say, you say it to Woodruff when he gets here. Don't make me the one has to give you grief."

Culp nodded. The only thing that had felt more strange than having his gun seized was being advised of his rights by Mitchell.

Culp slumped even lower, then leaned forward and spit on the floor. Police cars are made for prisoners, which means that there are no window or door handles in the back seat, so fuck 'em, if they were going to make him sit in the back like some puke, then they could clean out the goddamn car. Assholes. Come on, come on, don't be an asshole. He sat up straight again and took a deep breath. He wished Bartell would turn around so he could look him in the eye, but Bartell continued staring straight ahead through the windshield.

"Sorry, Tobe," Culp said.

"Yeah, sure."

A moment later Woodruff arrived. The first thing he did was get in the back seat next to Culp and read them Miranda, first Bartell and then Culp, even though Tobe Mitchell said somewhat indignantly that he'd already done that. Woodruff said he was advising them for the same reason Tobe had, because only Bartell and Culp knew what had happened and both lieutenants wanted the two patrolmen to understand what they were saying before they said anything. Then Woodruff moved Culp into his car, leaving Bartell alone with Mitchell.

By the time they got to Woodruff's sedan, two other cars had pulled up with more detectives: Sam Blieker, Butch Durrant, and Phil Jacobs. Woodruff told Culp that those three would stay at the warehouse and work the crime scene while he went to the station with Culp and Bartell and got their stories.

"I'm going to tell you something else," Woodruff said before driving off.

"I feel like I've already been told quite a bit, without anybody having to say anything at all," Culp said. "If you know what I mean."

"I know what you mean," Woodruff said. He'd started wearing glasses in the last year, large teardrop lenses in a spare golden frame. His hair looked even more blond than when he was young, but if you looked close, you could see that the lighter shade was really gray, almost white. "But I don't want to have to rely on you picking up vibes to get this straight. I've known you for ten years and you're a good cop. I shouldn't tell you this, but I'm telling you. Get a lawyer. When we get to that station, I'm going to ask you a lot of questions, and if you've got any brains, you'll get a mouthpiece before you tell me squat."

"What's the first thing you think, Frank, when a guy gets an attorney? You think he's guilty."

"I didn't say that."

"I know you didn't. I'm talking about just as a matter of course. You're a cop and when some guy asks for a lawyer, you write him off as guilty."

"I didn't say I thought you were guilty of anything. Christ, I don't even know what happened."

"I don't need any ambulance-chaser."

Woodruff sighed and rubbed his eyes, then pulled on his sheepskin gloves. "Just think about it. Okay? At least consider it before we get downtown."

With that, Woodruff got out of the car and had a few words with his three subordinates. Then he came back and they started downtown.

Chapter 5

□ □ □

"He should've run away," Bartell said, looking across the interview table at Woodruff. "Doesn't figure. He should've just booked and that would have been the end of that."

Woodruff removed the tape cassette from the recorder, then pulled off his glasses and lay them on the table beside his elbow and shrugged. "Stupid, maybe." Woodruff was a deliberate man, past forty now, but with a kind of boyish face, upon which wrinkles looked like furrows of well-tanned wax. "Maybe he was too drunk, too drugged-out to do the smart thing. We'll have a blood alcohol on him tomorrow, after the autopsy. About drugs, it'll be a little longer."

First thing tomorrow Woodruff would start a complete criminal history check on George Rather. A fingerprint check with the FBI was already underway, compliments of the arrest at Roosa's, but that took at least two weeks. That meant that they wouldn't get a report back for a week at the inside.

According to reports from Blieker, Durrant, and Jacobs, the woman that George Rather raped and cut was named Nadine Howard. Dini, she called herself. At the time Woodruff talked to Bartell and Culp, she was in St. Francis ER getting the hole in her lung repaired. While they were at it, the doctors also set her broken arm and applied other miscellaneous bits of medical technology to her assorted damaged parts. Woodruff had ordered up a rape kit on her. That should put the icing on any probable-cause questions surrounding the shooting, as if sticking her and holding Bartell at gunpoint weren't enough reasons to check George Rather into the Slab Inn.

"We want to get everything documented as completely as possible," Woodruff had explained as soon as he and Culp met Bartell at the station. Woodruff never left any doubt as to who was in charge of the situation, which suited Bartell down to the ground. Things may have turned to shit, but it had all been George Rather's doing, and Woodruff didn't want any doubts creeping in just because some dick who was rousted out of bed in the middle of the night didn't have the presence of mind or the energy to anticipate what those doubts might be and nip them in the bud. Tomorrow he'd arrange for ballistic samples from Culp's service revolver and from the .44 Ruger Blackhawk that Rather had carried. He also said he'd want test rounds fired from Bartell's gun, too, even though it had not been fired that night.

"What chance do they give the Howard woman?"

"Piece of cake," Woodruff said. "She'll be back uptown sucking down schnapps by next week."

Rather had nabbed Dini Howard at gunpoint when she was between her car and her front door, then walked her the quarter mile to Corso from the stucco hovel she rented on California Street. Ike Skinner knew Dini Howard from business he'd done with her in the Rankin Strip bars, and he told everybody that she was not exactly uncharted territory, as far as her experience went with men and other tragedies. Bartell had guessed as much about her back at Corso. She had the puffed red hands of an alcoholic, and beat-the-shit-out-of-me eyes. That didn't mean she deserved getting mauled and possibly dead.

"Rather was living in that warehouse," Woodruff said.

"Near as I can tell, he moved in after he got out of the county three days ago on that mess from the cafe."

"Funny he'd take her where he lived," Bartell said. "I mean, if he meant to kill her, which it looks like he did."

"Yeah. Funny . . ."

"He could have taken her on inside her own house, where it was warm."

"She's got kids there. Maybe he cased the place and knew that. Who can figure a guy like that?" Woodruff said.

Bartell looked at his watch. It was nearly five in the morning, almost two hours after his shift ended. The shooting had occurred at about half past midnight. He'd phoned Helen around two o'clock, after the dust had settled, once it was clear that he would be much later than usual, later even than if he'd holed up somewhere with the other Maggots for a beer, which happened now and again. "We about done now?" he asked Woodruff. Even the hardest of the hardcore Maggots were home by now, even the divorced and the divorcing.

"As far as I can tell, yes." Woodruff stood and slipped his glasses in the pocket of his blue chamois cloth shirt. It was strange to see Woodruff without a jacket and tie.

"Why don't you head home and get some sleep?" Woodruff rolled down his shirtsleeves and buttoned the cuffs, which made Bartell feel like a job that the lieutenant had just done. "The only thing left I need is for you to stop in sometime tomorrow and read over your statement and sign it. It ought to be typed by the middle of the afternoon." He shuffled his notes into a manila file folder.

Bartell stayed in his chair as Woodruff stepped around him toward the door. He hunched forward and put his elbows on his knees and stared at the floor. It felt as if his body were shrinking, being ground away to dust between fatigue and the echo of George Rather's voice: *I ought to blow your ass up.* And he thought about the other cops, the rest of the Maggots, about how he and Culp had become the objects of sudden attention, along with something else—was it wonder?—that made it nearly impossible to talk about the incident with any kind of substance.

Several of the Maggots were milling around the briefing room when Woodruff, Bartell, and Culp passed by on their way to Detectives. "You done good," Juju Watson had said, parroting a TV cop show from several seasons ago. "Dumped the douche bag," said Randy Heidmann, nodding his great walrus face and offering Culp a high five. Culp didn't say anything back and stared up Heideman's hand until he lamely dropped it.

"Open season now, boys," Ike Skinner boomed down the hall after them. "Open season on assholes. That's the way to fill a tag, gents," he said, as if they—well, mostly Culp—had left the station empty-handed and come back with an elk.

What the fuck . . . Bartell still felt himself falling farther and farther from all those guys, as though he had failed. He didn't know how Culp felt, but he felt like an old dog who'd been given a nice meaty bone, then booted out of the house to gnaw on it alone.

Maybe Culp didn't feel so bad, though, since he'd rescued the day, rather than been suckered by it.

Who could say?

How do you talk seriously to a man who might just have saved your life?

Or might have killed a guy who was in the process of giving up.

Killed.

None of the stationhouse philosophers used that word.

Nobody said *killed*.

And nobody said *dead.*

"You think he'd have shot me, Frank?" Bartell felt his breathing grow more labored in the long silence before Woodruff answered.

"I don't know. That's not the answer you want to hear, but I'm telling you, just between the two of us, I don't know."

"We were talking about New Mexico, about going on the run to New Mexico, and he said he had family down there. And about his kids. He had those pictures, see—"

"You told me."

"—and all of a sudden, see, I felt like I knew the guy and he wouldn't shoot *me. I* was telling him to put the gun on the car. I think that's what he was doing."

"But Culp couldn't know that. All he knew was the gun started up."

"I know . . . Maybe if I'd told him just to drop it on the ground."

"Maybe."

"But I was convinced—"

"*I'm* convinced he *might* well have killed you," Woodruff said with surprising sharpness. "When I said I didn't know, that cuts both ways. The guy was a criminal. An asshole."

"I know."

"And he stuck that woman like a melon."

"Yeah."

"He had a gun."

"And he *might* have shot me."

"That's right," Woodruff said, still talking from the doorway behind Bartell. "He might have. And if you or Paul had been carrying a walkie-talkie with you, you wouldn't have had to go back to the car and you wouldn't have had the confrontation at all. Maybe he'd have hot-wired your car and you'd both feel like idiots."

Woodruff was in the neighborhood, but he wouldn't quite come out with it: Had Bartell behaved in such a way, a wrong way, and put himself unnecessarily at risk? Had he been careless? Whenever a cop is killed, a bulletin goes out to every law enforcement agency in the country. Incidents are hashed over at coffee and in patrol cars and at officer safety workshops all over America, and the final implication, the bottom line, is always this: The cop should have seen it coming and stopped it.

"The thing went by the numbers," Woodruff said at last. Was he on the level, or just letting Bartell off the hook? Bartell didn't know.

"I know it did on paper," Bartell said. "But I'm not talking about numbers. I'm talking about inside my head."

"I'm talking about that, too. What I'm telling you is you can't start playing games with this thing. You do that and it'll eat you alive."

There hadn't been a police shooting in Rozette for almost eight years, over two years before Bartell came on the department, so there wasn't any real cultural apparatus among the other cops to deal with what Culp and he were going through. Shooting people was something a cop did when he had to . . . *if he reasonably believed that such force was necessary to prevent imminent death and serious bodily harm to himself or another.* That was how Montana's deadly force statute read. *Reasonable.* That was the word they always gored you with. And *imminent.* There was another word to hang your guts on. How imminent had Bartell's death really been? Not very, it seemed now. But was that perception accurate, or simply a safety valve, a mechanism that was required if he were ever to be able to walk into another piece of nasty business? Culp was right. Bartell thought too much. But the real point was that he'd gotten himself into a position requiring rescue, punched a ticket for George Rather, who was dead, and for Paul Culp, who had to live with killing him.

"I *knew* he wouldn't shoot," Bartell said. "You know what I mean, Frank? You know all those times a guy *should've* been shot, but you knew, you just *knew* somehow that it wasn't the time to shoot. You've had those times, Frank, I know you have. Every cop has."

"Sure. And maybe every cop that gets shot dead knew the same thing just before he got it. So what?"

"But if I didn't have that control, then I must've screwed up. You think I screwed up, Frank?" Bartell was surprised by how badly he wanted an answer. Not just an answer, but an answer he could believe.

"It's like you said, Rather should've hit the ground running. Things always go down like that . . . ways you can't figure . . . it's *always* like that. If you hadn't handled the guy like you did, stringing him along like that, somebody would be over at your house now, talking to Helen. And tomorrow I'd be watching Doc Molyneaux post you instead of that guy in the morgue."

"Where's Culp?"

"He's waiting in my office. I've got a few more questions for him. You want to talk to him first, before you take off?"

Bartell didn't want to talk to Culp. Tobe had given both of them the next night off, and after that Culp went into his regular days off, which meant that Bartell might not see him again for nearly a week. He knew he should talk to Culp, but what was there to say? In a moment of precise calm just after the shooting, they had knelt over Rather's body and Bartell thanked Culp and Culp said, "Jesus Christ, Ray, he had you dead to rights. What happened?" He sounded very businesslike.

What happened?

After that the roof fell in and they hadn't had a chance to talk alone since. While they were waiting in Tobe's car, Bartell could feel Culp staring at the back of his head. But he never turned around. He just looked straight ahead through the windshield. Bartell remembered now thinking how warm the lights looked over downtown, and how the world was big and dark and wild when you looked at it from the center of something terrible. He was never afraid of the dark, even when he was a kid on all those ranches out there in the belly of Montana, where there was no light save the moon and stars, even then he was never afraid of the dark. It was as though night had always been a place where you went after the sun was gone, a new country that you could explore and learn. But the night wasn't a place anymore, there in Tobe's car. Night had become a *thing*.

Bartell leaned back in the creaking wooden chair in the interview room. The pale blue walls were scuffed and smudged, and the blue all-weather carpet was scarred with tracks left by live cigarettes, which crawled over the floor like fossils of extinct worms. Bartell looked behind him at the door, but Woodruff was gone. *I had him*, he thought, *goddamnit, I had him through it and now he's dead anyway, but I fucking had him. I know it, son of a bitch. I know it.*

He didn't talk to Culp.

* * *

Bartell poured three fingers of unblended Scotch in a tumbler and looked through the arched door at Helen, who waited for him in the living room. The furnace belched from deep in the basement outside Jess's room and the house began to shudder with heat. He held the tumbler up to the kitchen light and contemplated the whiskey's color, marveled at it actually, that perfect amber tint which, like the manners of a well-trained dog, never falters, at least until the dog starts taking off your fingers one knuckle at a time. Bartell drank very little, but his old man was an absolute missionary of booze, so Bartell had a keen appreciation for the psycho-medicinal properties of whiskey. He swirled the Scotch deftly around the inside of the glass. He held the glass to his nose and smelled the peat, the fast cold water from a Scottish glen, the debris of centuries wedded artfully with the freshness of a new storm off the North Sea. Magnificent. Then he poured it all down the sink.

"I thought you wanted a drink," Helen said when he sat down empty-handed across the room in a rocking chair.

"I did."

Helen couldn't understand how whiskey could be therapeutic even if you didn't drink it. She tucked her legs more snuggly under her on the couch.

"I couldn't get back to sleep," she said. Jess's hairdryer whispered from the bathroom and Helen looked at her watch. Helen leaned toward the door to call to Jess, but held back. "I kept tossing," she said, turning back to Bartell.

"I know."

"Even when you said it was okay, I just rolled around for an hour, then finally got up and got dressed." Helen laughed, that high, nervous gasp of hers that used to drive Bartell nuts, until he learned to tune it out. "Once I got my clothes on, I tried falling asleep on the couch. It didn't work, so I wrote out the bills."

"Jesus, that could be more traumatic than the shooting."

Helen laughed again, but Bartell hadn't intended to be funny. She tugged at the sleeves of the bulky Icelandic sweater Bartell gave her two Christmases ago. Even all that tastefully knitted yarn failed to hide her figure. Her thighs and hips were still trim and snug inside her jeans and her blond hair tossed sleepily from her head like the nest of some delicate Amazonian bird. Sometimes Bartell forgot that his wife was a beautiful woman.

Bartell wasn't sure how much he would be able to tell her about the shooting. He locked his fingers behind his neck and rocked steadily. He had turned the rocker to face another chair and now he propped his bare feet on the chair in front of him.

"I wish you wouldn't . . . do that . . ."

Bartell looked at her for a moment, then shook his head, sighed, and put his feet down.

"It's Jess. I get mad at Jess all the time . . ."

Bartell waved her off and closed his eyes. There must be something about motherhood that puts a certain tone in a woman's voice, a scolding tone that makes everybody within earshot feel about three years old.

He used to tell Helen everything that went on at work. Even before he was a cop he was like that. But over the years Bartell had taken on an odd air of privacy. Most of what he told her now was about what went on inside the department, as though the street were now simply an unchanging, chaotic given.

"I feel," he said, his eyes still closed, "I feel like I've left too many things undone. Like I get to a certain point and then I just walk away."

"But last night—"

"I don't mean just last night, I mean all the time." He meant everything all the way back to when he'd abandoned school after drawing a high number in the draft lottery. He meant before that, even, when his mother climbed on a bus and he felt like he'd allowed his father to let her go. "Like everything I do turns out to be *almost* okay." He'd once told Helen about this feeling, years ago before he stopped talking to her about things that mattered. He smiled now; he'd *almost* made her understand.

"I think you did the right thing," Helen said. "The way you kept the man talking like that."

"I should be out right now with Culp. Unwinding and working this goddamn thing out."

"Why don't you get some sleep, then call him this afternoon? I know you, Ray. I know that to you, what Paul thinks will matter more than what really happened."

"I hoped I was more subtle than that."

"Try again," Helen said. "I've been washing your socks and underwear too long not to know at least that much."

"I'm real good at talking people out of things," Bartell said. "At explaining everything."

"What's wrong with that?"

"Talk my way around all problems, professional and domestic. Is that all it takes for a well-adjusted life? A good line of bullshit?"

"You know better than that."

"You always picture yourself doing something like what Culp did." Bartell rocked slowly and watched out the window, where a school bus crawled by over the icy street.

"Killing somebody?" Her voice matched the incredulous look on her face.

"Give me a break, okay?" Bartell rubbed his face with both hands and yawned. "You know. Riding in on a white horse and all that crap. Handling things. I mean, I know it's stupid and corny, but it's still something in the back of your mind, the kind of thing that helps bring you back when you get too cynical."

"Nobody expects you to ride a white horse." Her voice had that soothing, crisp tone she used on Jess, another variation of her motherhood voice. "Anyway," she went on, "you always told me that was a bad state of mind for a cop to carry around."

"It is. But it's no goddamned fun always being Pancho, goofing around waiting for Cisco to save your ass."

"I think your ego's getting in the way of your good sense."

"Could be. It just sticks in my craw that I did it right, that I had things worked out, handled, but I still came out the goat."

"You're sure he was putting the gun down?"

"Yes."

"What would you have done if you were Paul?"

"Goddamn, I don't know. I really don't. And that scares the hell out of me, too."

"Because you could have been wrong about this Rather . . ."

"And I might not have shot," he finished for her, feeling like he'd just sat down on a ice pick.

"But Paul knew." Her voice sounded so distracted it put him on edge even more. "I mean, he knew enough about what appeared to be happening . . . what could happen . . . to shoot."

"Whose side are you on?"

"It's not a matter of sides," she said, exasperated.

"Thanks," Bartell said acidly. "It's a good thing you're not a psychiatrist. We couldn't afford the malpractice."

She was right, of course, which only made things worse. Why was it that those things of greatest personal value can rarely be discussed without rancor? Jesus Christ, he was in a lather about what Culp did, when he should be content to be alive.

Bartell looked up when he heard Jess come into the room. She was wearing a baggy Seattle Seahawks jersey, blue jeans with frayed cuffs, and a pair of down-at-the-heel Nikes. Bartell could tell in a flash that Helen was displeased; Helen's displeasure had an almost tangible quality, an aura, that let everybody know they were in deep trouble.

"Will you be in the newspaper?" Jess asked.

"I threw those shoes in the trash," Helen said.

"I got 'em out." Jess didn't look at her mother. "Will you?"

Bartell had told Jess over breakfast what had happened. She'd seemed a little excited, but more sleepy than excited.

"Probably," he said.

"Like *People* magazine?"

"You can't wear those shoes in the snow."

"Mo-ther, please."

"Ray—"

"Not like *People* magazine." He waved Jess over to his chair and gave her a hug. "Now hit the road. You'll be late. And hug your mother."

"Come on!" Jess protested.

"Do it," he ordered.

"We'll talk about those shoes tonight," Helen said as Jess leaned down.

"There ain't anything to talk about."

"There *isn't* anything to talk about. And yes there is."

"Yeah, yeah, yeah." Jess bounced out the door and Bartell watched her walk away down the snowy street.

"She reminds me of you," Bartell said to Helen.

"That bad?"

"Not bad." He tried to think of the right word as he watched Jess knock snow from a bank of evergreen hedge. "She just insists on being who she is. That's why the two of you fight all the time."

"You mean domineering."

Bartell started to flare, but when he looked back at Helen, he saw that she was smiling. "Give me a break," he said. "One brush with death a day is enough."

Bartell asked if Helen wasn't too tired to go to work, but she said she was too keyed up to sit around the house all day and would be better off at the office. She was very conscientious about her obligations to Dr. Melvin MacKenzie, the general practitioner, whose practice she'd managed for years. But Bartell was afraid it was his infectious gloom that she saw as the true problem with staying at home. He couldn't blame her.

After Helen left, Bartell sat back down in the rocker. It was after eight o'clock, but the sun was just beginning to break over the mountains behind Bride's Canyon. It snowed by fits and starts. Across the street a pair of crows danced among the branches of a tall, snow-laden spruce. From time to time they swooped down from the tree and stood in the neighbor's yard, like bits of punctuation on a page without words. What words would Bartell have written on that cold page? *Afraid?* That's a terrific word, a pertinent word. *Stupid?* That isn't a bad word, either. *Alone.* There. That's the best word of all, a word fit to accompany a stolid black crow. Or perhaps he should pass up words altogether and just run out and lay down and scoot his arms and legs in short arcs, carving angels in the snow, like kids do. Or like the dying do in their contortions. Jesus Christ, there wasn't any fucking place to go. He went out back to the new room and chucked a pair of logs into the woodstove. He switched on the TV and found a rerun of a college basketball game on the twenty-four-hour sports channel. He showered, dressed in old clothes, and lay down on the couch, where he spent the next several hours dodging in and out of dreams. A crow circled a police car. The car raced over snow, heading for another unnamed disaster. The siren screamed *Caw! Caw!* The driver—he saw from afar that it was Ray Bartell— kept doubling back to start over, never learning where he was supposed to go. Just before noon Bartell jumped awake in a sweat. The lithe basketball players had given way to sumo wrestlers, who charged and butted like bullish gods. He sat up and looked out the window. It was late afternoon. It had stopped snowing.

Chapter 6

□   □   □

The next weeks were even more dismembered than usual. At home Bartell tried his hand at chores, a sure sign that all was not well. First he finished installing wood trim in the infamous new room, a devastatingly minor chore he'd stalled off for nearly two years. For his next feat he reglued the wallpaper in the bathroom, which Jess steamed loose every time she took one of her thirty-minute showers, a daily ritual since puberty had blindsided the family. He was getting ready to start painting the living room woodwork when he gouged his hand with a screwdriver while opening a paint can, then barely caught himself on the verge of throwing a gallon of white paint across the living room, then caught himself again on the verge of tears. So he slacked off, started sleeping till midmorning, then getting up and fixing lunch for Helen.

Bartell spent his afternoons before work downtown at a gym in the basement of the old Lennox Hotel, pumping weights and brooding. Pumping weights is not a good pastime for a man in a bad mood; it isolates and constricts the mind which is already in disrepair. Running is better when you feel like a kicked dog, since it tends to release the mind by playing tricks with its oxygen supply. Bartell tried running, too, four miles a day, until he convinced himself that the city's blanket of wood smoke, one of the rewards of hearty Western living, was coating his lungs with creosote. So he trudged back to the weights, until he pulled a muscle deep in his shoulder and had to lay off altogether. For two days he could hardly lift his arms high enough to pull his hair out.

Infirmities, he growled to himself. Destruction and doom. Weakness. Analgesic creams were the answer. He cajoled Helen into several applications a night on the principle that it was her duty as a member of the health-care industry. Three days later, after willing himself healed, he plodded back to the Lennox and succeeded in extending the pain up into his neck. He finished out the week sleeping trussed up in a cervical collar, which had been prescribed by Melvin MacKenzie himself.

"Take it or leave it," MacKenzie shrugged. The arrogant son of a bitch, what did he know about failure? Some doctors lost all their charm when you asked them to treat you for free. Helen told him that night she was embarrassed by his behavior. Bartell told her to drop dead and ended up spending a night on the couch.

Then back to the Lennox. If you hurt, it meant you were alive, and Bartell was distinctly alive. If he were a samurai, like Ike Skinner had suggested, he'd have been out at the next available dawn, carving his guts out.

On his nights off Bartell sat close to Jess on the sofa and endured her favorite TV shows. Later he'd lay quietly in bed, listening to jazz on the radio and not sleeping. He remembered talking to Juju Watson a couple of years ago about dreams, and Juju told him he always had bad dreams for a couple of weeks after something awful happened at work. Bartell had never paid much attention to his dreams, but it came back to him after the shooting, what Juju said, and he waited for the bad dreams to start, but they never did. In fact, after the dream about the crow, he couldn't remember dreaming at all, even though they say you dream all the time. During those little bits when he slept, it was like he was dead. He woke up once with Helen under him, but as soon as he awakened, it was over. She didn't say anything about it the next day, which he guessed was good, but she acted like she was waiting for a corpse to start to smell.

The job was a real treat, too. Bartell turned into a fiend on the traffic circuit, pinching everybody in sight. At disturbances he had the fastest handcuffs on the department. You want a break? A break, you say? We don't give any breaks, we give justice. So saith the Lord God Bartell. Amen.

"How have things been with Paul?" Helen asked one night after putting her book down and switching off the lamp on the nightstand.

"Culp's fine, I guess." Bartell cocked his knee, then tucked the blanket under his chin and folded his arms over his chest.

"Have you talked about what happened?"

"Lots of things happen. We talk all the time. Sure."

"Not that. I mean the shooting. Did you ever talk about that?"

Nearly three weeks had passed since the night at Corso. Bartell thought about all the long nights after in the car with

Culp. "Yeah. Sure. I thanked him and he told me he was glad it worked out okay."

"And?"

"And what? And nothing. He did what he did, I did what I did, it was a clean job, and that was the end of it. End of case history."

Helen lay on her side, her head propped in her hand. "You never talked about it, I mean *it*, how you both felt?"

"That's considered bad form." He closed his eyes. It was amazing. When you closed your eyes, you could be anywhere: a hotel in Seattle, or better yet, a line cabin in the Belt Mountains. It would be early June, still cold at night because of the altitude, but warm under the sun. Outside, the horses stand tethered between a pair of lodgepoles, their heads hung low with sleep. It's early, just before dawn. About five feet from the end of his bunk, the wood-burning cookstove sits cold, half buried under dirty dishes and rank, empty cans. To his right Cash lays snoring, whiskey-soaked air whistling noisily through the iron-gray beard that hides his mouth. It's the best time of day, an hour before first light, when you can go back to sleep, or half sleep, and wait for the wind to cut loose just before daylight. Sometimes you hear a calf bawl, or a coyote yip, but mostly it's just dead quiet, the world getting ready to try you on again, but for another hour you can lay back and say to hell with it. Then of a sudden the horses kick up holy Ned and Cash is on the way out the door, feeding a shell into the old .45-70 bear tamer he always keeps close by.

"What is—"

"Ray?"

He was sitting on the edge of the bed. Helen shook his shoulder again and asked what was the matter.

His shoulders ached and his bladder felt heavy as a wagonload of rocks. After a stumbling trip downstairs to the bathroom, he slid back under the blankets beside Helen.

"I think it was a bear."

"What?"

"A bear was after the horses and the old man was on the way out to kill it." He didn't know if the dream was the beginning of the end, or the end of the beginning.

"You all right?" She snuggled her head under his chin. Her hair tickled his nose.

He nodded and closed his eyes and squeezed Helen's shoulder. She hooked her knee over his thigh and pressed closer. "I tried to say something to Culp, but I couldn't. I mean, having a guy . . . save your life . . . lot of baggage goes with a thing like that."

She slipped her hand under his T-shirt and scratched his ribs. He kissed her, then slid his hand under her nightgown and slipped the gown up over her shoulders and leaned into her.

"Been a hundred years," he said. In the glow from the streetlight her skin looked amber.

"The lay of the century," she said.

Helen tucked herself under him and he flipped the blankets over their heads. A moment later the blankets slid away and he buried his face in the gap between her neck and shoulder and held on. Sometime later in those still moments just before dawn, the coldest, cleanest part of the day, the bear lay dead on a broad mat of juniper and Cash Bartell was busy cutting out its claws, which were worth money down in Great Falls.

Paul Culp was friendly to anybody who spoke to him. A week after the shooting, he drove to Kalispell to visit his boys, but Glenna, his ex-wife, said they were on a ski trip with her husband. Culp figured she was lying, but he decided not to cause trouble and drove back to Rozette.

He worked all his shifts, and after work he went straight to his apartment. He seldom went out, except to get a bite to eat at the Cloverleaf and have a chat with Nails Hogan if the old guy was around. And he went shooting. A hundred rounds every other day or so at the police range.

About once a day Lucky Brisco stopped up to see how he was doing. Lucky was even fussier than before about knocking.

"You need some therapy," Brisco said one day. His jowls sagged heavily against his collar as he scowled across the table at Culp. His white hair, cropped close to the bone, looked like spikes of frost.

"A fuckin' headshrinker," Culp snarled.

"No, I ain't talkin' about no goddamn witch doctor," Brisco said. "I'm talkin' about *therapy*. The old-fashioned, normal kind. A good drunk. A woman. Something like that. *Therapy*."

"You're just full of suggestions."

Lucky Brisco grinned, an act of considerable strength, considering the normal bulk of his face. "Not just suggestions . . . but help." He reached inside his jacket and pulled out a bottle in a bag. "Cuervo Gold. You can leave the bottle in the bag while you drink, or take it out. Depends on your mood."

"You know that's against my rules," Culp said.

"That's the point. Anyhow, it's not like you're a drunk."

"No. It's not like I'm a drunk." Culp went to the sink and brought back a pair of glasses. He set one of the glasses in front of Lucky Brisco.

Brisco turned the glass bottom up. "Now me, on the other hand, I'm not a drunk, either, but I do have a stomach with a hole in it. This stuff'd have me puking blood before sundown."

"You're pretty considerate," Culp said, breaking the seal and pouring. "For a slumlord."

"Just a little Mexican sunshine on a winter's day." Brisco stood from the table and zipped his jacket. "How's it going? Tell me the truth."

Culp looked up at Brisco without expression and knocked back a jolt of Cuervo, then poured another.

"I figured," Brisco said, walking toward the door. "You remember when I killed that kid."

Culp didn't personally remember, since it happened before his time on the department. Still, it was a sort of fraternal memory he had come to share.

"Must be thirty years ago," Brisco said. "Kid run a stop sign on a Saturday night, then run from me, I guess because he was afraid of gettin' caught drinkin'. Wedged his Chevy between two big firs on the way up Yellow Pine." Brisco shook his head. "I coulda just let him go. A fuckin' stop sign."

"That how you got the hole in your stomach?" Culp looked at the old copper. If he was on the prowl for absolution, he'd come upon a dry fountain. If he was dishing out empathy, then he was about fifteen years too late for Culp.

"Son, that wreck was just one drop in a whole storm of acid." Brisco laughed and pulled open the door. "Now, I'm trusting you to do the right thing." He laughed again and stepped into the stairway. "It was a two-tone blue Chevy," he said, his face looking like pale mud. "His dad's car." Then Brisco headed down the stairs before Culp could think of anything to say.

Culp took the second drink, then poured a third, then a fourth, the Cuervo boring him out but good. He felt warm for the first time since last August.

Culp wondered if people at work were afraid that shooting Rather had brought back too many memories for him to handle. Anybody who did direct his curiosity in that direction would be right, but probably not for the right reasons. What hit Culp the hardest was not the remembered horror or the fear, which he did feel, but in small doses. No, the real sledgehammer was the intense familiarity of it all, the rush of close death, the *freedom* of being alive. He had forgotten that sense of freedom over the last decade and a half, and now it occurred to him that such freedom could be a very dangerous thing. He'd gotten glimpses of it in the police department, especially during training exercises after he'd agreed to take a position on the SWAT team. But glimpses were one thing. Now he felt stalked by a ghost.

Was that ghost really the ghost of Paul Culp?

Culp carried the half empty bottle to the front window and looked down into the street over the top of Lucky Brisco's eternally flashing sign.

Could that really be Culp there in the mud behind a dyke, praying for choppers?

The guy lugging ammo through the hot wet green squeeze of heavy bush?

For some guys, seeing a special car or hearing a special song made them remember how it felt to be young. For guys like Culp, it took a killing.

Goddamn, it was strange . . . no, not just strange, but absolutely, totally goddamn fucking *weird*, because Culp realized that what bothered him most of all was not the lost necessity to do the terrible things he had done then, but the fading ability. Were he to attempt that sort of madness now, he'd be the one who ended up dead.

Culp read in magazines and newspapers and saw in all those new high-tech big muscle war movies that he was supposed to be angry. Culp wasn't angry. He had never been angry. He had been—still was—unbearably sad. But never angry. A few years back the government relocated several hundred Vietnamese and Laotian refuges in Rozette. Far from objects of hatred, such people were, for Culp, figures in a museum. A museum of his own life. Removed from heat and rain and jungle and mud and fire, the Asians were simply people, artifacts cast in the same ghostly mold as Culp himself.

It was getting dark and the bottle was almost empty and Culp was almost on his ass. The drunks were starting to roam up and down Woody Street outside his window. Culp studied the street, looking for a two-tone blue Chevy. He saw a green Buick convertible pull in across the street, looking like it was being driven on eggshells. A fat, balding man got out of the Buick and hitched up his pants and turned up and down the street, like he was looking for a chance to misbehave, looking for somebody to tell him a story, a good, funny story that would make him laugh until he cried and keep on laughing until he stopped. But now the street was empty. The man stepped up on the curb, then hesitated a moment, like he was trying to decide, then walked with a rolling, seaman's gate that could have been a limp to the door of Harold's Club across the street, where he shouldered his way inside.

Culp set the empty bottle on the windowsill and staggered back to his bed, where he wrapped himself in several blankets and began to shiver. Mexican sunshine wasn't much help. Booze was supposed to dull the senses, but right now Culp felt nearly blinded.

When he was a kid, he used to see guys from the American Legion when they marched in parades. Guys carrying flags and old Springfield rifles and wearing blue cunt caps with all kinds of badges on them and they were the same age then as Culp was now and now all those guys were starting to die of old age. Where would they have the next war? The war that would produce the survivors who would make Culp old?

Culp tilted his head back and looked up at the shelf where the gun lay.

He didn't want to cause anybody any trouble.

Those old vets, you always saw pictures of them trying to fit into their dress uniforms from 1919 or 1945. Even 1952. Ike jackets or wool OD blouses with brass buttons and campaign ribbons and bellies that reminded you they'd been boys when the uniforms were issued.

But when you saw guys from Culp's war, it was in jungle fatigues. And more often than not, the fatigues still fit, which didn't mean at all that they hadn't been boys when they got them. It's just that fatigues are big and baggy, one size fits all, fits a lifetime. Culp had burned all his old uniforms, except for the field jacket, which he wore nowadays hunting and fishing out in the woods. Even so, whenever he had a mental picture of himself, he was in jungle fatigues and flip-flops, smoking a Marlboro and drinking a Bud on a boat heading upriver. That was the Paul Culp that Paul Culp knew.

Jesus Christ, he didn't want to hurt anybody ever again.

Culp took a deep breath and willed his eyes closed and was soon swallowed up by the fire inside.

By the first week in February, both Culp and Bartell found their two shared shifts a week nearly unbearable. Although Culp was senior and technically in charge of all their calls, over the years they had developed a rapport. Bartell knew beforehand how Culp would want something handled, and Culp in turn trusted and supported Bartell's judgment. So it was strange, the way Bartell started deferring to Culp in ways he hadn't since their first months together three years before. Bartell sensed that this suited Culp, but he wasn't sure. Culp didn't care one way or another.

When the January pinch record came out, Bartell was top man on the department, a first in his career. Even though most of the pinches were two-bit traffic, Tobe Mitchell was pleased. Tobe put a lot of stock in a guy's pinch record, because the overall pinch record of a shift was closely watched by the chief and his accomplices in the administration. When the shift was writing a lot of pinches, it meant they were doing a good job, and when the shift did a good job, the Shift Boss did a good job, too. It was all very logical.

Eight days after the shooting, Woodruff had called Culp and Bartell into his office. He finally had the FBI report on George Rather, who turned out to be a guy named Sam Armstrong, who was extremely wanted in Arkansas for cutting his wife and her boyfriend into lunchmeat.

"That closes the book," Woodruff said. "A detective in Jonesboro named Crego sends his thanks. He's had that case around his neck like a yoke for two years. Him and his partner, a guy named Fullerton. Said they knew it was Armstrong all along, but it looks like he went on the bum to hide out." Rather/Armstrong turned up from time to time, Crego had said, through just the kind of misdemeanor fingerprint checks that had caught him out in Rozette. He just knew the system, it looked like, knew he could risk a few days in the bucket, then be gone before the background panned out.

"The whole thing makes sense, just like he told Ray that night," Woodruff said. "He just got trapped here by the cold. Too cold to hitch a ride or hop a freight out. He must've been on the dodge long enough to know he could risk a few days on a misdemeanor, before the ID on the prints came back. A felony pinch, though, like for the woman, and he'd of got his ticket punched clear back to Dixie."

That put a whole new wrinkle on things, since any dirtbag looking over his shoulder at the electric chair would surely never surrender. Unless the guy was just plain tired of running, which seemed entirely plausible to Bartell. In any case, he decided more emphatically that he should apologize to Culp. Bartell didn't know why he didn't just do it, but he didn't.

Chapter 7 □ □ □

By the first of March, Bartell had made up his mind to break up the partnership. He didn't know how that would go down with the rest of the guys on the street, splitting with someone like Culp, who had always been popular and respected, and who was now heroic to boot. It didn't help that Bartell himself saw those same qualities in Culp.

But he had to do something. All through the shifts he worked with Culp, Bartell wore those few moments at Corso like a straitjacket. When he worked alone, he felt naked. He wasn't sure which was worse. Maybe a break with Culp would lead him to some middle ground.

It would be easy. You make partnerships, you break them.

Happy trails, pard.

That's the ticket.

Bartell could have done it, if Captain Bud Haller hadn't met him and Culp at the door one afternoon with a smile on his face and a song in his heart.

"Sit down, boys," Haller said, leading them into his office. He smiled toward the two straight chairs against the wall beside his desk. His smile made Bartell want to check the chairs for electrodes.

Haller looked about three sizes too big for his desk. One wall, a long window, fronted the general area of the station, so that anybody who wandered through could see that you were in The Captain's Office, a situation that always proves to be about as enlightening as striking a match on the gates of Hell, since you are either in trouble or sucking up to prevent trouble, both inflammatory circumstances for the sincere young policeman looking to mind his own business. Culp and Bartell took a dose of humiliation when Juju Watson strolled by the window, grinned, and pointed down at his crotch, then mouthed a kiss at them. Luckily, Haller was looking the other way; he might have thought Watson had a good idea.

Bartell wasn't sure why they were kneeling at Haller's throne. Hell, maybe they were about to suck up and didn't even know it. The victim's always the last to know. The only escape from Watson's brand of harassment was to draw the curtains, but Bartell was afraid that if Haller did that, he'd feel buried alive. Better to be mauled in semipublic.

"You know, boys," Haller began, still smiling expansively, "a lot of the boys think their old captain's like a mushroom." Haller paused and gave Culp the expectant look of a man who's just fed somebody a straight line.

"So?" Culp stared back at Haller, not about to give him any encouragement. *Feed a snake*, Culp thought, *take care of it, pet it, be nice to it, and give it a home and it'll still haul off and bite your ass.*

"A mushroom," Haller repeated. "A captain's like a mushroom. Don't you get it?"

"You mean they're fat and full of air and go *plop* when you step on 'em?"

"No!" Haller roared. His neck began to swell and he raked his fingers through the thin gray hair that he combed from low on his skull and balanced gently over the top. "I mean lots of guys think a captain's like a mushroom 'cause he sits in the dark and feeds on bullshit!"

"Oh," Culp said flatly. "I guess there's that, too."

"It's a joke." Haller rubbed his right index finger between his collar and neck. His watery blue carp eyes were brimming with ambushed dignity.

"Oh," Culp said again, reflectively. "Sure. A joke, Ray." He aimed a wandering eye at Bartell and winked. They both started to laugh, something they hadn't done at the same time in the same place since the shooting.

"Culp, you are a shitheel."

"And you are—" Culp started.

"The captain," Haller reminded him with noble good humor. "And no matter what they tell you, son, it's a lot nicer on the top of the heap than under the bottom of it. And you know why? Because shit always rolls downhill."

"Unless it floats," Bartell said.

"Yes," Haller said, searching for his misplaced dignity. "Well. Enough of this rude scatological humor—"

"What?" Culp hated to give Haller enough line to spit the hook.

"Shit jokes. Enough of that. I've got something in the mill for you guys. And believe me, I'm not sitting in the dark on this one."

Bartell was far enough down that he decided to take Haller on faith, though God knew that faith in any of the big shots around the Rozette P.D. was a pretty delicate item. Maybe for a change the captain would be half right . . . or half sane.

What Haller had was a proposal. The duo had been an item of primo interest to the local news hounds lately, what with Culp's daring rescue of his partner from death at the hands of the Depraved Rapist and Killer. That was to be expected, given Rozette's size and the scarcity of police shootings in these parts. People are bound to be interested when the local boys in blue start trading bullets with the baser elements. Until now the department had done a decent job of shielding Culp and Bartell behind press releases. Helen Bartell had clipped out the two or three stories that ran in the *Free Independent* and filed them away in her recipe drawer, as if newsprint could age into fine parchment in the manner that rotten milk matured into cheese.

But Bud Haller's proposal was of a more distressing chemistry.

"You guys know Quentin Davies, right?" Haller asked, dredging a pack of cigarettes from a desk drawer crowded with multifarious vitamins, dietary aids, and other assorted death preventatives. Haller tapped out a smoke and twirled it from finger to finger in his right hand before setting it on fire.

"Quentin Davies," Bartell said, tensing back a grin. "Isn't he the owner of a pro football team in California?"

"I thought it was a prison in California," Culp said. "Got to have something to do with something in California, it has such a hip ring to it."

"Culp," Haller said, "your wit is exceeded only by your sense of humor . . . whatever that means."

Quentin Davies was the news anchorperson for KROZ-TV, one of the two stations in Rozette. According to Haller, Davies had pitched an idea for an hour-long documentary on Bartell and Culp, an extravaganza of sincerity about the rigors of police work and the bond that grows between partners. Ordinarily, this would have been an easy punch to duck, but Davies had started with the mayor and worked his way down, and by the time it landed on the wide-open chins of Culp and Bartell, it was a real knockout.

"Who does this guy think he is?" Bartell said. "Geraldo Rivera?"

"Actually, he's more the Barbara Walters type," Haller said, connecting for a change.

"And who's picking up the tab for all this nonsense?" Bartell couldn't imagine anybody laying down cash money for such a lame-brained idea, the story of two hick cops who had filed a miserable specimen of Homo sapiens under *C* for *Corpse*.

"A federal grant," Haller said. "What else? Some kind of community service thing, killing a dozen birds with two stones, if you get my drift. Hell, I don't know, I don't even care."

"We don't have to put up with this shit," Culp said.

"The chief thinks it's a good idea," Haller explained. He sounded very enlightening.

"We don't need this bullshit at all."

"The assistant chief thinks it's a good idea—"

"I'll file a goddamned grievance—"

"The detective captain thinks it's a good idea—"

"I'll own this city—"

"And I think it's a good idea."

"—my attorney—" By then Culp was so wired he could hardly talk.

"What are we supposed to be," Bartell said, "cops or TV stars?"

Haller shrugged innocently, "I didn't know there was a difference. You know what they say."

"No," Paul Culp said. "What the fuck do they say, Bud?"

Haller cleared his throat majestically. "Birds of a feather come home to roost."

Quentin Davies probed his salad with a knife and fork. He was the only guy Culp had ever seen who attacked raw vegetables with the solemn ferocity most people save for meat. Davies was in his late twenties, nearly ten years younger than Culp. His dark, wavy hair was prematurely thin, but the spaces were filled in artfully by a blow dryer. Culp had seen Davies on KROZ News several times, though he was never a regular viewer. Davies was the kind of guy who impressed you with his articulation, with the poised way his blue eyes fenced with the camera, with his cutting sophistry. Quentin Davies was the kind of guy who would be surprised that a guy like Culp knew a word like *sophistry*. But then Davies was a guy who would have trouble believing that anybody else knew anything.

"You two guys have become something of a local legend." Davies pressed a napkin to his lips, then wadded it up and dropped it onto the excavated salad. He glanced around the sparsely crowded restaurant, as though anticipating recognition. Most people who are unused to the company of cops feel strangely, intensely watched when they tag along with all that leather; you sense it in the way their eyes get the heebie-jeebies and you know they're just itching to jump up and shout to everybody that they haven't done anything. Davies, though, seemed acclimated to the heat of eyes warming him. "I hope I'm not embarrassing you."

"I can live with it," Bartell said. The role of humoring Davies had fallen to him, since Culp's conversation up to that point had been rendered in a series of animalistic grunts. Bartell shuddered to think how Culp would come across on a sound track. *Caveman* came first to mind. Bartell wondered if he should inform Davies that the taciturn Culp had once uttered the longest epithet ever to cross the lips of an English-speaking person: *Goddamnedhippiescrotebagsonofabitchfilthymongreldog.* Now that would be a real piece of investigative community service journalism. Bartell smiled in spite of himself.

"What is it?" Davies asked, brushing imaginary dandruff from his shoulders.

Bartell waved him off. "Community service," he mumbled, clipping off a smile. "Just warms my heart, that's all. Right, Paul?"

Culp made another caged noise deep in his chest.

"Well, we've got lots of bucks on this one," Davies said. "Big bucks, and the station's giving me lots of time. That's money, too, you know."

Davies planned to spend three full shifts with them, starting the next week.

"You'll need a full week?" Bartell tried not to sound anxious one way or another.

Davies nodded, a gesture that made his carefully balanced hair quiver like a helmet of blackberry jelly. "I hope so. I wanted more, but your captain put a lid on things. I might ask you guys for a little more after that, to fill in some blanks. But I won't know about that till it happens." He sipped carefully from his cup of herbal tea, then made some notes inside the leatherette notebook beside his plate, "An hour is a lot of air time. I just hope the week will fill it."

"You'll be in the car with us?" Culp asked. It was the first time since meeting Davies that Culp had managed to formulate a complete sentence.

Sometimes, Davies told them. Sometimes he and the film man would be in the back seat of the car with them; others, they'd tag along in KROZ-VAN-6. In any event KROZ-VAN-6 would always be close by, in case the cops . . . er, officers . . . needed the back seat of their car to transport somebody to jail. They did that sometimes, didn't they? Take people to jail? Yes, of course they did. That's what police work was all about. Conrad Stark was the film man. Jerry Hoerner drove KROZ-VAN-6.

"And we run the show," Culp said.

"Absolutely," Davies agreed.

"None of this eyewitness news bullshit," Culp went on. "We tell you to clear out, you clear out. You got to understand most of the time nothing happens, but there's lots of times when something *could* happen."

"I know." Davies sounded almost giddy.

"I ain't kidding around about this," Culp said sharply. "I don't care what kind of deal you cut with the department. I got enough troubles on this job without one of you guys getting hurt on me. Or me getting hurt on account of you being in the way. Get in my way and I'll feed you that camera one piece at a time and then I'll start with the van."

"I accept that," Davies said crisply.

"He accepts that," Culp said.

"Yeah, that's what I hear," Bartell said.

"You guys are terrific," Quentin Davies said. "Look, I know you were just involved in a bad scene, a really bad scene. Hell, if it weren't for that, I wouldn't even be here. But still, this isn't a big city with murderers behind every lamp post. We all know that. That's the point. That's the way I pitched it to the funding people when we checked out the grant. Everybody knows what it's like being a cop in a big city. They see that every night on television. What we're after here is grassroots police work. What it's like being a cop in a smaller place. This is community action television." Davies started slapping the tabletop gently with his hand for emphasis and Bartell began to feel as though he and Culp were an audience, cannon fodder for the big Q.D.'s ego. "We want a real story, that's all. Realism. A real story about real cops in the town we live in."

"Where you from?" Culp asked.

"Pennsylvania," Davies told him. "By way of the University of Montana J School down in Missoula."

Culp nodded and sucked at his mustache. Bartell felt smug, but not too smug. He wasn't from Rozette, like Culp, but at least he was from Montana.

"What does that matter?" Davies asked.

Culp waved him off.

"Who's going to see this?" Bartell asked.

Davies leaned forward confidentially. "It'll be run on KROZ, of course, since those are the people I work for. But just between the three of us, I think I've got my finger on the pulse of a bigger market . . . a *much* bigger market."

"A network?" Bartell said the word innocently enough, but instantly felt as though he'd entered into a conspiracy.

Davies only smiled brazenly and said, "We'll see."

Bartell looked over at Culp, whose face was turned toward the window. It was amazing. In the space of a few hours, the two of them had been pulled back kicking and screaming from the brink of a breakup and now they were about to become, if Davies could be believed, part of a tradition. No longer would they be just a couple of guys who shared the same car and the same grief for twenty short hours a week. Now they were partners. *Partners!* Like Coke and Cola, bullets and guns. Drug and addict.

"So it's set. We start the first of next week," Davies said.

"What do you think of that?" Bartell nudged Culp with his elbow and forced a smile.

"I think this whole goddamn business eats shit," Culp said.

"Love it!" Quentin Davies said. "But you'll have to tone it down a bit for the local broadcast. We can edit some, but too much editing makes a pretty rough copy."

Culp turned away from the window and brought both eyes, the wandering one and the true one, to bear on Bartell. "Great steaming *piles* of shit."

"Is he like this all the time?" Davies asked Bartell. He looked as goggle-eyed as Culp.

Bartell thought about Davies's question more seriously than he would have expected, and then he said, "Yes." And then he took a last swallow of cold coffee and he and Culp slid out of the booth and left Quentin Davies with the check.

Chapter 8

□   □   □

Quentin Davies looked like a million bucks in his L. L. Bean parka, his aviator glasses with the bright, nonprescription lenses, his wide-brimmed safari hat cocked rakishly over his right eye. Culp and Bartell stood with their haunches against the front fender of their freshly washed and waxed police car, watching Captain Bud Haller do his imitation of a policeman for Davies and his cameraman, Conrad Stark. The three were filming a lead for the pending Culp/Bartell saga, tentatively titled *Brothers in Blue.*

". . . Yes, Quentin, we're all extremely proud of Paul Culp and Ray Bartell. Their professionalism is the standard of this department, as is the professionalism of all our officers."

"Don't he look good?" Bartell said quietly to Culp.

"Medium rare," Culp agreed. "With American fries and Texas toast."

The interview was taking place on Ross Avenue, near the front of the police station, rather than at the more frequently used back door. That way, the back door of Nails Hogan's retreat for gentlemen wouldn't interfere with the view. Bartell figured that decreased the likelihood of retakes, since the camera wouldn't have to stop if somebody happened to fall out the alley door of the Cloverleaf and deposit his liquid lunch, in one form or another, on the multicolored snow. You can't be too careful with cinematic values, you know. The sky was a putrid, late winter gray, the ground still frozen under dingy slush, save for the occasional section of brown, matted grass littered with cigarette butts and chewing gum wrappers.

"Haller still looks like a detective," Culp said, reaching for his Copenhagen. He was referring to the not-so-distant past, when Bud Haller had been boss of detectives. There were all kinds of rumors about why he'd come back into uniform. The one concerning his dealings with a certain spouse of a certain plainclothes officer was the most vigorously denied. "It's an aura they get," Culp said.

"Police shootings are rare in Rozette, Captain Haller," Davies prompted, then shoved the microphone back under Haller's considerable chins.

"We live in a good city, Mr. Davies. This is a city of solid people, who have a healthy relationship with their police department. And we like to think that the department itself is to some degree responsible for that. People here, as a rule, know they don't have to shoot first and ask questions later; they know that when a policeman shows up, he'll be levelheaded and fair."

"Yet Paul Culp and Ray Bartell found themselves called upon to make that ultimate, split-second decision."

"It's the kind of thing," Bud Haller solemnly intoned, "none of us wants to be faced with."

"Yes," Quentin Davies said, turning squarely into the camera, "the kind of thing no policeman desires, but all must expect. They were checking out-of-the-way places . . . late at night . . . doing their job. It's the kind of job that sometimes forces upon policemen the undeserved rap that all they do is drive around doing nothing between too frequent and too lengthy stops at a favorite restaurant. But on this night . . . a cold, typical night in Rozette, Montana . . . Paul Culp and Ray Bartell found fear, injury . . . and death . . . waiting for them in the shadows of the Corso Lumber Mill. But the story doesn't end there. In a way their story only began that January night in the snow. Because there . . . in that split second of danger between the boredom of routine patrol and the helter-skelter of interviews and reports that followed . . . Officers Paul Culp and Ray Bartell found something much more important . . . they found a special feeling of comradeship . . . a comradeship shared only by those rare men . . . who have put it all . . . on the line."

With that Davies twirled the mike on its cord and let it drop to his side. He turned and shook hands briskly with Bud Haller. Conrad Stark stood up behind his tripod and massaged the muscles in the small of his back.

"I don't think I'm going to like this," Bartell said.

"Go with the flow, son," Culp said through his teeth, his eyes wandering wildly. "Go with the flow."

Conrad Stark was a gum chewer. He wore a New York Yankees cap mashed down over the wild bushy red thing he called hair and he chewed gum absolutely without pity for any living creature that might have to ride around with him inside a police car.

"How do you hold that camera still, son? All that chomping and what," Culp asked Conrad Stark when Stark popped another cube of Hubba Bubba between his punishing jaws.

Conrad Stark answered, but it was impossible to understand what he said.

"This man is an absolute genius," Quentin Davies said. "Graduate of the USC film school. An artist with videotape. He could have made a real name for himself in Vietnam . . . but of course the war ended before he graduated."

"Maybe El Salvador," Bartell suggested. "Lebanon." If you really want to be famous, there's never a shortage of wars.

"Low public interest, low exposure," Davies said. "Times change."

"Nicaragua."

Conrad Stark shook his head.

"The trouble with reporting all these current wars," Quentin Davies said, "is there's no clear public sentiment on who ought to win."

"Sounds subtle and complex," Bartell said.

"Incredibly," Quentin Davies said.

Culp offered Conrad Stark his Copenhagen, but Stark shook his head and blew a huge bubble, which burst and hung like pink skin over his raging beard.

Bartell looked over his shoulder at Davies, who sat splendiferously behind Culp. Conrad Stark peeled the gum from his beard, fed it back into his mouth, and busied himself tinkering with the object of his genius. Behind their car, the plain white KROZ-VAN-6 followed, a large, bland mechanical dog at heel.

City mechanics had removed the screen from the car that Culp and Bartell would use, so that the back seat could easily accommodate Quentin Davies and Conrad Stark and their equipment. The inside of the car was also clean, the rubber mat vacuumed and scrubbed, all the dust and cigarette ashes wiped from the doors and dash, the seats rubbed clean, and the inside of the windows polished free of smoke film. All in all, it was a revelation: police cars didn't have to be honey buckets.

Mitchell's Maggots had been briefed earlier on what was up with Culp and Bartell and their star machine on wheels. "Don't fuck around" was Tobe Mitchell's dictum on the whole dazzling affair, a sentiment shared by no lesser lights than Captain Bud Haller, the chief of police, and the mayor himself. Such counsel from the top, while not especially elegant, was probably the best that anybody could have offered.

Privately, Culp and Bartell were told that Davies and Stark would spend about four hours a night with them, at various times during the shift, for the next week and a half. Their guidelines were maddeningly simple: Davies and Stark were to be given a good story, but not exposed to any risks. Nor would any fuck-ups be exposed to Davies and Stark. Everybody was glad that the two coppers had volunteered for such a dangerous assignment. It was truly above and beyond. If the department believed in giving out citations, Bartell and Culp would have been first in line to draw a pair. Of course, citations are strictly unheard of, since all of Rozette's policemen are equally above and beyond, and to recognize some would only offend others.

"You understand," Bartell said to Davies, "we could ride round for a long time andnot have much going on."

"We're aware of that," Davies said. "But you're used to this kind of work. I imagine things that seem routine to you guys will have quite a bit of film value to us."

"I'm not talking about routine. I'm talking about nothing. Really. Just nothing. Just driving around."

"Don't be so negative, Ray," Davies said, squirming in his seat. "I'm up for this. Really jacked. This is going to be first class. You just watch."

That was how it all began, with Bartell's apprehension, Davies's mania, Culp's brooding silence behind the wheel, and Conrad Stark's jaws going *chomp, chomp, chomp.*

And it continued that way. For nearly thirty minutes.

Then, at about 4:30 p.m., they were dispatched to an alarm at one of the banks, Rozette National, on Townsend, two blocks east off Defoe. Culp accelerated slightly in the rush-hour traffic, but didn't get especially excited.

"Aren't you going to go?" Davies asked, leaning over the front seat and talking into Culp's ear.

Bartell was surprised that Davies had picked up the dispatch, since it usually takes several days of listening before people are able to comprehend police radio gibberish. It was possible, though, that Davies spent a lot of time listening to a radio scanner at his office, the better to pick up stories with, my dear.

Culp glared over at Bartell, silently instructing him to educate Mr. Davies in the facts of life.

"It's a screw-up at closing," Bartell explained. "We get three or four a day, when places open, when they close. A clerk screws up the alarm sequence. That's probably all it is. In six years I've had maybe half a dozen good alarms."

"I know," Davies said impatiently, "but you can't be sure, I mean one hundred and ten percent positive, that that's what it is. Shouldn't you at least turn on your lights?"

"Look at the traffic," Bartell said. He tried to explain that with everybody bumper to bumper, the lights wouldn't help that much, since nobody had anyplace to go to get out of the way. If anybody got hurt while a police car was running hell-bent for election through all that traffic, then the cops would be responsible. Period. "We aren't going to put people at that kind of risk for a job like this. Hell, we're only four blocks from the bank anyway."

"Sure. I guess not." Davies slumped back in his seat and sulked. "Did you get that, Conrad?"

"Get what?" Culp said.

"That brilliant exercise in bureaucratic flim-flam."

"Got it," Stark said. *Chomp, chomp, pop!*

The camera had been so quiet Bartell hadn't known he was being recorded. Now he felt as though he and Culp were being blackmailed with their own good judgment. He turned to explain further that even if the alarm were legit, you didn't want to make a dramatic arrival and panic some criminal, make him stay inside the bank with a bunch of citizens. Losing federally insured cash was one thing. Hostages were something else. Unfortunately, Bartell wasn't allowed to explain this theory on bread-and-butter police work.

Bartell first heard the siren, a thin wail like a fine wire between his ears, as Culp was jockeying for position at the light on Rankin at Defoe. A second later he could tell that the siren was approaching from the south on Defoe, and when he looked to his right, he saw the red and blue lights streaking across the Defoe Street Bridge, parting the bumper to bumper traffic like a Red Sea of squealing brakes and wrenched sheet metal. Deputy Chester Boyles smiled and waved as he blew the red light in front of them, not a foot from their bumper—on *Bartell's* side of the goddamn car! Bartell had his retirement speech all set.

"I think it's the big one," Chester said over the radio.

"You hear that!" Davies shouted. "Get that, Conrad!"

The tape was already rolling.

Culp swore, then hit his own lights and siren and punched the gas.

"*Stupidgoddamnedassholelamebrainedshitheadbastardidiotfool!*" Bartell was too busy to count letters, but he was fairly certain Culp has just broken his own world record for a single-word obscenity.

"Keep rolling, Conrad, we can edit that later!"

Snap crackle pop!

By now Culp was acting out of pure self-defense. Bartell watched the cross streets, calling out when it was clear for them to pass, but by the time he could shout "Go!" Culp was already gone.

Bartell looked over at his partner, but his view was blocked by Conrad Stark's camera, which intruded between them like the snout of a mechanical hog.

They caught up to Boyles within a block of the bank, and when Chester whipped into the empty parking lot behind the bank and spun his car through two complete three hundred and sixty degree spins before skidding to a stop on the ice, Culp was right on his ass.

A middle-aged man in a gray suit walked slowly toward them, picking his way through the slush. Culp and Bartell got out of their car, and when Bartell looked to his left, he saw Chester Boyles leveling a shotgun at the man in the gray suit.

"That's Walter Grimes," Quentin Davies said. "I met him when I did a story on interest rates."

"Hands over your head, dirtbag!" Boyles shouted.

"I work here," the man said lightly. "I'm a vice president."

"I said reach!" For emphasis, Chester raked back the slide on the shotgun.

"Chester?" Walter Grimes said. "Is that you, Chester? For God's sake, it's—"

If God was watching, he was too entertained to intervene. Chester Boyles fired the shotgun into the air and the man in the gray suit dived into the slop.

Bartell heard the sound of skidding tires behind him and turned to see KROZ-VAN-6 drifting broadside toward them.

Duck . . . look out . . . son of a bitch . . . Noooo!

There was a second blast from Chester's shotgun, which drilled a wild pattern of oo-sized holes into the side of the van. Jerry Hoerner dived out the door, his hands clinging to sky.

"Cut!" Quentin Davies called.

Conrad Stark popped another bubble and Bartell caught himself reaching for his gun.

An hour later Culp and Bartell found themselves once again in Bud Haller's sanctuary. It had not been a pretty sight. Two police cars had caused four car crashes and sent a beer truck through the front window of Finch's Fireside Lounge, which started a near riot once the patrons realized that the end of the rainbow had just come crashing down at their feet. All this for a response to an alarm that anybody with half a brain knew was false. A shotgun had been fired twice for no damned good reason. A respected bank official had ruined his suit and his health and was, at that very moment, talking to his attorney. A television van was filled with buckshot holes. No, it was not a pretty sight at all. And it was all on videotape, thanks to the absolute genius of Conrad Stark.

"Cop's gotta take chances," Chester Boyles had said later for the camera. "I thought of all them innocent women and children in that bank there and I just didn't have no choice."

Bud Haller slammed his fist on his desk. "What in the goddamned hell did you people do out there?" Sweat oozed from the folds of skin that framed his eyes. Haller's glasses kept sliding down his nose, and he continued to jam them back into place with such force that Bartell was afraid he'd knock himself unconscious and he and Culp would have to answer for that, too.

Culp tried to explain that they were only trailing in the wake of Chester Boyles, trying to keep tabs on the wreckage, so to speak, but Bud Haller was too wound up to hear any of that.

"It was sooooo goddamned fucking simple," Haller said. "Just drive the car, Paul. That's all you had to do. Just drive the car. Write a few tickets. Oh, sweet bleeding Christ! Now you've got the chief nervous as a whore in church."

Bartell wondered out loud if that meant they'd be calling off the whole dismal mess.

"What a lovely idea, Officer Bartell." The light of angels flickered briefly behind Haller's eyes. "There's only one problem. Mr. Quentin Davies and his keepers have the whole catastrophe on tape. And you know where that videotape is now? I'll tell you where it is, Officer Bartell. It's wrapped right . . . around . . . my . . . nuts!" Haller stopped to catch his breath.

"I guess that means we're still movie stars," Bartell said.

Haller glared at Bartell, then his lips began to twitch. "Chester really did all that?"

"It was the goddamnedest thing you ever saw," Culp said.

"I was his training officer, you know," Haller mused. "Ten years ago, when he broke in with the city and I was still working the street. It was like riding with a stick of dynamite. Ker-fucking-boom! And Walt Grimes in the muck. The prick. He turned me down for a loan one time. I'd love it, if I didn't have to be the captain,"

Bartell had never seen Haller go soft before. There seemed to be a long-buried core of good humor trying to burn through the sludge. It was, however, soon smothered.

"You've gotta haul Davies and that other worm for *two* weeks," Haller said, "That's the new deal. No questions asked, no backsliding. Your job, Officers Culp and Bartell, which you have accepted, is to make sure that son of a bitch doesn't want what he thinks he wants, and then give it to him. You got that?"

"Simple," Culp said, reaching for his jacket.

"Exactly," Bud Haller said. "So simple it makes my teeth hurt."

It was an attorney's wet dream. Walter Grimes was suing the sheriff's office and Boyles, while Boyles was suing Rozette County, Sheriff Riley Salk, and the county commissioners for trying to fire him, a gesture that would exhaust the law enforcement agencies in the area to which Chester might extend his invaluable services. The city filed cover-your-ass charges against Rozette National for not clearing the ice from the parking lot and for failing to train its employees—vice presidents included—in the proper and established alarm procedures. In the meantime KROZ and the *Free Independent* threatened counter suits that had something esoteric to do with freedom of information regarding the videotape, and a man who rented a fifth-floor office in the bank building was hauling everybody's butt into court because nobody wanted to pay for the huge thermo-pane window that Chester Boyles destroyed with his warning shot. The city wouldn't pay, because police department personnel on the scene had the good sense not to fire any shots, no matter how badly they wanted to shoot Chester Boyles. And the department itself had demonstrated good faith—to say nothing of good sense—by canning Boyles over a year ago and now he worked for the county. The county wouldn't pay because Chester Boyles had screwed up, which made it his own personal lookout. Chester Boyles, through his attorney, said that the bank should pay because it was their alarm. Rozette National wouldn't pay because Walter Grimes should have stopped walking when Chester Boyles told him to, especially since the tape revealed that Grimes knew it was Boyles on the business end of the shotgun, and anybody who knew Boyles knew what that meant. And Walter Grimes wouldn't pay because he'd ruined a four-hundred-dollar suit and suffered a close brush with death at the hands of a lunatic masquerading as an agent of the law and he didn't think it was fair, not a goddamned bit fair for him to pay one red cent. The only thing anybody knew for certain was that the country club would be holding special membership elections once all the lawyers' fees were collected. Somebody suggested that all parties join in a suit against God for negligence in creating the day. But they couldn't find a volunteer to serve the papers in Heaven. Maybe they should conscript Chester Boyles for that errand, somebody— rumor had it that it was Riley Salk himself—suggested, but the suggestion was quickly withdrawn. The papers would scorch, along with Chester's vile carcass, before he got within pissing distance of Paradise.

"You want to be careful about these things," Tobe Mitchell counseled Bartell and Culp when they got together early one morning for an emergency post-shift session over brains and eggs at the Cloverleaf. Tobe daubed a glob of gray matter in the yellow yolk and shoveled it into his churning mouth, then squirted more ketchup on the eggs and hash browns. Bartell felt the bottom drop out of his stomach, Culp stirred an ice cube into his coffee, then leaned his head against the Paris green wall and closed his eyes.

"These assholes'll bury you," Tobe said, choking momentarily.

And just how, Bartell wanted to know, were they supposed to be careful, when Davies and his camera seemed to draw trouble like shit drew flies.

"I'll see to it you don't get sent on hot calls," Mitchell said, conveniently ignoring the fact that cops usually don't know which calls are hot until somebody strikes a match. Hell, the Rather shooting, the source of all their grief, was proof enough of that.

"I don't like it," Culp said. "I feel . . . Christ, I can't even tell you how I feel. Just kind of sick, I guess. Raped."

"Look," Tobe said, growing uncharacteristically serious as he spread grape jelly on his toast and mopped it through the remains on his plate, "you guys've had your backs broke with this thing. And I mean the shooting, not all this other horseshit. And I won't try to shit you it'll get better."

Culp squirmed in his seat and raked his hand through his mop of hair. His wandering eye seemed to have settled on the door to the card room behind Tobe, while the other fixed on Tobe himself. "So you're saying because we did our job, we shouldn't go on doing our job."

"I guess so," Mitchell said. "I don't know. I've never shot nobody. Never been shot at myself. I'm just—"

"I've killed guys before," Culp said in a surprisingly casual way. "In Vietnam—"

"Then you should—"

"But I never had my face rubbed in it. Not like this, not in public."

Bartell felt as though he were standing before a door that had just cracked open. "So what are you saying, you saying you think I put you through this shit on purpose?"

Culp took a deep breath and shook his head. "It was a fluke." He shifted an eye to Bartell. "Christ, how do you think we'd both of felt if I wasn't there to do it? It could just as easy have been the other way around. I mean, shit, that's the one part of it all that helps."

Helps, Bartell thought. Helps what? "With that kind of help—" he started, then stopped when he saw Culp's wandering eye start to pull into focus on him.

"You saying you don't think it's a help, being alive and all, like you are now?"

"No, you're right," Bartell said. "It'd be pretty bad if you hadn't been there." He felt like a little boy, trying to explain some delinquency for which a friend had paid the price.

"You're out of your goddamned mind," Culp said.

Bartell heard himself start to laugh.

"Look," Tobe said, "it's been a long time since the cops hit somebody in this town. The administration is all concerned about a bad PR rap. That's what this whole thing's about. You know that."

"Sanitizing me and Paul, you mean," Bartell said.

"You're goddamn right," Tobe said. "I think it sucks, but I don't have an answer. You'll just have to get through it. Everything don't have a solution." Mitchell squirmed into his coat and reached for his wallet. "All I know is you guys are good cops and I don't want to lose you."

"You're embarrassing me," Culp said, before Bartell had a chance to say the same thing.

"Tough shit," Mitchell said over his shoulder as they walked out the back door and across the vacant police department parking lot. "There ain't no solution to that, either." With that, Tobe Mitchell cocked his hip and farted.

"Jesus Christ, Tobe." Culp backed away. "I ain't had my shots this month."

"You could charge admission for that one," Bartell said.

"You boys be careful," Tobe said, limping toward his pickup.

And so for the next two weeks, Bartell and Culp did as Bud Haller had ordered and Tobe Mitchell advised. They drove around with their hands discreetly covering the proper place. They wrote a few traffic tickets, shepherded the bums around the freight yards, and waved at the drunks at bar closing. Fortunately, the world cooperated with their ruse, presenting them with two weeks of nearly unsullied calm. If he smelled a rat, Quentin Davies never mentioned it. He sat quietly in the back seat, prompting them with questions as the hours dragged by and they cruised the city, like moths dodging a thousand tiny hidden flames.

Chapter 9

As he pulled away from the last stoplight in Kalispell, Culp looked up into the rearview mirror and nursed the swelling in his lower lip. No matter who she was married to, Glenna still had a mean mouth and a roundhouse right to match. Culp had driven over again to see his boys, but this time the boys were in Seattle with Roger for a Sonics game.

"This Roger, he's quite a fellow," Culp had said to Glenna. At first she wouldn't let him into the big cedar house any farther than the vestibule, but even from that remote vista, it didn't take a genius to see that Roger wasn't exactly on the slide. The TV that sat about half a mile away at the far end of the sunken living room was bigger than the bathtub in Culp's flop over Lucky Brisco's.

"You should call first," she said. "You always come bouncing in and I never know. It's no wonder the boys are never around."

Glenna was a leggy woman as tall as Culp, with jet-black hair that was just starting to turn salty. Though her hips had filled out from carrying the two kids, she still had a gangbusters figure. She was about a 9.5, Culp decided. But an even 3 if you knocked off points for congeniality and charm. Near the end of her term as Mrs. Culp, Glenna had taken up aerobic dance. Culp had halfheartedly wondered at the time if she was getting herself in shape to make a move. That day in Kalispell, she looked like she hadn't stopped moving since. She wore black wool slacks, a gray silk blouse, and jewelry, gold jewelry that rippled like damp fire against her breasts.

"I was thinking," he said. "Maybe I could come in for some coffee . . . a beer, maybe. It's a long drive over."

"This is a modern town, Paul. We have restaurants for that sort of thing. And taverns, too. But of course you know all about those."

"It's a long drive back." He hesitated, unsure of how much to tell her about the past weeks. She knew about the shooting from news reports and from his last disastrous trip to Kalispell nearly a month ago. But he hadn't really talked to her, told her how he felt about the whole thing. He hadn't talked about that to anybody; he didn't have anybody who would listen, "I won't take a long time." He looked down at the cobblestone floor and felt, with quiet surprise, humiliated. "I won't get out of line." He was still more surprised when she accepted.

The house was even bigger than it looked from the street, a multistoried palace that worked its way down the side of a hill. From the living room, where Culp sat waiting for Glenna to serve coffee, he looked out over the roof of a lower wing. The roof was covered with cedar shakes. The leading edge of each shake had been painted green, resembling moss. Through the late afternoon winter dusk, a grove of blue spruce rose up toward the house from the coulee below.

"Kenny and Pete will be back tomorrow," Glenna said, placing a pottery mug on the glass table at Culp's left hand. The table separated the two matching wing chairs in which he and Glenna sat.

"They drive over?" It seemed odd that the boys would be out of town on Wednesday, a school day.

She shook her head. "Flew. Roger has a lawyer friend who owns his own plane."

"That can be pretty tough, a private plane in the winter, the kind of weather we get out here."

"It's a big plane. A twin, with a pressurized cabin. Weather's no problem. We all—three couples of us—flew in it to Mexico over Christmas. It's very nice."

Culp looked around the room as he thought about flying in a private plane to Mexico to escape the cold. He wasn't usually one to notice a job of interior decorating, but in Glenna's place, you just couldn't help it. The room was done in white, with red and gold accents. The pure white carpet was nearly ankle deep, yet a bright rug covered the carpet between the two wing chairs and the deep white sofa across the room. Behind him, the huge windows opened on a view that seemed to stretch all the way to Canada. To his left a fire simmered in a fieldstone fireplace.

"All along," he said, "back when we first busted up, I thought Roger was just some DJ in Idaho."

"He was. I never lied to you about any of that."

What she had left out, though, was that Roger was a DJ on his father's radio station, and now his father was dead. These days Roger could afford to live far away from the family's three radio and four TV stations. Culp was surprised Roger had to mooch an airplane off his friend. One thing was sure. Roger's bankroll could buy a lot of aerobic dance, and from the look of things, it was worth every ounce of sweat that had ever glistened on Glenna's well-tanned skin.

"Maybe I should have called." It made Culp's guts feel like twisted wire to admit that Glenna could be right about anything. "It was just a spur of the moment thing. Guilt, I guess, maybe. I never got to talk to the boys since all that mess at work."

"If you'd just called, we could have flown them down for a weekend." Glenna stared distractedly out the window.

"I work weekends."

"I forgot." She etched the nail of her little finger along the line of her lip.

Both Culp and Glenna ignored the fact that Roger had taken the boys out of school for a basketball game.

"Anyway," he said, "I got no place to put them up. Except with Pop."

Glenna sighed and started to squirm.

"Don't worry," Culp said. "I didn't forget how you feel about that."

Staying with Culp's parents was part of what started the fight on his last attempt to see Kenny and Pete, Glenna had lived with Roger long enough to acquire specific ideas on what was a suitable environment for children, and neither a hovel above a junk shop, nor a rundown bungalow in Ragtown qualified. Culp might have visitation rights, but he didn't have an attorney who owned an airplane, so the threat of interminable hearings and rehearings forced him to get *along* when he would much, much rather have gotten *down*.

Across the room oil portraits of both Kenny and Pete hung above a low bookcase containing perhaps a dozen bronze figurines. Both of the boys wore their hair longer than Culp liked. Kenny's, in fact, was nearly as long as Harry MacDonaugh wore his over ten years ago when he and Culp worked undercover drugs. MacDonaugh was stabbed and nearly killed the same year Kenny was born. Kenny was the older of the two boys. Culp was back in uniform two years later, when Pete was born. He'd lived away from the boys for nearly six years. They barely knew who their father was.

"What time do the boys get back?" Culp took a sip from the mug, which was still hot. He rested the cup on his knee.

"Early."

"Maybe I could stop back tomorrow."

"They have to go straight to school."

"I could get a room. Come by in the afternoon."

"I'm sure you're too busy for that." Glenna stood up and straightened the crease in her wool slacks.

"We've had some great battles, haven't we, sweetheart?" Culp smiled at her as he stood. He'd known her for six months before they were married. Sometimes it seemed as though the marriage had never existed. There were days, though, when he was convinced it would never end, not until one of them was cold and stiff and underground. Maybe not even then. He looked at the portraits again as he set the mug on the table. It was as if he were looking at two versions of himself. Both boys were blond, like him. Both had a look that said they saw the world slightly out of whack. Culp figured they'd grow up like him no matter what Glenna did. It must drive her nuts.

"How come we ever got married?" he asked as he walked to the door.

"You got me pregnant. I can't believe you forgot that."

"Of course I remember." He felt as though he were walking on air. "But we still didn't have to get married. Not really. You know that. So how come we did?" He was walking ahead of her, getting the bum's rush. He didn't care.

"Maybe I was stupid."

"There's never been any doubt about that." He pulled up on the cobblestones and turned to face her.

That was when she unleashed the roundhouse right that caught him full in the mouth and he started to laugh. She drew back to throw another and he caught her wrist and stopped laughing.

"You're a bitch, too. But I never let that bother me."

Glenna spit at him and he pushed her against the wall and walked out. As he walked down the sidewalk he could hear her screaming after him. He didn't hear the words because he didn't care what the words were. They were the same words she'd called him before, the same words he'd used himself on more people than he could remember. He could still hear her when he got to his pickup, but he never looked back. He tasted the blood in his mouth and swallowed it. He remembered the gun under the seat of the truck. He carried the gun whenever he traveled out of town. Then he drove away.

What the fuck. Culp sat the bottle of Jack Daniels on the floor beside his chair and looked out the window at the mountains across Flathead Lake. The cut inside his mouth stung whenever he drank, but he figured that meant that the cut would be thoroughly disinfected by morning. The Swan range lifted high out of the dusk and into the sunlight far away across the flat gray water. He should go there someday, go into those mountains and see what they are like. Lots of places he should go someday and someday he'd go to every goddamn one of them. What the fuck.

After the bout with Glenna, Culp made it as far as a little town called Lakeside, which is about fifteen miles outside of Kalispell. He pulled into a bar called the Chalet. Every wide place in the road in Western Montana had a bar called the Chalet. In Eastern Montana they had bars called Stockman's. He bought the bottle, then took a room in a small motel on the lake. The motel was sandwiched between a marina and an apple orchard. From his window he could see the orchard, the lake, and the Swans. He couldn't see the marina, but then he didn't give a shit about boats anyway.

A bottle of Jack and a room with a view. What a life.

Culp took a last sip, then capped the bottle and set it on the nightstand as he made several well-balanced steps toward the door. He had had some drinks and now he was hungry. He remembered a café just across the highway from the motel.

If the café did any business at all, it was well past the evening rush by the time Culp sidled through the door. He settled into a booth out of the draft from the door and ordered a chicken fried steak. He was the only customer. The waitress hung around a heartbeat too long, wanting to talk. She was about thirty, in the last stages of being pretty.

"You look like you've had a long hard ride," she said to Culp.

"You might say that. Yeah." He stirred ice into his coffee and smiled up at her.

"Well, we all got 'em, I guess."

"What's that?"

"Troubles. We all got our share of those." She set the glass coffeepot on the table and put her hands in the pockets of her checked apron. "You from around here?"

He shook his head. "Rozette."

"You're a long way from home." She had what they used to call a button nose. Her hair was parted in the middle and worn long and straight in a style that had gone by the wayside about ten years ago. "You over here on business?"

"Pleasure," he said, running his tongue against the cut inside his lip.

"Made a few of those myself."

"What's that?"

"Pleasure trips to a torture chamber." She smiled and glanced back at the kitchen.

"My name's Paul." He stuck out his hand. She took it.

"Nancy." She shook his hand with more than a little strength.

"Paul and Nancy." He coughed and reached for his glass of water. He must be drunker than he thought. "Sorry."

"We close in about twenty minutes," she said, taking back her hand. "You were lucky. Another twenty minutes and you'd have had to go hungry. Or go back into Kalispell."

"Then I'd have been hungry," he said.

She smiled at him again, then busied herself filling salt and pepper shakers, getting ready to lock up. Culp heard the sounds of cooking from the kitchen. Probably made the cook madder than hell, having to warm everything up this late in the game. Well, that was just too damned bad. He watched Nancy bend over the tables. She had strong hips, but not too heavy, and the lines of her legs moved with sureness under her skirt. Sometimes, when she reached especially far, her hair fell across her shoulders and brushed the tabletop and when she stood, she brushed her hair back over her shoulders.

A few moments later a low buzzer sounded from the kitchen and Nancy brought him his food, but Culp didn't seem to be hungry anymore.

"It won't taste as bad as it looks," Nancy said. She stood at the end of the table, laughing. Her face didn't look nearly so tired when she laughed.

"It's not that . . ."

"I didn't cook it. You don't have to spare my feelings." She draped a towel over her shoulder and glanced expectantly at the empty seat across from him. "You mind?"

"Help yourself."

She sat down and they talked. She asked what kind of work he did and he told her he worked for the City of Rozette. He didn't tell her he was a cop. People always have cop stories and he liked her too well to take a chance on what kind of cop stories she might dredge up. Nancy was from Ohio. She used to be married to a guy who was stationed at the Air Force radar station at the edge of town. The station had been closed a long time now, and her marriage closed with it.

"He went to Spain," she said. "I was only seventeen when we came out here and I was only nineteen when he left."

"You passed up going to Europe?"

"He was going to send for me, you know? I was working here, saving, and he was getting ready to reenlist. That way the service would have moved me over. Then he got busted. After a big brawl at the bullfights and he stole a car when the cops came. Then he, ah, he was trying to get away and he ran over this little boy." She looked down at the table and gave up a small, tight laugh. "Well."

She'd brought up a cop story on her own. Christ, he was doomed.

"We got divorced while he was still doing time." She looked up and shrugged and chewed on her lip. "I'm sorry. None of this is really your headache."

"I'm sorry about your bad times." Culp hoped he sounded on the level. She was too nice a woman to string along.

"I haven't seen him since he got on a bus here in 1974." She thought for a moment as she took a sip of Culp's coffee. "He was a real bastard, anyway. I could've ended up stranded someplace a lot worse than here. I like it here."

"You could go home to Ohio."

"Who wants to be stranded in Ohio?"

"Kids?"

"Like I said. Who wants to be stranded in Ohio?"

They kept on talking while Culp pretended to eat. Somewhere along the line, the cook shut off most of the lights and shouted from the back door that she was leaving. Nancy didn't say anything back to the cook and Culp heard the door slam.

Culp wasn't sure just how it had happened that she went back to the motel with him. He sobered up as they talked and soon it was nearly midnight. Now he sat in the window of his room and listened to the shower. She wanted to shower to get the restaurant smell off her. He watched the low chop work at the ice that banded the lakeshore. To his right perhaps half a dozen deer wandered into the orchard and began pawing at the snow. He imagined that he could hear the water and the deer, but the night was infinitely silent. He was startled when Nancy leaned over his shoulder and kissed him. Her wet hair tickled his bare chest.

"I was watching the deer," he said. He pulled her around and onto his lap. She had wrapped herself in a blanket, which she opened and folded around his shoulders.

"They come down in the winter and browse the orchard," she said. She was warm and damp inside the blanket.

"Like Eve chowing down on the apple," he said.

"Exactly." She kissed him again and took his hand and placed it between her legs. "The thing you've got to remember about Eve," she said, "is if she had it all to do over again, she wouldn't change a damned thing."

With that Culp carried her to the bed and they busied themselves learning just what it was that the deer were looking for out there under the barren winter trees.

"You can drive all the way up the mountain," she was saying. "The radar domes are still there, even though they don't use them. I think there's still a microwave station or something still working up there. But that's all." She lay on her back and across her flat belly, Culp could see into the orchard. The deer were gone, pushed out by a fresh wind that promised new weather by morning. That was what got her to talking about the mountain. The wind. "You can see for miles and miles and when there's overcast, it's like a white blanket with all these mountains popping up through it."

Culp was unbearably sleepy. He hadn't enjoyed a woman as well or as long as Nancy in over a year. Now that the whiskey and his blood were on the ebb, his head felt as heavy as the mountains far across the lake.

"Don't you ever wish you were in Ohio? Back in your home?" He remembered what she'd said earlier about Ohio, but it seemed too unlikely that someone could abandon her home without a care, as Nancy said she had done.

"What's there that I need?" She turned on her side and faced him. Her breasts fell against his arm but he was too drained to be stirred. "Folks have split, brother's moved away, too. Nothing but fights, the memory of fights, and anticipation of the fights to come."

"What'd you do all that fighting over?"

"Things. Just things, that's all." Culp thought of Glenna.

"But you should be past that now. You're old enough to lead your own life."

"I know." With her fingertips, she traced the line of his eyebrows, nose, and lips. "And I'm leading it here." She traced his ear. "Leading it with you."

"You don't know who I am, do you?" He couldn't keep his eyes open.

"You're Paul. You're a good lover. Is there something else I'm supposed to know?" She continued tracing.

He wanted to tell her who he was. Not that he was someone special, just *who he was*. That was all. Such a simple little thing. Tell her he'd shot a man and now he felt bad about it. Nothing, really. Just say the words. Words he could say to anybody, except that he couldn't say them to anybody, but he wanted to say them to her, say that and everything else, except that she kept tracing his features and he was too tired to speak. He started to lift his head, but she told him to be still and he drifted away.

When Culp awoke a moment later, the room was light and she was gone. Her scent was still in the bed, but her place was cold. On the nightstand he saw a glass with a quarter inch of whiskey in the bottom and a quarter moon of lipstick around the rim and beyond that the orchard was bright under several inches of new snow.

Culp sat up and without hesitation reached for his pants beside the bed. He pulled out the wallet. At last he hesitated, remembering her hand on his under the blanket, the power of her hips and the gentleness of her fingers afterward as they lay talking. Then he checked the wallet.

Nothing was missing.

She'd told him the way to the old radar station, and he found the abandoned gray buildings without difficulty. He drove on past the lower area and headed up into the mountains, past several cabins and trailer houses tucked away in the trees. After several narrow switchbacks the road opened out into a broad hanging valley and on the floor of the valley he could make out under the snow a wide beaver pond, with a thread of open water meandering across the expanse of snow-covered ice. The valley was perhaps a mile deep and then the road pitched upward again in a grove of enormous firs.

The road was plowed but snowpacked and when Culp turned into the first corner after the firs, the truck fishtailed. He stopped, got out, and engaged the front hubs so he could use the four-wheel drive, then went on. It was snowing and ahead he saw the belly of the overcast, which finally engulfed him as he drove on through a series of long grades for another eight or nine miles up the side of the canyon. Finally the road leveled out somewhat along a divide, before steepening in one last assault on the peak.

Just before the road crested out at the locked gate of a chain-link fence, the overcast cleared and Culp was momentarily blinded by the sun reflecting off the clouds below.

Lord God, she was right. Snowy peaks sixty or seventy miles away reared through the clouds and all below was a cold gray cauldron. Above him three radar domes squatted like white mushrooms beside a low tan blockhouse. The snow was stacked seven or eight feet high along the road and the trees were sparse and gnarled and laden with snow. Nancy said sometimes the clouds . . .

Nancy said . . .

Culp had a vision of himself, a scared little man checking his wallet in a lonely room, and his eyes stung and the wallet felt like fire on his hip.

Chapter 10

The premiere, Jess called it, which made Bartell even more nervous. Jess was blond, like her mother, and she had Helen's knack for pointed commentary. Sometimes it seemed to Bartell that Helen had simply cloned herself, without his participation at all.

Bartell had been on TV once before, a short crime prevention interview a couple of years back. Lock your doors, draw the curtains. Leave a light on. That sort of thing. The basics. Nothing earnest, like get a Rhodesian Ridgeback trained to rip out a guy's balls on the way up to savaging his throat. Nothing truly sincere, like sleep with a .45 cocked and locked under your pillow. Just be careful. And then he picked his nose. Not really picked it, he insisted, as Helen and Jess sat in the living room and howled. Just scratched it. On the outside. But he did it in profile, on the side away from the camera, so the effect was disastrous. All the way up to his second knuckle, like he had the deepest nose in the world, the Berkley Pit of noses. That was what television got you. The sons of bitches.

The three of them sat in scooped, orange leatherette chairs inside the labyrinthine confines of KROZ and waited for Culp. Across the room Quentin Davies busied himself adjusting a video recorder and monitor.

The last few weeks hadn't been any great shakes on the home front. Because he worked the early night shift, it wasn't unusual that Bartell became a stranger around the house. Helen and Jess were both gone during the day, and he was already at work when they got home in the afternoon. But it had gotten worse since George Rather, when Bartell fell into the Great Silence, a silence which he supposed now was a subconscious effort to make others believe that everything was all right. The weather had been foul for a week, rain and snow mixed, which put a damper on his afternoon jogging, and his shoulder was still too crippled to handle workouts at the Lennox. So he moped around the house and ate. Toast. Breakfast cereal. Sandwiches. His belly felt like a mudslide creeping over his belt, but when he looked at himself in the mirror, he looked the same, not thin, not fat. Just the same old usual Bartell. On his nights off he sat in the front room alone, poring through old issues of *Sports Illustrated*, which Helen brought home from MacKenzie's office. (Christ, what kind of diseases oozed through those ragged pages after months in a doctor's waiting room?) Sometimes he caught himself staring at Helen as she ate, or washed the dishes in the evening, or dressed in the half-light for work, while he pretended to sleep. She reminded him of a person he used to know, or a person who used to know him years ago, before he found it necessary to learn other things, to become someone else. But what was it that he'd learned being a cop and studying *Sports Illustrated*? Reggie Jackson's batting average two years ago? The muzzle velocity of a .357 magnum at various loads? The texture of snow blowing under headlights on a deserted street? What good was any of that? Bartell remembered his grandfather, Milt Edmonds, during the years he spent with him over in Lehman City, Montana. Old Milt knew lots of things, too, but he couldn't tell you any of them. He just worked all day and listened to the radio in the evening and went to bed and did the same thing all over the next day. But what did old Milt really *know?* He never said, never told you how a man was supposed to settle. Cash couldn't tell you how it was done because he'd never settled himself. Neither had Bartell's mother. Was it in the blood, then, a genetic itch always out of reach? Or was the biology more crude, a matter of gray cells giving up the ghost until your brain decayed enough to give you a little peace and quiet?

"You ever wonder where you'd be if you weren't here?" Bartell had asked Helen one evening after she'd interrupted him in the middle of a dogeared article about last year's Super Bowl.

"I used to pretend I lived on a houseboat," she said. "On a tropical lagoon."

"With some hot dog, I bet," he said. "Some guy like Tom Selleck, with a big mustache and a hairy back."

"Maybe yes, maybe no," she said, snuggling down next to him on the sofa. "It's good for you to wonder."

He had wanted to tell her about his own daydreams, but he couldn't remember what they were, it was all so confused, the house and job, Jess, who was getting so old now it terrified him. If he went on the bum, what photographs would he take along?

Then he realized that he wouldn't have any to select from, since the family didn't own so much as an Instamatic. So the next day he bought a pocket camera and shot up half a dozen rolls of film, driving everybody around the house nuts, before he finally put the thing away.

Paul Culp showed up alone for the screening. He wore mud-blotched khaki pants and a faded GI field jacket with an Airborne patch on the shoulder. When Bartell said hello, Culp only nodded, then smiled at Jess, punched her on the shoulder, and called her Ace. Culp was subdued, even for Culp. He looked as though he hadn't slept for days.

"You maintaining?" Bartell asked quietly.

"Been to Glenna's," Culp said through his mustache. "Then I met this gal . . . discovered a mountain."

"I'll bet." Bartell chuckled and was surprised to see that Culp was serious.

"When's it gonna start?" Jess said, squirming in her seat on Bartell's other side.

"In a minute," Helen said, exasperated. "It'll start in just a minute."

"In a minute, in a minute," Jess mimicked sarcastically. And in an aside to her father "See? She's always—"

"Enough!" Bartell snapped. Maybe he was too aware of Culp, who sat pitched forward, as if balanced on a thin, sharp wire. Bartell wasn't about to referee a mother-daughter shouting match in public.

Quentin Davies rescued the moment when he turned and faced them. Davies looked surprisingly harried. His slate-green knit tie was jerked loose from the collar of his pale-green shirt. His scalp glistened through the gaps in his hair.

"Remember, these are just rough cuts," Davies told them. "There's no continuity or anything, no voice-over by me. Just raw tape. I wanted you all to get an idea of what we're dealing with here." Then he switched off the lights from a remote control panel, started the tape and sat down. A few seconds later the dark screen jumped to life. Bartell listened to himself explaining why they weren't foaming at the mouth to get to the infamous alarm at Rozette National Bank.

Culp: *"Look at that stupid shit!"*

(The picture swings wildly past the back of Bartell's head and settles erratically on Chester Boyles's car as it leaps off the bridge.)

Davies: *"What's he—"*
Bartell: *"Chester. Holy Christ, it's Chester."*
(The image bounces and sways as Culp turns in pursuit. The soundtrack is cluttered with excited voices and engine noises, sirens. Shifting focus . . . surprised faces, traffic, fury.)
Boyles: *"On the ground, dirtbag!"*
(Boyles lays a shotgun over the hood of his car. Walter Grimes. Grimes gestures with his hands, his voice too faint to hear.)
Boyles: *"I said on the ground!"*
(Boyles again, shotgun at forty-five degree angle. Puff of smoke, distant, toylike sound of a shot.)
Culp: *"Goddamnit, Chester!"*
(Grimes: prone in the slush. Then, in a crouch, Bartell, left hand on the fender of the car. The frame jumps, sweeps to the white van, jumps again with second puff and pop, fades out with zoom in on Bartell's gun hand.)

"Who was that?" Jess asked.

"A maniac," Paul Culp said.

"Was it really a stickup?" She was almost breathless. "You never told me about any stickup."

"No." Bartell put his hand on her knee and squeezed for her to be quiet.

"You never—"

"It wasn't a stickup. Just watch now." After a pause the screen was active again.

Bartell: *"There's one. See him . . . in the weeds behind the shed."*
Culp: *"Might as well move him before it gets dark."*
(A bum laying on the ground, line of green and red-brown boxcars in the background.)
Culp: *"Get up."*
Bum: *"What's wrong now?"*
Bartell: *"Lemme see some ID, pard."*
Bum: *"Got a food stamp card. Food stamp card enough?"*
(Bartell takes the card, shows it to Culp, then leaves the frame.)
Culp: *"Can't sleep here, Kermit."*
Kermit: *"Can't stay no place."*
(Culp points to a sign on side of shed that says "No Trespassing.")

Culp: *"Gotta hide better, stay outside the city. Spokane's that way."*

(Culp points, presumably westward, down the tracks, toward Spokane, Seattle, Japan.)

Kermit: *"Ain't no fuckin' jobs. Bulls don't want you on the trains, then you guys . . . Fuck, I don't know . . . what's a man s'posed to do?"*

Culp: *"I don't know, Kermit. I don't know . . . just don't do it here."*

Kermit: *"Who're them guys?"*

(Kermit points at camera and squints.)

Culp: *"TV folks. They're makin' a movie,"*

Kermit: *"Movie of this?"*

Culp: *"You got it, Toyota."*

Kermit: *"Crazy. Whole fuckin' world's fuckin' nuts."*

(Kermit takes a step toward the camera and bends forward.)

Kermit: *"Lookin' for some kinda freak show?"*

Culp: *"Take it easy, Kermit. This might make you a celebrity."*

Kermit: *"Fuckin' perverts."*

Culp: *"I said settle down."*

Kermit: *"I guess I ain't s'posed to say that . . . can't say that with that thing here."*

Culp: *"What's that?"*

Kermit: *"Fuck. Can't say that . . . can't say . . . that word . . . on television."*

Culp: *"I don't give a fuck, Kermit. Say any fuckin' thing you want."*

(Kermit straightens up again and spruces his gray hair back over his ears. The two men wait for Bartell to return. Artifacts: old socks and gloves, bread sacks, wine bottles, potato chip bags, cigarette butts, tin cans, ashes from a campfire, plain white cans that say BEER. Bartell enters the frame, hands over the card.)

After the scene with the bum, there were two more similar incidents, along with four quite ordinary traffic stops. Bartell felt Jess squirm. He looked at his watch: Seventeen minutes. Davies would have to write Pulitzer-class copy to salvage this mess. Bartell found watching bits and pieces of his job even more boring than doing his job. He decided he wouldn't need an agent. Then another scene appeared, a scene filmed after dark with an existing light inside the car, the camera moving easily from Bartell to Culp and back, their faces, seen in profile, alternately exposed and hidden in the shadows from passing streetlights.

Bartell: *"Nice night out."*

Culp: *"Early spring. Yeah. I'll take all of this they got."*

Bartell: *"You want me to drive awhile?"*

Culp: *"It's okay. This seat's not busted down like some of the other cars. My back's okay tonight."*

Bartell: *"You seen that Jeep, the one Skinner bought?"*

Culp: *"He should've waited till after the divorce. Now it's community property."*

Bartell: *"I learned to drive in a Jeep. Old surplus job belonged to some ranch my old man worked on."*

Culp: *"My old man used to get off the day shift at Corso, load me and my little brother up in this big old green Buick he bought third hand. Go fishing."*

Bartell: *"Yep."*

(Pause.)

Culp: *"Over on the Joseph River up toward the log camp at Bittercreek."*

(Pause.)

Bartell: *"Good country."*

Culp: *"Road wasn't paved any then. No traffic. He'd let me sit on his lap and steer. Then when I got older, he'd get out at one hole, let me take the Buick on up to the next, and wait for him. Scared my brother to death. I couldn't hardly reach the pedals or see over the dash. But he'd stick it in low and let me drive that big old car anyhow . . . get your ass arrested for a thing like that now."*

Bartell: *"You remember the first time you shifted into second gear?"*

Culp: *"Oh, hell yes . . . yeah . . . it was like—"*

The screen went blank and Quentin Davies switched on the lights. "Sorry about that last," he said. "The tape ran out on you, Paul."

"Flying," Bartell said, turning to Culp, who looked as if he'd been sleeping. "You said it was just like flying."

Culp nodded. "Like growing wings." He remembered floating through the snow down the mountain above Lakeside that morning. He'd looked for Nancy at the cafe, but she wasn't there and the old battle-ax behind the counter wouldn't tell him where he could find her. Hell, he didn't even know her last name.

"When're you gonna teach me to drive?" Jess said.

"Someday."

"Movie stars," Helen said good naturedly. "I won't even be able to get you to do the dishes now."

"You do the dishes?" Culp said.

"He didn't pick his nose," Jess said.

Quentin Davies laughed uneasily. "I think you can see what we're faced with here." He turned his chair around and faced them confidentially. "This is pretty much the best of all we shot. I ran it by my producer and the funding people this morning. Then called the chief. They, uh, we—"

"You're shitcanning it," Culp said, shrugging an apology to Helen for the language he'd used in front of Jess.

"Well, not exactly." Davies and crew had over twenty-five hours in the project, and time being the money that it is, nobody was willing, exactly, to can the whole works. But an hour, well, an hour is a *long* time. A very long time, practically forever. Especially when you have to rely on fate to supply the action and move things along. Davies went on: "You know, this adjustment is no reflection on the story we set out to tell, the story of you guys, what you did, the way you work. It's just that—"

"It's a boring goddamn job," Culp said. "We told you that from the start."

"You both seem obsessed with bums," Davies said.

"It's our job. Not to let them homestead," Culp said. "It takes up a big chunk of our day."

"Oh, I know that," Davies said. "And don't think I'm not sympathetic. It's just that on film—"

"On film they look like thugs," Helen said.

"I didn't say that."

"That's okay, Quentin," Bartell said. "Sometimes it makes us feel like thugs, too. Everybody wants the sidewalk clean, they just don't want to know what the broom looks like. That's part of what cops get paid for. So people don't have to know."

"It wasn't just me," Davies said. "Your own chief, I think, had in mind something with more positive values."

"Sure," Bartell said, reaching for his coat. "Everybody has his résumé to consider."

"There was one piece of luck, though," Davies said. "I went to J school with a guy who lives down in California now. I dubbed a copy of the tape from the bank alarm and sent it to him. It looks like one of the big departments down there—West Riverside— will be using it for a training film. Staging that kind of realism would have cost them a fortune. Not bad, eh?"

"So where does it go from here?" Helen said. Jess had gotten up and was examining the video machine.

"Well," Davies said, "Conrad and I shot quite a bit of tape over at the mill, where the shooting took place. We'll open with that as general background. About two minutes. After that we've got some stuff—what you saw, plus some more, really just more of the same—but it's not a bad mix. Nuts and bolts stuff, plus the human interest bit you saw there at the end, if there's time. Lord, we're buried in human interest."

"I thought that's what you wanted," Helen said.

"Oh, of course. Absolutely. It's just that it has to have balance, too, to move. We think what we have will work just fine, now that we've altered the magnitude of the project. We want to use it in our regular community affairs slot . . . a fifteen-minute slot early on Sunday morning."

"Will you do any more filming?" Bartell asked. He felt both relieved and diminished.

"Nothing on location," Davies said. "But we'd like to set up a time for you both to come back down here to the studio. For interviews. To help with the character and time aspects."

"Why should they?" Helen said. Even Culp was surprised by her tone. "I can't sleep nights because all Ray does is toss and turn and mumble in his sleep. Jess walks around the house on pins and needles because she's never sure if he'll blow up. He and Paul have both been used enough."

"We never meant—"

"Sure you did. You. The department. It's just another line."

"I think that's a little unfair," Davies said. "The chief himself— "

"The chief wants things to look good," Helen said. "The chief wants smiling policemen guarding crosswalks. He doesn't want wrinkled uniforms and rolling in the dirt and shooting people. He doesn't want people to see his policemen talking to guys who might be a bad influence on teenagers."

With that, Helen walked out of the room, taking Jess with her. Fifteen seconds later Bartell, Culp, and Davies were still staring at the door, when Helen came back.

"My husband and his partner aren't thugs," she said to Quentin Davies. "There's no reason why they should spend a minute explaining that to you or anybody else."

Then she left again for good.

"Let me know if you want to trade her in," Culp said.

"I guess that's a wrap," Bartell said to Quentin Davies, then followed his family and partner outside.

Chapter 11

□   □   □

The snow banked higher and higher along the road as Bartell drove deeper into the mountains, and it was still snowing. He spotted the lights from Bittercreek logging camp around the bend just ahead. He'd worked there once or twice before for Ike Skinner, so he knew the terrain and the routine. After getting through the locked gate, he drove to a large shop, where he pulled his truck in out of the weather, then went into the adjoining office and turned on the lights and heat. Then he went back to the truck and carried in a jug of coffee and a stack of magazines.

The camp was owned and operated by Corso, the same old and honorable company that had slapped a lock on its Rozette mill and, along with it, the town's future, adding nearly seven hundred ex-employees to the rolls of prospective vandals at the company's remote operations. Bittercreek was situated at the end of a narrow blacktop road along the Joseph River. There were several dozen houses along the road to the camp, mostly small prefabs and trailers. No matter how you cut it, though, the camp was isolated. That's the reason Corso liked having a guard around at night.

"You've got to forget about it. Just forget it." That was what Helen had said earlier, just before he left the house. She was talking not just about the shooting, but the newly unveiled television spectacular starring Officer Paul Culp and Ray, his rescued sidekick. Bartell assumed that Helen had started the discussion because he was not behaving well. Successful wives, he thought now, see behind all your faces.

"I know what you'll do," she said. "You'll go out there tonight and sit by yourself and brood until you fester."

"Never hurts to have an active mind." Bartell tried to smile, but his face didn't feel like he'd succeeded.

"Unless your mind runs in circles." That was her answer. "When a dog catches his tail, all he does is fall down."

"Is this the beginning of your well-being lecture?"

"I know what it is, why you can't let it go." Helen's acumen and practicality were legendary; everything had to mean something, and by Christ she knew what it was. "You think if you can learn all about some one thing, take it apart and put it back together, learn it inside and out, it'll give you some sort of special power regular people don't have."

"That's crazy." He couldn't believe it. A woman who knew she knew it all had just accused him of trying to know too much. "Really crazy."

"You're telling me."

"This is the well-being lecture. I knew it. Son of a bitch."

"You're not the one who has to live with you when you get morose like this."

"Consider it therapy." Bartell opened the door to leave and the cold wind backed Helen away. *Focused Gloom*, it's called. Something they developed in Vienna."

It couldn't hurt, could it? To spend the night out and shake off the town smell. Town. That's the place where people melt you down and cast you into something that fits their needs. And where you let them. Bartell thought of his father, who had made a life of breaking horses and telling people to go fuck themselves. And here was his son Ray, diddling away the night on the company dole. Instead of breaking horses, he felt like he'd been trampled by one.

Bartell rubbed his eyes and reached for the coffee. He was stuck in the camp until five a.m. A lot of cops worked night watchman after they retired, since their pensions wouldn't come near to supporting them. Nights like this could consume Bartell's future, and here he sat already, glancing at a tail that waved in the corner of his eye, thinking about that tail wagging there while he tried for all he was worth not to start chasing. Maybe Helen was right, maybe his being wasn't exactly well. He leafed through an old *Field and Stream* and tried to maintain his balance.

Bartell pulled his red mackinaw closer around his shoulders and debated turning up the heat. Outside the office snow filtered through the light of mercury lamps. Beyond the compound the Joseph River elbowed its way from one side of the dark canyon to the other. People everywhere, except in suburbs, have a habit of calling their home God's Country, as though God had some ridiculous need to state a preference and settle down. But those few people on the Joseph could have a point. Bartell smiled as he remembered talking with Culp about learning to drive while Culp's old man fished his way through the lessons. As he let his mind wander, Bartell realized that he couldn't tell if he was remembering the real conversation with Culp, or the film they'd watched yesterday with Davies, the conversation Davies would probably dump because it was only human interest and because that idiot Conrad Stark couldn't chew gum and keep tape in his camera at the same time.

Ray Bartell and Paul Culp, immortalized together on the silver screen. If Bartell broke up the partnership now, he'd look like the biggest jerk in the world.

Bartell tried to focus his attention by studying the compound, which was jammed with white and blue logging trucks, over a dozen, and several buildings, also white with blue trim.

All right, Officer Bartell, man of a thousand answers, what does being a video vaquero have to do with a real badge and a real gun? With real death? Expectation, perhaps. Expectation coupled with a need to understand what it is that scares the piss out of you when you drive alleys with the lights out hours after everybody's gone to bed and then a guy steps out of the middle of nowhere right next to your door and you wonder what he's been up to out there in the dark. Expectation and need, motives so common he'd forgotten them until that night at Corso, when he'd looked down the barrel of a gun and there they were.

You could ponder these weighty questions forever out here in the great woods, shut up in a strange building at the heart of a cold storm. Ah, the thrill of life on the cutting edge of masculine sentimentality, that particular spot where a freezing river runs forever through the exact center of the night.

Bartell pulled on his red-and-blue-plaid Scotch cap and a pair of gloves and left the office for a fast tour around the compound. It was nearly two in the morning and the snow hadn't slacked off at all since he'd arrived four hours before midnight. Snow had drifted nearly to the hubs of the logging outfits. He tried all the doors on the blue and white buildings and found them locked. He walked the ten-foot chain-link fence and looked for unusual tracks in the snow. You can't ever tell where people will come from. Think about things and plan forever, and what does it get you? How does it change anything? How does contemplation stop a gunshot from inside a car on a traffic stop you only made because you were pissed off at your old lady and wanted to give somebody a bad time? Can reflection ever divert a man from stepping up to you in the snow?

Bartell tried to stamp the cold out of his feet and recalled watching the video yesterday. Now, standing here shivering under a roiling black sky, he felt preposterous, as though he were only posing as a policeman.

"We looked so improbable," he'd said to Helen that evening at dinner.

"What's that mean?" Jess asked.

How do you explain the obvious? That was one of the tougher knots of raising a child. "It means Paul and I don't look like what we are," he said finally. "Or like we really aren't what we're trying to look like."

"Oh," Jess said. "Maybe we should move to California. I bet it's more dangerous there." She nodded confidently as she chewed her food. "Ka-pow!" She fired her finger at him. "Then you could be real cops. Like on TV. Ka-pow! Ka-pow!"

"Has she had her medication yet today?" Bartell said sarcastically to Helen.

"Your dad's a real policeman now," Helen said, "He's going to be on TV, isn't he? That proves it."

Bartell looked at his wife and rolled his eyes. Of course, he knew now that if he didn't want to crash headfirst into the well-being lecture, he'd have to learn to keep his mouth shut.

Jess shook her head and looked confused. "But people don't get shot all the time here. That's what I mean. It's not *dangerous*."

"Dad told you about the man a few weeks ago. You saw the TV thing with us yesterday."

"Sure," Jess said. "But . . . you know."

"She's as crazy as you are," Helen said. "I just don't understand this whole bit with danger."

That was the point, wasn't it? Her question was his answer. Still, it didn't make him particularly comfortable to have a twelve-year-old call his bluff.

Bartell slipped into a shadow between two logging trucks and stood with his back to the wall of the tire shed and looked out across the cold, white camp, where nothing moved.

At five a.m. Bartell bundled up again and pulled his truck out of the shop. He saw another pickup parked just outside the gate, out of view from the office. Bartell checked the gate and found it locked, though tracks in the fresh snow indicated that someone had tried to enter the camp during the night, sometime after two o'clock, when he had last been outside. Bartell unlocked the gate and walked through. He wrote the license number of the truck on the palm of his hand and noticed that the driver's window was down, despite the weather, and an empty beer can sat on the dash, along with five or six country and western cassette tapes.

Bartell followed a set of tracks through the snow. The tracks led away from the truck, across the hard road, and into the dark trees. For a moment Bartell stood on the crown of the road. Then, feeling the shoulder holster thump like a heartbeat against his ribs, he slid down the far bank and headed through the woods toward the river, following the tracks.

He heard the thin sigh of the Joseph drift up through the trees and the beam of his flashlight bounced onto clear, untrampled snow just past a large fir. Bartell stopped and swept the area with light, wondering what could have happened to the man who made the tracks. His neck started to tingle.

Then he turned and saw, without warning, the dark figure slumped against the trunk of the fir.

"Hey!" Bartell said once he'd caught his breath. "You okay?"

The man, who wore a heavy brown canvas coat, didn't answer.

"Wake up!" As hard as he could, Bartell hit the sole of the man's cowboy boot with his flashlight. "Wake up, bud!"

"Whaaa . . ." The man groaned and lifted his head slightly, very slightly.

"Wake up."

"Betty Jean . . . that you there, Bet. . ." The man tried to focus his eyes on Bartell. "Hell, you ain't Betty Jean."

"I'm not Betty Jean." Bartell played the light back and forth from the man's bearded face to the cold, limp hands on his lap. "You can't sleep here, bud. You'll freeze your ass, you sleep out here."

"Screw you, then," the man said. "Betty Jean . . . best goddamn jitterbug in Montana."

"Come on. You'll freeze."

"Hah!" The man probably worked at Bittercreek and was just getting a head start on the day.

Bartell shut off the light and shrugged. He took a step back and thought of Helen at home, sleeping, her arm perhaps reaching across an empty bed while here he was, freezing his ass off while he passed the time with a drunk out here in the middle of God's country.

The man began to snore. Bartell stepped away and turned toward the river.

Then he stopped and reached inside his mackinaw and pulled out his gun. He turned and leveled the gun at the sleeping man.

In the moonlight, amplified by snow, he could barely make out the sights on the gun. The man was just a blurred figure in the background.

That was the way they'd all look if you used your sights properly, just a blur in the background beyond the muzzle.

Bartell shuddered. He heard a high, distant ring in his ears and the gun dropped to his side of its own tremendous weight.

Bartell wedged the gun back into the shoulder holster and started for the river again. He'd coax the drunk back to his truck in a few minutes. Right now he wanted to take a look at the Joseph, which sounded like heads of grain rattling in hot, steady wind.

Chapter 12

□   □   □

Spring. The days lengthened, the sun seemed to take forever finding its way completely into the sky. Low, broken clouds hung against the mountains like a ragged T-shirt. Culp looked over at Bartell, who, as usual, was driving. Neither had said a word in the hour since they'd cleared from briefing. In fact, they'd hardly spoken since the Quentin Davies show aired over three weeks ago.

After months of winter and early darkness, it suddenly struck Culp as strange to see evidence of daytime life around him.

Children waved for fun instead of because they needed help.

Dogs barked and nobody cared.

Nobody was drunk.

Because it was spring, Rudy's Tires had gone into the business of selling boats, too, parking a pair of Yukon houseboats on the lot. All of the car dealers had flags set loose in the breeze and bare-bones prices smeared on the windshields of cherry used cars. Bicycles were thick as fleas, reminding Culp of a picture he'd seen once of a street in Beijing, curb to curb with a million Chinese clattering around on bicycles. They drove past a McDonald's on the Rankin Strip. Knots of kids hung around the lot. Girls brushed their hair, using the mirrors of cars, while boys leaned on the fenders and smoked cigarettes. Red and blue and yellow and green cars. Colors. Everything had color in the daylight, color faceted by intermittent rain beaded up on new wax jobs. Flashy pickups with roll bars and fog lamps. Camaros. Z-cars and Trans Ams. These kids, where in hell do they get the money? Burglary, probably. Selling drugs.

Bartell turned off on a side street and drove along the brown, swelling Holt River. Culp watched a long cloud slink over the top of Bride's Canyon and settle like a long flat gray cat into the valley.

How was it that spring always happened? They'd been lost on nights and now it was April and night was delayed. Rain smudged the mountains in just about any direction you cared to look, but for now, it was not raining on Paul Culp. He lowered the window and sniffed the air, which was warm and fecund. He wouldn't need his leather jacket until after dark.

Bartell was trying to think of something, anything, to say when they got a call. Ambulance and Fire rolling to 480 Harkins. Heart attack. No life signs. They were less than five blocks away.

This was no bogus alarm, no Chester Boyles special. Bartell kicked it in the ass and bottomed out the car on the first humped intersection he crossed, hoping to Christ that the ambulance, or at least the fire truck, got there first.

But he and Culp were first on scene. Bartell let the overhead lights run to mark the right house, then ran ahead of Culp across the soggy lawn to the stucco house in the middle of the block. He heard the fire truck's siren and saw the lights a couple of blocks away.

The door was locked. Bartell pressed the bell with one hand and pounded on the door with the other.

Just as Bartell was gathering himself to kick in the door, a young man wearing large glasses pulled it open. "I think he's dead."

"Where?"

"Family room. This way." The man pointed, Bartell and Culp followed quickly through the house.

The man lay flat on his back in the middle of the room, still and thick as the furniture.

"He's my grandfather," the young man said. "He just passed out a minute ago, he said he was feeling fine."

The man on the floor appeared to be in his late seventies. His head tilted back. His mouth was open. His eyes were open and unblinking. Bartell felt his throat for a pulse. The skin was still flaccid and warm, raspy from the trace of beard that glistened like frost. He found no pulse, but the man's skin wasn't blue yet. Bartell felt the trachea gurgle against his fingers.

The siren stopped. Bartell looked up at the young man with glasses. "Go tell them it's a code blue." The man started back through the house. "Step on it!" Bartell shouted after him. Then, "I got the chest." He started to look at Culp for approval, but finally ignored him.

"Airway's good." Culp knelt beside the man's head. "Go."

"One . . . two . . . three . . . four. . . five . . ."

Culp held the man's nose between a thumb and a forefinger and breathed into his mouth.

" ... one ... two ... three ... four ... five ... "

Culp breathed again.

" ... one ... "

The firemen dumped their gear on the floor across the man's chest from Bartell and one of them unwrapped a long pale green plastic tube. He attached one end to a mask and an air bag, and the other to a small green oxygen bottle. He adjusted the oxygen flow, then pressed the mask over the man's mouth and nose so that they could ventilate him mechanically. With that, Culp got to his feet and moved aside.

" ... four ... "

"Pupils look bad," said one of the fireman.

"You don't have to count now," said another fireman, looking at Bartell. "Not now we got him bagged."

"I can't get a pulse yet," said the first fireman.

... *two* ... Bartell kept counting to himself, to keep the rhythm correct.

Bartell settled into a routine and the room grew quiet as everyone waited for the ambulance. He bent over the man and applied firm, rhythmic pressure to the rib cage just above the solar plexus. From time to time the man's chest would growl under his hands and he would breathe one or two gasps on his own. Once he even lurched and the mask slipped aside. The man's breath smelled damp and cavernous, as though this special air had been stored inside his body for decades. His teeth had a dull, dry look that Bartell had seen too often before, a look he could describe only as useless. The fireman adjusted the mask and gave the bag two quick squeezes. Bartell began to sweat. Sweat rolled off his nose and chin and eyebrows in large drops and splattered over his hands and the man's red shirt. Bartell had the odd sensation that he was raining.

Intellectually, Bartell knew that sooner or later the man's ribs would break under his constant force, but he was unprepared for the first faint pop, a rib tearing free of the sternum with a distinctive snap that reverberated up Bartell's arms, through his shoulders, and down his spine.

Bartell heard a second siren, which was followed soon after by a racket from the front of the house, and a moment later he was surrounded by two ambulance technicians and the crew nurse. One of the technicians checked the mask and took over for the fireman. The other technician used scissors to cut away the man's shirt and immediately after that, Bartell placed his hands on the man's bare chest and the technician attached three electronic monitors in a triangle above them.

. . . five . . .

"Stop." The nurse touched Bartell's hands. "I want to check the monitor to see how he's doing."

Bartell straightened up and sat back on his heels. He stripped off his jacket and tossed it behind him. The air felt good against his bare forearms, which were glazed with sweat.

"Nothing," the nurse said. "Go."

Bartell leaned back over the man's chest. He felt a second rib give way.

The nurse was in charge now. "Let's hang an I.V., get some bicarb into him." Someone handed her a needle and Bartell held back momentarily so that the man's arm would stop tossing and she could find a vein. The nurse probed the man's arm with the needle and soon a dollop of dark venous blood ebbed out onto the man's arm and onto the floor and she attached a plastic tube to the needle. The other end was connected to a plastic bag filled with clear liquid, which a fireman held above them.

"You want a break?" Culp tapped Bartell on the shoulder. "I can spare you."

Bartell looked back at Culp, then down at the man's chest. By now the chest bore an indentation, as though Bartell's hands belonged there. He looked again at Culp and tried to focus on his face but his eyes wouldn't function properly. He could no longer associate voices with any particular face. Bartell shook his head and looked back down at his hands. To hell with it. He'd never stop . . . *three . . .*

The nurse touched his hands again and he stopped while she studied the monitor. "The bicarb's not working. Let's go with the lidocaine." A technician handed her another large syringe and she injected the drug through a port in the I.V. Several seconds later she stopped Bartell again and checked the monitor.

"He's fibrillating. We'll have to shock him."

"At least he hasn't puked yet. I hate it when they puke."

Bartell looked around to see who had spoken, but by now the room was crowded with people, including several who might be neighbors.

"Yeah."

The monitor emitted a low beep each time the man's heart pumped and Bartell tried to time his actions with the signal but soon realized that the monitor called out only when he leaned onto the man's chest. There was a high, thin whine as the defibrillator charged.

"What's his name?"

"Clear!" the nurse called out. Everybody pulled back from the man, even those who were not close enough to touch him, and the nurse rested a pair of plastic paddles with shiny metal surfaces on his chest. The man heaved up slightly and then settled back.

"Hold the bag higher."

"No good." The nurse glanced at the monitor. "Start CPR again." She looked at Bartell and blinked her eyes.

Bartell continued to work. By now his T-shirt was soaked and matted against the back side of the ballistic vest he wore under his uniform shirt. The vest, a flexible shell, trapped heat and each time he pumped, heat gusted up along his throat. His hands were wet and slick from the sweat that kept dropping from his face.

"Get ready to move him," the nurse said.

Just then a man dressed in black leaned over Bartell's shoulder and Bartell started to move aside and give him room.

"Go ahead," the man said softly, so softly that Bartell may simply have absorbed the words rather than heard them. The priest pressed a mark onto the man's forehead and spoke an indecipherable utterance of grace and then he was gone and they tried once more without luck to shock the heart back into its own rhythm.

"Time to go."

"Roll him over a little. That's it."

"I'm on the feet."

"The shoulders. Somebody get under his shoulders."

. . . four . . .

"Lift. There."

"Get him strapped down."

"Move it."

"Watch the I.V. It's tearing out."

Inside the ambulance Bartell braced his shins against a bench and the gurney and maintained his balance and his work while the ambulance swayed through traffic. The technician continued to squeeze the air bags and the nurse fought to keep the I.V. in place despite the constant movement. Bartell felt a curious sense of vertigo as he stood in the moving vehicle and looked occasionally ahead through the windshield.

When they arrived at the hospital, they lifted the gurney to the ground. An emergency room nurse stood across from Bartell. "I've got him now," she said and Bartell stared at her. "It's okay." She seemed to know what Bartell was thinking.

Bartell nodded. "Three . . . four . . . five . . ." he said aloud and stepped back.

" . . . one . . . two . . ." said the nurse as they wheeled the man inside.

Bartell stood alone in the parking lot. He sat down on the back of the ambulance and found a clean white towel in one of the cabinets. Bartell wiped his face and the back of his neck. He got a sudden chill, a cool breeze against his clothes all soaked with sweat. He got up and went into the reception area, where Culp was waiting after following along with their car.

"The thing is, Ray," Culp said as he drove away from St, Francis, "you got to decide if you're going to be a saint or a jerk."

"Like you?" Bartell said, before he could catch himself. After that it was one very long night.

The next day Bartell slept until well past noon and called in sick. A mental health day, he told himself. Getting in a car with Culp that night would be very bad for his mental health.

The man's name was Arthur Cartright and he was dead. Bartell supposed that he had been dead from the very start. After two cups of coffee Bartell managed to shoulder his fatigue aside. He changed into running gear and set out for the Holt River, where runners over the years had worn a trail along the south bank up into Bride's Canyon. True to its early promise, the day had turned off bright and warm. The air felt good against his bare, blanched legs as he ran, synchronizing his breathing, inhale, exhale on every third step. One . . . two . . . three . . . in . . . one . . . two . . . three . . . out. For a while he kept confusing his own rhythm with the earlier five-beat sequence on Cartright.

You always go wrong, trying to make sense out of things. In all the times Bartell had used CPR, the technique had worked only once, another time he'd been first on scene at a medical. That time it was a woman, who'd taken her percodan with Jim Beam chasers, trying to check out on her own personal cloud. Bartell found her on the floor of her basement apartment. No pulse, no respiration, the same sad old story. He'd started by himself, the same five-beat cadence, with the woman's drunken boyfriend trying to breathe for her, and Bartell without enough time to keep the son of a bitch out of his way. When the ambulance arrived a moment later the woman was alive again.

So how do you figure bullshit like that? A guy wants to live—and dies—and a woman wants to die, but somehow the magic works. Bartell looked down at his hands as he ran. He couldn't imagine being a surgeon, having life and death reside in those hands each time he did a job. He wondered if the magic ever stopped for such men. How could you live without that magic?

And that was the funny part about running, too, for since he'd taken it up five years ago, Bartell had learned more about how his body worked than he'd known before. Oh, he wasn't a fanatic, but he did his share of browsing through the appropriate magazines whenever he passed a stand in the supermarket. Diet and shoes. Those were the two big-ticket items in the running biz. And heart rate. Mustn't forget heart rate, since that was really the name of the game. Make the old ticker tick. Flushing the peanut butter out of his arteries, Bartell called it. Breathing in, breathing out. Hypnotic. Relax. One foot after the other. Let the ticker do its job, so nobody has to put his bloody hands on it, break your goddamn ribs. Was it a sign of prosperity when health became a hobby?

Bartell reminded himself to check Arthur Cartright's obituary in the next day or so, see who the man was.

After about half a mile Bartell broke a sweat, and soon after that he turned right just before the footbridge onto Leeds Island Park and struck the path east along the river. Considering the day, he was surprised not to have come across many other runners. The sky was a bare blue bowl over the mountains, the day dead calm. It must have been almost seventy degrees, though the temperature dropped significantly along the river, and the path was soft after rain the night before.

One after the other, left and right, out and back. Breathe . . . breathe . . . breathe.

Big . . . Fucking . . . Deal . . .

Hypnotic.

Bartell looked at his watch. He'd been out for thirty minutes. If he turned back now, considering his modest pace, the total distance would be about six miles. But it was always hard to turn back, like stopping the globe and restarting it in the opposite direction. As he approached a broad green bed of ferns, Bartell planted his left foot and pushed off back toward home.

Slowly the earth resumed its original plodding pace and Bartell knew he'd soon be back. Just keep picking them up and putting them down. Watch the river. The river is always good, the river pumps through the country like the rivers inside Bartell's heart. He passed a long cascade and tried to outrun the water, but the river never tired and he soon settled back into the shell of his own motion. The path was washed smooth by the rain. A set of tracks, his own, ran toward him down the center of the path and slowly, inevitably, Bartell followed them back, those footprints like miniature graves settled in the soft bare ground.

Bartell was just getting out of the shower when Helen and Jess got home. Jess had gone to a friend's house after school, and Helen picked her up on the way home from work. The house erupted once Jess walked in.

". . . and they've got a video game, too," Jess said, plunging forward into a brief handstand.

Bartell and his wife exchanged the standard courtesies. How was work? Good to have you home. What's for dinner? The basic amalgam of home life, which means nothing unless nobody bothers. Bartell settled into the rocking chair in the front room, the old part of the house. He drew his blue robe closer around his middle and reknotted the sash.

". . . and they're only three hundred bucks, Melanie says. So why can't we get one?"

"Because they turn your brain into rice," Bartell said patiently. It was his standard rejoinder to a long-standing argument.

". . . and they've got this new game"—Jess fell from still another handstand—"about World War II, with bombers and machine-guns and everything."

"Reducing World War II to a video game is pornographic," Bartell said.

"What's pornographic?" Helen called from the bathroom.

"Huh?" Jess said, her face once again upside down.

"Never mind," Bartell said. "If I have to explain it, you wouldn't understand anyway."

"You filled the bathroom with steam again," Helen said, straightening her plaid skirt, the new cotton one she'd charged that time she bumped the Visa over the limit last spring. "All the wallpaper's peeling off."

"That's life," Bartell said, wishing he hadn't.

"Watch this," Jess said. She spun through a series of cartwheels that carried her to the television set in the next room and she was quiet, as though someone had punched her Off button.

"That bad?" Helen asked. She sat across the room on the couch and tucked her legs beneath her on the cushion. They were, Bartell realized, in positions almost identical to those they had occupied when he told her about the shooting at Corso last winter. Their bad news mode, he told himself.

He knew that he could tell Helen about Arthur Cartright, if only he could get started. At first he laughed, feeling indiscreet. And then he told her, simply and directly, as he had told her so many things over the years. Just the facts, please. Thank you very much.

"We get people like that at the office," Helen said when he had finished. "People who could die, I mean." She'd worked at MacKenzie's medical office longer than Bartell had been on the department, so he wasn't unveiling any experience that was exactly new to either of them. It was just tiring.

"I'm afraid I'll never know when somebody needs it," Helen said. Dr. MacKenzie kept all his people trained in CPR, in case somebody dropped dead at his office. So far, though, Helen had never needed to try it out.

"You'll know," Bartell said. "You just take one look at the guy and the first thing that goes through your head is, Jesus Christ, that son of a bitch is dead. That's when you know." His legs felt heavy from the run, as though his feet were growing to the floor. "I want to go out tonight. All of us. I want to eat something spicy that I can taste."

Helen nodded and Bartell crossed the room and kissed her, placing a hand on her breast.

"Knock that off," she said, pushing his hand away.

Bartell went upstairs and dressed. On the way downtown he told Jess about what he'd done the day before. She wanted to know if it would be in the newspapers, like the shooting had been. She'd clipped out those stories and taken them to school. It wouldn't, he said, thinking of how Quentin Davies would react if you tried to fob off death by natural causes as news. It probably wouldn't even qualify as human interest.

They ate Mexican food and Bartell drank two bottles of dark Mexican beer. Helen drank coffee and Bartell glanced guiltily across the room each time he drank, beginning to worry that somebody on the department would see him out drinking when he was supposed to be sick. Before long even Jess was subdued. By the time they got home, the house was chilled and it was snowing outside, a nervous, spring breath of snow that hung in the air and never seemed to reach the ground, though the ground was turning white. Spring. Mountain springtime. Bartell stoked a fire in the woodstove, then sat down in an armchair and draped a thin wool blanket over his legs and watched television.

"I finished my homework," Jess said, anticipating the inevitable bedtime question. Grades were not a happy topic of conversation in the Bartell household. "Math. I did it at Melanie's." Bartell smiled. At Jess's age the only mathematics that truly interested her was the mathematics of a telephone number.

"I can't get her to take dancing lessons," Helen said after the girl was in bed. "We had a big fight over it the other day."

"You always have big fights." Bartell felt himself backing away. Sometimes it seemed like half the fights he had with Helen were over the fights Helen had with Jess. He didn't need to open a second front tonight. Not tonight.

"This was different," Helen said.

"Maybe she just doesn't like to dance." Robert Wagner and Stephanie Powers were laughing together as they drove through snowcapped mountains in their bright yellow Mercedes.

"She should do things like that, though."

"Did you?"

"No. That's the point."

"You can't force her. She's too old for that."

"We have to persuade her. That's your job."

A short time later Bartell and his wife went to bed, too. Helen turned on the radio instead of the little black and white TV he'd bought her for their last anniversary. He hated that TV and she knew it. She set the alarm and put her glasses in the drawer of the nightstand so the cat wouldn't knock them onto the floor during the night. Bartell lay awake reading for a while, a novel about a man who was working some elaborate revenge against his former employers at the CIA, The Company, as everybody in the spy business called it. Soon he put the book down, turned out the light, and rolled onto his side. He belched the last of the Mexican beer and felt his body fall steadily back into sleep and then his left arm snapped forward in an involuntary jerk.

. . . one . . .

Chapter 13 □ □ □

The bums were back. Not just the hardcore who'd gotten stranded in Rozette after it turned off too cold to lay up inside a boxcar, but great smelly flocks of bums, bums humping around the Burlington Northern yards under bedrolls bound up in rope, bedrolls dangling plastic water bottles and clothes and transistor radios: bums under hats, baseball caps, cowboy hats, watch caps, hats that used to be fedoras when somebody wore them on the El from Arlington Heights to work in the Loop in 1955; bums wearing bandannas that used to be red or blue, clipped around yet another dusty neck with a rusted Concho; bums inside coats and vests with pockets bulging with spoons and knives. Prince Albert and Top and papers and pipes; bums carrying blood donor cards, Social Security cards, birth certificates, discharge papers, V.A. medical cards, and lint; bums talking about death, about good rides across Nebraska, partners lost in a jail someplace in Idaho, yard bulls and cops, how to beat the cops, hide your campfire, stash your outfit where you could find it next morning when you get out of jail; bums talking about vintage Thunderbird and Mad Dog, about some guy named Mojave Slim got heaved out on a trestle someplace you forgot the name of—bones now, like all the rest of them; talking about free meals and cashing food stamps, about missions where they made you be sober to eat, or made you listen to some Bible thumper rant and rave about Glory before they let you eat, missions where they cut you off after three, four, five days, a week; talking about good tattoos, San Diego for ships, Seattle for a girl's name, dragons in Bangkok; talking about America; talkin' 'bout the Devil, Big D gonna getcha. Talking. Always talking.

Quentin Davies, my child, where are you now?

"I love the springtime," Ray Bartell said. He put his sunglasses in their case and dropped the case in the pocket of his leather jacket. In the four days since he'd driven through a snowstorm to Bittercreek, the weather had turned off warm. Not just warm, but that special first warmth of spring.

For Culp spring meant mud. It shouldn't bother him, the mud. He didn't have to walk in it or sleep in it anymore, but when spring came, mud for Paul Culp became a state of mind.

"Maybe Quentin Davies was right," Bartell said.

"How's that?"

"Maybe we are thugs. You ever think about that? Rousting these guys the way we do."

"You turning into some kind of bleeding heart on me?"

"Commie pinko bleeding heart," Bartell said, smiling. "Maybe it's the spring. The golden-eye ducks are gone, you know." Golden-eye ducks are small and shy and for them, winter in the south is defined as Montana. With the thaw they head back into Canada. At night golden-eye ducks gather in rafts in the backwaters of the Holt and you can spotlight them and in an instant they dive as one, leaving only a flash of silver water.

The sun was completely down now, leaving nothing of the day except a jagged orange ribbon behind mountains and clouds to the west. Soon that would be gone, too. "Makes me feel like a shepherd," Bartell said.

Culp didn't say anything. He was thinking about George Rather, who was really Sam Armstrong, wife-slayer. When you've seen one bum, you haven't necessarily seen them all. These days, whenever Culp remembered Rather, it was more likely than not in terms of marksmanship, a technical kind of memory that took him step by step through the shooting, without any sort of emotional snares. The car bounced along down an alley between a pair of soot-smudged brick warehouses and the tracks. Half a dozen bums stared at the ground as they passed. That's right, Culp thought. Stare at the ground, you sons of bitches, don't you sons of bitches be looking at me.

"Don't climb on a cross for that trash," Culp said finally, knowing he'd drilled Bartell in the heart of his empathy. And who knew? Maybe he was also doing a sales job on himself.

Bartell bounced easily in the seat, riding the bumps. He thought about Helen, alone at home on a Friday night. Jess was staying over at a friend's and Helen had the blues. With the girl getting older, both she and Bartell were starting to see the end of the line, the years after Jess left home and Helen would be stuck alone in an empty house nearly every night.

"I'll be the old lady on the corner who always has a light on," she'd said tonight. "Just one light in the back room. Waiting for somebody to call me on the telephone. We should have had more kids."

"If we'd had more," Bartell told her, "then sooner or later you'd have been saying, Oh, Lord, the last one's gone. And by then we'd be too old to have fun and get over it."

"You call this having fun?"

"We'll travel someday."

"We both work," she reminded him. "We can't travel, because we both work. And if we don't work, we can't afford to travel."

"You're just feeling old. You're still a beautiful woman."

What good was that, she wanted to know, when you sat home alone every night.

Of course, they didn't sit home *every* night. Last Thursday they had gone to one of the seasonal music programs at Jess's school. Jess played the clarinet. Her current boyfriend manipulated a trombone in the back row. His name was Chad, a wretched opportunist if Bartell had ever laid eyes on one. Bartell enjoyed seeing all the parents. Over the last seven years he'd developed a nodding acquaintance with perhaps twenty, whom he and Helen saw three times a year at school programs. Oh, he saw them once in a while outside the school, whether driving or jogging. Or in Singletree Mall he might brush elbows with one of the fathers, an accountant, in the fishing department of the sporting goods store. Or spot another, a dentist, secreting an ice cream cone from Baskin-Robbins. Bartell didn't really know these people, just knew who they were, as he supposed they knew who he was. The older you got, the harder it was to hide in your town. Every year at the school programs these people were a little more aged, a little more beaten down by the onslaught of their children, as he and Helen undoubtedly were, too. The bleachers hurt his butt more this year, it seemed, despite more built-in padding on his posterior. During a quiet passage in the seventh- and eighth-grade band performance, he could hear the soft pit-pat of twenty or thirty adolescent toes marking time, an unalterable stampede of children. After the performance Jess complained that Chad's family—everyone in the miserable lot, father and mother, grandparents, but especially the mother, who hated Jess's guts, she just knew it—had spent the evening glaring at her. Bartell remembered glaring at Chad (the rutting imbecile) and said, "Of course they did." Someday, Helen was right, someday soon this would all be over.

"You going to pause tonight?" Culp asked. He meant was Bartell going to drink beer with the rest of Mitchell's Maggots, whom Old Tobe had personally invited to come sit at his feet.

"Why not?" Bartell said. Helen was already in a funk; what did he have to lose? Nights with Old Tobe were the modern equivalent to painting up and dancing around the fire. The only thing missing was raw meat and the sacrifice of virgins. The closest they'd ever come to that level of celebration was the night Tobe himself had them over to his house for elk steaks. Tobe's wife was out of town, and Chester Boyles, still among them, had promised to bring along a virgin, and swore later that he had found two in his travels that night, but had ruined them before the party started.

Maybe it was getting crossways with Helen earlier. Or it could have been the lingering strain between him and Culp. Whatever it was, Bartell felt like so much baggage during the greater part of the shift.

The bar crowds were fairly small that night. At the corner of Ross and Rankin a squadron of chopped scooters outside Leech's Tap numbered scarcely a dozen. A block north on Van Valkenburg, there weren't enough bodies inside Conroy's to field a decent rugby team. *Rugby Players Eat Their Dead.* That was one of Bartell's favorite bumper stickers. He saw it on a beater Volkswagon bus behind Conroy's.

Bartell liked bars, though he seldom patronized them. He liked the way bars have their own people. Bikers at Leech's, jocks at Conroy's. Fundamental booze hounds at the Bismarck and hippies at Angel's. And he liked the way bars were often named for a person, like you were going to somebody's house, where all your friends would be and you could relax, safe from all the animals outside, who were in their own bar and equally glad to be safe from you. There were two clusters of bars on the north side, those near the Rankin Strip, where the crowd was relatively young, and the places farther north on Hartsell between Lawrenson and the tracks, where the main attractions left open were Wally's Lucky Lady and the Bismarck. Hartsell Street used to be a regular anthill, when the mills were running full bore and the railroad still carried people. Now, most of the Hartsell Street crowd were either old men who still lived and drank by long defunct train schedules, or young Indians who could not forget ancient days of wild, unlimited vision and wind.

And Culp. Culp still lived in that hole over Brisco's next to the Bismarck. Lived up there like some Lord of the Down and Out. Who could figure it?

Sometimes in the bars there were disagreements among friends over who got the woman that night, or who was the best point guard in the NBA, or who pocketed the stash after Stardust rolled the last stick. But those were family things, like brother complaining that sister breathed too loud on a long car trip, things usually settled by the time the cops arrived, or before they were even called. At least that was the case with bars, which Bartell distinguished from night spots, joints that featured loud bands and available women confronting available men. Cripple Creek was the most notable of these, a sprawling tin shed on the south side, where the parking lot rained beer bottles at closing, where the rest rooms were crammed with hotshots trying to smoke seeds and stems or suck up a line of trampled flake, so crammed you couldn't take a decent piss, so you pissed in the parking lot, maybe *that* would turn somebody on, like casting for big steelhead over in Idaho.

Culp turned into the Super America station at McLean and Flynn a block off the Rankin Strip. Bartell checked them out and locked the car door behind him. Culp needed Copenhagen. Maybe he needed somebody to talk to, too. Bartell hadn't been much help in the conversation department, and one of Culp's fishing buddies, a big bald man named Harold, was on shift at the SA.

Culp and Harold exchanged pleasantries about business while Bartell examined the rack of peanuts, cookies, and other fixatives. By now he knew most of the clerks in the all night stop and robs, the Mini Marts and Circle Ks, the quickie self-service gas and snack shops, like SA. For the next fifteen minutes Harold and Culp traded lies. Then they were back in the car, burning the city's gasoline for a few more hours, another installment on a lifetime. Wasn't this police work fun?

Just before one o'clock the radio crackled out their call number.

Bartell: "Go ahead."

Disturbance at three thousand Garden. Two men fighting outside. Unknown weapons. South units are busy, can you handle?

Bartell said of course they could, darlin', though he didn't actually call the frigid voice *darlin'*, because that would have been *very* bad form. Then he asked the Duroc where the complainant might be found. They were a good mile from the call. Culp switched on the overheads and aimed the car toward the center line on the Defoe Street bridge.

See the woman in Apartment 2. Doris Bachmeuller.

They made good time in the sparse early morning traffic, considering that the car did not have wings. Culp sharpened up his high-speed driving skills by floating through several turns on the way to Garden, a narrow dirt street that wrapped around the base of Hollow Ridge on the southeast edge of town, through a neighborhood that had never developed enough that you could say it was deteriorated. Culp braked the car in the 2800 block and turned off the overheads and the headlights. A moment later the street dead-ended in a parking lot. They got out in front of a long, low, green shingle building, the only building in the 3000 block.

The back of the building butted up against the mountains. The gravel lot was only half full of vehicles, old cars and pickups, half of those sitting on blocks like the mounted remains of dinosaurs in a museum of natural history. A field of straggling weeds crowded at the lot. The air was still and cool, slightly sharpened by a hint of ozone. Bartell saw a light come on inside Apartment 2. He and Culp made their way slowly for the door.

A woman stumbled out onto the cement step, then stumbled on toward them across the gravel. Bartell could smell the booze when she was still ten feet away.

"Doris?"

The woman nodded and fell toward him and he caught her under the arms. She had kinky black hair, wore a white sleeveless blouse. Her arms were thick and lifeless as sausages. Her left cheek was the size of a tennis ball, pinching closed the eye above it.

"What happened, Doris?" Bartell asked. He held her from one side, Culp held her from the other. Bartell guided the three of them back toward the apartment, intending to take her inside and find out the skinny on these two assholes who were supposed to be pummeling each other in the lot. When the light from the open door went dark, Bartell looked up and saw that it had been eclipsed by a man big enough to block out the sun itself if he took a notion.

"So she really called you," the man said.

Acting as one, Bartell and Culp lowered the woman to the ground, balancing her there like Humpty Dumpty. If things got out of control, they didn't need to have an armload of cold-cocked woman in the way. A few seconds later Doris Bachmeuller groaned loudly and fell back, her head making a hollow thump on the ground.

"Bitch," the man said. "Never figured she had the guts to call."

"What happened?" Culp said. He figured this behemoth was sure as hell guilty of something, but Culp didn't have to advise him of his rights until he was in custody, and he was about as close to custody as he was to the moon.

Bartell felt as though they were stalking Godzilla. The man's face was buried behind a black beard and black hair that fell to his shoulders. Bartell was sure he was seven feet tall, though that was probably an exaggeration. Probably six-ten would cover him.

"Caught her chippin' with some asshole." The man shrugged and his shoulders squeezed against the doorjamb. "Chippin' with a goddamn Indian. Right here in my own goddamn bed. You ain't gonna bust me for that, are you? Not for thumpin' a goddamn wagon-burner."

"I don't know about that," Culp said, wondering if they could just run the man over with the car. "But I think Doris here ought to see a doctor. Why don't you go call us an ambulance, Ray?"

"Screw her," the man said. "She don't need nothing 'cept another knot on her head."

"I'll tell you, pard," Culp said, taking another step for the man, "she was mine, I'd at least get her looked at. Might save you a few bucks later on, infection, you know, bullshit like that. Go on, Ray."

The man didn't argue and Bartell turned nonchalantly for the car.

"And you might have another car stop by," Culp said quietly, smiling at his moderation. What they really needed for this bearded wild man was an air strike. Bartell walked back to the apartment door, checking along the way to make sure Doris was still drawing breath.

"Where is that Native American gentleman, anyway?" Culp asked.

"Hell, I don't know," the man said. "Crawled off someplace, I guess, you know how them people are."

"I'll tell you, Mr. Bachmeuller—that's your name, ain't it?" Culp asked.

The man nodded.

"What's your first name, anyhow?" Culp stuck his hands in his hip pockets and cocked his head sheepishly.

"Buck."

"I'll tell you, Buck, we're kind of stuck with this thing here."

"I ain't going to no fucking jail. Not for whippin' a prairie nigger and a whore."

"Well, I don't know about jail, Buck, but we're gonna have to head downtown and sort this thing out. That okay with you?"

By the time Bartell got back from the car, his toes were numb and he gripped his flashlight tightly behind his back to keep his hands from shaking. He wasn't afraid, but he knew that Buck Bachmeuller was big enough that they'd have to hurt him, hurt him bad, to get him under control if he went on the fight.

"Come on, Buck," Culp said. "Let's go over to the car and sit down." He reached out slowly and took Bachmeuller by the elbow, as if handling a snake. Bachmeuller jerked his elbow away and Bartell shifted his weight forward on his feet, but then Bachmeuller squared his shoulders and walked ahead of them to the car, taking the opportunity to spit in the general direction of Doris as he passed. Bartell and Culp looked at each other. Culp's eyes got big as headlights and he let out a deep silent sigh.

"Now, Buck," Culp said, "I know you ain't gonna like this, but I gotta put a set of cuffs on you. Okay?"

"How come? If I ain't busted, how come—"

"It's a rule, Buck."

"What kinda rule?"

"Just a work rule. You've gotta job, don't you?"

"Damned right."

"Then you know about work rules. You know what them sons of bitches are like."

"No shit," Buck Bachmeuller said, offering his wrists behind his back. It took Culp an awkward, tense moment to fit the cuffs over Buck Bachmeuller's wrists. Close up under the streetlight, Bartell saw that Bachmeuller's forearms and the front of his white undershirt were spattered with blood. "I'm busted, ain't I?" Buck said.

"Yep," Culp said, "you're busted."

"Figures," Buck said, nodding his head like a bull contemplating a china shop. Then Bartell opened the back door of the car as if going to jail were the most natural thing in the world and they were just paying old Buck the courtesy of giving him a lift. Buck Bachmeuller squeezed inside. Bartell slammed the door and he and Culp fell against the back fender.

"Jesus Christ," Culp said.

"Yeah," Bartell agreed. "I'll second that."

They were still catching their breath when another police car pulled up and Juju Watson got out.

"You got a permit for that?" Watson asked, looking in the back seat. Watson's kinky blond hair looked like a halo under the orange artificial light. He adjusted his aviator-style glasses on his nose and took a closer look at Buck Bachmeuller.

Culp laughed, then said they'd better look around for a mangled human. Bartell checked once more on Doris Bachmeuller, this time taking the trouble to straighten out her legs, which had twisted up under her like pretzels when she fell. She was comfortably alive, as near as he could tell, breathing regularly as a clock, snoring, in fact. Down the street, he saw the red lights of the ambulance.

They found the Indian, who turned out to be Lawrence Kills White Man, under a blocked-up green Ford Galaxy at the end of the lot, where he apparently had gone to hide. His face looked like somebody had driven over it with a lawnmower. With the help of the ambulance crew, they slid a backboard under him, dragged him out, and hauled him to St. Francis, along with Doris, his star-crossed lover. In the weeds near Apartment 2 they found an axe handle, which was splintered and matted with blood and long straight black hair. They took this for evidence. Buck Bachmeuller, they took directly to the county lockup downtown on Weaver Street.

"You know, Paul," Bachmeuller said as he changed into jail coveralls, "it's a hell of a thing when a fella can't even beat shit out of a Indian."

"Hell of a thing," Paul Culp said.

"They was humpin' right there in the house, you know."

"Yep."

"Goddamn women," Buck said as the jailer turned a key on him.

"Good night, Buck."

"Yeah. See you, Paul. See you, too, whatever your name is," Buck Bachmeuller said, crinkling his gargantuan frame onto the small jail bunk and closing his eyes. "See the both of youse when I get out."

"Son of a bitch gave me the heebie-jeebies," Bartell said, cracking another beer, his fifth or seventh, he had lost track. Only four of the Maggots turned out, Bartell and Culp, who genuinely needed a drink, along with Tobe Mitchell and Juju Watson. Skinner and Proell sent their apologies, making it known that they had female encounters of the erotic kind on tap.

"I talked to him, though, didn't I?" Culp said with uncharacteristic smugness. "Talked that prick right into the bucket slick as snot, slick as Ray here coulda done."

Bartell nodded. He knew what Culp was hinting at.

"The world," Tobe Mitchell intoned, waving his forefinger in prophetic drunkenness, "is full . . . of assholes . . ." Tobe flung his empty Budweiser can in a poorly arched hook shot toward the green plastic garbage can between the refrigerator and the water fountain. The floor around the can was littered with misses.

The Maggots were laying the night to rest in the Police Union Barracks. They were called a union because Rozette tended to be a union town and calling yourselves a union simplified getting charitable donations from the working crowd. The barracks part applied to a large second-story hall on Hibbard Avenue across the street from the Federal building. They called it the barracks because some old captain years ago had a military bent. The lease made it possible for the brothers in blue to engorge themselves with alcoholic beverages at a neutral site, which was nice, since it meant that the Maggots wouldn't have to wake up somebody's old lady and kids to get the job of drunkenness done.

". . . and she's all changin', boys," Tobe Mitchell went on. When they convened formally four times a year, Old Tobe—he was always Old Tobe on these occasions, just plain Tobe on others, and never ever lieutenant—Old Tobe, who had in over twenty years, always sloshed over into the tales of years gone by, Fables of Olden Times, he called them. But they never talked about recent catastrophes, such as the George Rather catastrophe, for catastrophes needed years of careful aging before they became Fables of Olden Times, suitable for savoring on one of those nights when you marinaded your troubles in a blend of finest hops and choicest barley.

Instead, Old Tobe told them again about the night Tommy Parker (Christ, old Tommy died last year! Heart got him!) drove ten miles outside the city limits and spotlighted this big cow elk, knocked it off with his service revolver (as neat a head shot as you'll ever see!), then got a hot call and was racing eighty miles an hour back into town with five hundred pounds of slaughtered elk dripping blood out of the trunk of the police car when he hit an Angus steer standing in the middle of the goddamned road.

"Goddamned black cattle," Old Tobe said. "Why, hell, it's no wonder a guy runs 'em over, you just can't see 'em when you've got the lights off."

And Krueger. "Any of you guys ever work with Krueger? No, you're all too young, just babies. Well, you didn't miss nothing, I can tell you that. I worked for him plenty. He was an asshole. I knew him when he was just a sergeant and he was an asshole then. Then he made lieutenant and he was a worse asshole and after he was a captain he was a *real* fuckin' asshole. I think he's dead now, too. Must be, I ain't got no time off lately. Good thing, too, or I might've had to kill him." Old Tobe hooked an empty and sent Juju Watson to the icebox for another twelve-pack.

"You know a guy named Buck Bachmeuller?" Bartell asked Old Tobe.

"Sure, I know the hammerhead. What's he into now? . . . and Renaldo Dolan. The Mexican Mick . . . you guys are too young to remember him, too."

"Jail," Bartell said.

"Whassat?"

"Jail," Bartell said again. "That's what Buck Bachmeuller's into now."

"Jesus Christ, I didn't even know he was out. Anyways, Renaldo Dolan was a *great big* guy . . . like that goddamn ox Proell and—"

"Buck took a whack at his old lady," Bartell continued futilely.

"Wouldn't you?" Old Tobe said, stopping to irrigate his vocal cords. Telling a story of your own once Old Tobe got geared up for the Fables of Olden Times . . . well, you might as well try to leap tall buildings with a single bound.

"One day this taco-chomping Irishman, he gets it in his head everything's bugged. Won't talk to you, see, without there's a radio going, and he starts looking under chairs and desks, and after a year of this horseshit somebody . . . I ain't sayin' *who* . . . but *somebody*"—Old Tobe grinned like the Devil himself—"starts rigging up buttons with wires . . . stickin' 'em on the ceiling, behind the furniture . . . every goddamn place . . . even stuck one behind the crapper and that goddamn Renaldo Dolan even finds *that* one. Well, of course by then he's just . . . *wild!* . . . tearing everything apart and the chief of police—that was Schmitz in them days . . . a *real* asshole . . . if you think this guy we've got now is bad . . . anyway, Schmitz, he wants to know who *the fuck* is tinkering with Renaldo Dolan's circuits."

By now Old Tobe was sweating. "Krueger . . . Schmitz . . . Renaldo Dolan . . . Parker. All them guys is dead, I guess. Well, wait, somebody told me Krueger's still alive . . . he's just retired over on the Flathead." Old Tobe shrugs and opens another beer. "And him the only one deserves to be dead . . . just goes to show . . ."

Juju Watson looked at his watch, stood up, and stretched while Old Tobe rambled through the Fable of Hank Torgerson, which involved a midnight romp to Butte on a police motorcycle thirty years ago, before even Old Tobe donned the blue.

"Gotta go," Watson said finally. It was almost five o'clock and he was out of leash.

"Chicken shit," Old Tobe growled, his belly straining against the brass buttons on his uniform shirt. "Sit back down there, son." Old Tobe pretended to reach for his revolver, which was holstered on the gunbelt under his chair, in faithful observance of the time-honored rule known as Guzzle Without Guns.

Watson smiled crookedly and winked at Culp and Bartell and zipped up his jacket, then ducked out the door just ahead of a flying beer can, which was still rattling across the floor by the time Tobe removed another to replace it.

"Asshole," Tobe snarled, then laughed and fell into a coughing fit. "Aw, hell, he's a good kid. You're all good kids." He popped the tab, spraying beer on his chest, then looked down and carefully wiped his badge dry with his sleeve.

Culp looked at Bartell, scowled, and shook his head slightly.

Bartell said that he needed to head out, too, that his leash was so much shorter than Watson's he'd already damned near hung himself. He asked Culp for a ride home. Ordinarily, Bartell would catch a ride home with one of the guys on shift. But tonight he was too tanked. Riding home drunk in police cars made you fodder for a Fable of Olden Times for some new crop of cops in the distant gray future. So Bartell and Culp said their good nights to Old Tobe, slung their gunbelts over their shoulders, and ducked out the door just ahead of another dead soldier.

Outside the birds were already starting to sing, and Bartell's head began to throb as they walked down the alley behind Brisco's and climbed into Culp's hammered pickup, a relic of his property settlement. Bartell hated staying over late like this, getting stiff and throwing off the rhythm of the next day. His belly sloshed and his head drooped as Culp drove toward the Bartell homestead on West Fieldon Street. The sky was rimmed red in the east, time for decent men to go to work.

"Always wanted a big Cadillac," Bartell said. "Big goddamn El Dorado convertible with a red leather interior. Drive around in the country and listen to Hank Williams, Jr. Drink beer and throw out the cans, just toss 'em straight up in the air and let the wind take 'em."

"Worse ways to live," Culp said. He clipped the words, as though meaning that he had personally examined those worse other ways and was here to say that Bartell was nothing more than a fool chasing an idiot's dream.

Culp.

What the hell did he know?

Beat your Cadillac to death on dirt roads, knock the front end out of line on the potholes of life, yeah, that was one way, all right, the hard easy way, or was it the easy hard way, or maybe just a way, maybe, any old way to get by, beat your brains out on the road and run over a steer on the way back to town.

Bartell decided that he might be sick. He was about to tell Culp to pull to the curb, when Culp pulled to the curb in front of his house. There was already a light on in the kitchen. Culp shut off the engine and rolled down his window, like he wanted to talk.

At last, Culp did in fact say something. He said, "You thought you had him, didn't you?"

He meant George-A-for-Asshole-Rather. Bartell knew that was what Culp meant without even hearing him say so. "Yeah," Bartell said. "I sure thought I did."

"So how the fuck was I supposed to know?" Culp said. "How come I'm the asshole of all time just because I keep your carcass above ground? How come that is?"

"I never said . . ." What a fiasco. Bartell wanted to tell Culp how he felt, but he was too drunk to piece it all together, and if he'd been sober, they wouldn't be having this conversation at all.

"That's right," Culp said. "You never said nothing."

"So what was I supposed to say? *Thanks*?"

"Maybe."

"Right. Okay. Here it is. Thanks for making me look like a chump—"

"That's not—"

"—thanks for making it look like I can't do my job—"

"You're outta your mind."

"Thanks for making me look like I fucked up."

Culp shrugged and drummed his fingers on the steering wheel, "I can't help it if it looks like you fucked up."

"I never fucked up!" Bartell smashed his fist against the metal dash and pain shot up to his elbow. "Fuck!" He nursed his throbbing knuckles.

"You're a goddamn moron." Culp shook his head.

"Maybe," Bartell said, "but I had that guy through it. I may be a moron, but I never fucked up. Not that time, anyway." Bartell looked down the street, his street, where children would play in a few hours, once the neighborhood was again transformed by daylight into a civilized place.

"I killed a guy on account of you," Culp said. "That's bad enough. I'm not gonna have you making me feel like an asshole for it."

"You're not an asshole," Bartell said. He was starting to get dizzy. He felt his throat flush and he started to sweat in the small creases around his eyes. He rolled down the window and spit onto the sidewalk. "I never said you were an asshole."

"Well, I haven't made up my mind about you yet," Culp said.

"I think I'm gonna puke." Bartell looked up and saw Helen standing beside a clump of bushes near the back door of the house. She was still in her robe, but had thrown on her down jacket. She took a step or two toward the pickup, but stopped when Bartell made eye contact with her.

Bartell looked back at Culp. "So you think I've been an asshole."

"I said you were a moron. I told you I haven't decided about the asshole part."

"Thanks a lot. I'm really gonna puke."

"Then get out of my truck."

"We're not done talking."

"If you're gonna puke, we're done. Now get the fuck out."

"Not till you tell me I'm not an asshole."

"You haven't got time." Culp reached in front of him and opened the door. "See you."

Bartell faltered only slightly as he got out of the pickup. He walked the short distance to Helen and put his arm around her waist and pulled her close, but there was a stiffness in her back. He turned once to see the pickup weave delicately down the street.

"So long, prick," Bartell said after the pickup.

"What?" Helen's back stiffened even more and she pulled away.

"Nothing," Bartell said, "Forget it." He pushed her away, took a few steps toward the house, then turned aside quickly and threw up in the bushes.

Chapter 14

The breeze felt cool on Culp's belly and he was afraid that it would rain. It was sticky enough to rain and every now and then the imprint of the Hollow Ridge skyline flashed at the edge of town ahead of lightning. Culp could see the ridge above the roof of the Hong Kong Chinese-American Café and Noodle Parlor. He turned on his side in bed and propped the sticky pillow under his head. The Bismarck had been closed for over an hour and the alley was quiet. Moments ago he'd heard a shout, then the small, tight crash of a bottle breaking. But that was better than half an hour ago. It wasn't noise from the alley that kept him awake.

Maybe it was the rumor of rain he smelled on the wind. The dusty smell. The clap of a million fresh leaves. The sting of endless rain, the nightmare grip of clothes that were always soaked.

Culp felt short of breath. He got up and went to the sink and ran cool water over his head and felt better, felt the weight release from around his bare chest. He hitched up his undershorts and went back to bed. Thank God he didn't have to work tomorrow. He should have gotten out of town.

Gone back to Kalispell, maybe, looked up that girl Nancy in Lakeside.

When he heard the stairs giving way, he reached to the shelf above his head and took down the gun and padded across the room to the hinged side of the door and waited.

Culp didn't answer the first knock, and when the second came, he said, "What?"

"Paul?" A woman's voice.

"What?"

"Paul, please let me in."

"Who is it?"

"Please."

Culp crossed to the sofa and pulled on a pair of jeans. He started to replace the gun on the shelf, then changed his mind and held it against his thigh as he opened the door.

"Hello." Helen Bartell looked behind her down the stairs, as though checking to see if she'd been followed.

"What in the hell do you want?" Bartell had said his wife moved out. Came home from work the afternoon after the blowout with Tobe, threw some stuff in a bag, and left. It was a good thing Jess was old enough to stay alone at night, since Helen left *her*, too. Culp cut the conversation short when Bartell started looking for handholds to hoist himself onto another goddamned cross.

"I'm not sure. I don't know if you've heard—"

"I heard. Ray told me."

"Yes. I guess he would. He'd tell everybody."

"It wasn't like that." But of course, it was.

She glanced down the steps again. "Anyway, I've been staying in this cheesy motel and they don't have cable TV and all the stations went off and . . ." She stopped and shifted her weight from one foot to the other. "Oh, hell, can't I even come in?"

Culp stepped aside, then closed the door after her. He went quickly to the shelf above his bed, hoping he was being nondescript as he replaced the gun.

"Are you drunk?" He sat beside Helen on the couch.

"You know what happens to little girls who look under the bridge?" She kicked off her shoes and hitched her legs up under her. "The troll gets them."

"You're not drunk."

"I'm not drunk."

"It's three in the morning. People don't visit places like this alone at three o'clock in the morning, not if they're sober."

"We could get drunk."

"We could get in trouble."

"We could get in a lot of trouble." She frowned and leaned toward him slightly, then pulled back.

"Too damned much trouble." Culp said.

"I'm sorry."

"What is it you want?" Culp got up and walked to the window on the west side of the room. He could see lightning from that window now. The storm must be circling town to the south. He stood in the window and listened to the wind, but the direction had changed and the air was still and heavy in the window.

"I wanted to be with somebody."

"That's why they've got bars. Dim lights. Strangers. Things like that." He didn't know what she wanted, but he was afraid of what she might want.

"Did he tell you why I left?"

Culp didn't answer at first. He kept his back to her, kept looking out the window, watching the storm bulge toward the moon. Finally he said, "He was drunk. That's all." He figured she must be talking about the morning he'd brought Bartell home drunk and they'd had it out in front of the house.

"That?" she said. "That was just the lock on the door."

Helen squared herself and put her feet on the floor and crossed her legs.

"You got a secret, Helen?"

"I've got fifteen years of open book," she said, laughing. "Fifteen years of breakfast, lunch, and dinner."

"And that's such a bad thing?"

"You know what I am, Paul? I'm *Occupant*."

Culp shrugged. "So you get regular deliveries. That's better than no deliveries at all."

"We used to lay awake all night and talk about nothing in the dark. Now it's like . . . it's like I'm not worthy because . . . I'm not sure . . . maybe because I haven't suffered."

"So you come to me for a dose of suffering. Thanks."

"That's not true."

"You figure I'm the safest suffering you can come up with. We don't see each other much, but you know me, so I'm not risky, like some guy in a bar. But I work with your husband"—why couldn't he say he *was friends* with her husband?—"I work with Ray, so there's not much chance I'd push this farther than you want to go."

"That's not fair."

"Fair?" Culp looked at her and smiled. He could hear the thunder now, rolling off the lip of the cloud, which had now overtaken the moon.

"It's okay to admit it. You don't have fifteen years in me. You come to my house in the middle of the night on the make—"

"I'm not on the make."

"Sure you are. Maybe you just don't know it."

"So maybe I am." Helen got up and walked to the window and stood beside him and looked down into the cutaway behind the

Bismarck. "It stinks from down there," she said. "How can you stand it, living in this place?"

"I can't." Culp held her face in his hands and kissed her.

"That many years," she said, "you think of yourself as *we*, then all of a sudden you think of yourself as *me* and it's too much surprise. Like an overdose."

"Who you thinking of now?" Culp knew Helen's "we" didn't mean him.

"Maybe it's me that's the lock. Me feeling guilty . . . guilty about how much I want something you're not supposed to want."

"Who you thinking of now?"

"Me." She kissed him and he ran his hands up her back under her shirt and lifted the shirt over her head. Her back was cool, but her nipples stung his chest.

"So am I," Culp said. He stepped away and handed her back her shirt. "Thinking of you, I mean. Thinking of me, too." He shuddered once and scratched the back of his head and tried to focus his eyes, tried to ignore how beautiful she looked, her skin shiny from the heat as she stood half naked in that patch of light from the window.

"Maybe you should suffer on your own time." He went to the sink and drew another glass of water and drank and when he turned back to her, she was dressed.

"It's terrifying, how much I found myself wanting to hurt him. Not just hurt him, but make him see me. If I do it like this, I'd just end up feeling sorry for him. I could handle the hating myself, but not feeling sorry for him. Not now. I shouldn't have tried to use you for that."

"I'm sorry I couldn't cooperate," Culp said. "Believe me, I'm sorrier than you can possibly imagine. I'll be sorry for years." He started to laugh then and was glad to hear Helen laugh, too.

"Wouldn't it be lovely," Helen said.

Culp lay on the bed and clasped his hands behind his head and watched the lightning and listened to the thunder draw still closer.

"He has all these books," Helen said. "He ever tell you about those?"

"No."

"One of them, it's about this little town where he grew up. Over east of the mountains. There's some old murder story in it he reads sometimes. And poems. Books of poems."

Culp was surprised to learn that he knew a guy who read poems. "What kind of poems?"

"Poems about life and death. Simple little things like that."

They both started to laugh again and after a moment he heard a peculiar note in her laughter.

"So, you figure you'll go home?" he said.

"Probably . . . tomorrow, probably tomorrow. I'm not even sure why I left. Except I just knew I had to know how it would feel, know if it felt right, because I wasn't sure anymore that staying was right. Then, once I was gone, it scared me how important hurting him became."

"When I was a kid," Culp said, "I went with my old man, who was working on a remodeling job of some kind at the church we went to. I was about twelve or thirteen."

"I wouldn't have guessed you for a churchgoer."

"I was almost a preacher."

"What changed your mind?"

"Who knows? Anyhow, that's a whole other nightmare. But we were there, see, working on this building project. And there was another little kid there, too, he was only seven or eight. And he starts throwing rocks at me, see. I was sitting outside in the yard and this little bastard starts throwing rocks at me, really whacking me with them.

"Now, the crazy thing, see, is I didn't do anything. I just sat there and let him pelt me. I remember I kept telling him to stop, but I never did anything to *make* him stop. That's because I kept telling myself that I was bigger than him, so it wasn't right for me to do anything to *force* him to knock off hurting me."

"I can't imagine you being that way," Helen said.

"Well, I can't either, now. But I was like that then. And it wasn't that I didn't think I had the right to force somebody littler than me. That wasn't it at all, you know. What it was, was I liked getting hit with all those rocks, liked feeling sorry for myself."

"But you're not like that now."

"No. Nobody's going to hurt me like that now. I decided that a long time ago. But your husband, Ray, I think he's still a little like that."

"So how do I stop that?"

"You can't. Only thing you can do is refuse to be the one throws the rocks. Unless you really want to bust him one."

The breeze quickened and now Culp could hear thunder after the lightning. After each successive flash the gap narrowed between noise and light.

"Paul?" Helen said.

"What?"

"Can I come over and lay beside you? Not for any funny stuff. Just to be close to somebody."

"I don't think you better do that." Culp looked down at the beads of sweat gathering on his belly. If you don't want people throwing rocks at you, then don't let them pick up the goddamn rocks.

It was quiet for several minutes and then Culp heard her breathing, breathing long and drawn out, and he knew she was asleep. Culp stared at the ceiling and lay very still and after a few moments, his body felt numb. He thought of her sleeping nearby, remembered the sheen of her standing against him only an instant ago. He imagined his body moving beside her, imagined her legs drawing him inside. It wasn't long after that that the rain started.

Chapter 15 □ □ □

Within a week after Helen came back, Bartell no longer felt like eating his gun. Of course, there was never any real risk of suicide, the way Bartell saw it, because he'd always heard that people who decide to pull their own plug always get sort of . . . happy . . . once all the dust has settled and they've made up their mind. There was no chance that anybody would mistake Bartell for a happy man. Helen had been gone for five days, leaving him and Jess to fend for themselves. Then one morning she came back. Just like that, like she'd settled something.

One night in bed Bartell told her he was sorry he'd taken such a wrong turn. Luckily, she didn't ask him which particular turn he was tagging as wrong.

"If we could go anyplace we wanted," Helen said, "where would you want to go?"

Bartell didn't know.

"I'd go to Scotland," she said. "One of those wild islands in the North Sea." That was all she said. She turned on her side and faced the wall away from him and went to sleep.

The cops, as cops will, circled the corpse of Bartell's mental health like vultures. Not that Bartell had turned the details of his private life into a public spectacle. Hardly. But nobody has to send up a flare over a piece of roadkill; buzzards take wing all on their own.

Thomas Cassidy volunteered the names of several good divorce attorneys, attorneys into whose care he'd entrusted his personal fortunes many times. And Ike Skinner threw in some salve he had left over from a prescription. Bartell would need this, Skinner assured him, to cure the rash he would get from holing up a couple of months at Nails Hogan's monastery across the way from the cop shop.

"You gotta look decimated in front of that judge," Skinner counseled, even though Bartell insisted he was not even on the road to court. "Anyways, you'll *be* decimated once the papers are signed. Living at Hogan's crib is good practice for your new life. Take it from me. I sold off that new Jeep just last week."

Proell said he knew a woman on the south side who was reasonably fresh, fresh enough anyway to see Bartell safely over to the other side with relatively few medical bills. She wasn't exactly a beauty queen, you understand, but she wouldn't make you gnaw off your arm in the morning. You could take her places, too. In public. As long as you were careful to do it after dark, and to places where everybody was drunk.

Bartell took it all in stride and staunchly refused to ventilate his cerebral regions with 158 grains of lead.

The split with Culp was something else, at least as far as the other cops were concerned. It was a measure of seriousness that nobody talked to Bartell about that breakup. Nobody since their last night together, when Culp said he'd decided he wanted to go it alone for a while. He never said he wanted to be rid of Bartell; it was *alone* he was after. Tobe Mitchell went along. If Bud Haller screamed, nobody heard.

Bartell could hardly say he'd resisted Culp's decision to end the partnership. If anything, he was relieved, as though he'd been cut free of an emotional straitjacket. Any sentimentality he may have felt for what Tobe Mitchell might call Olden Times was rubbed out by the fact that Culp told Mitchell he was quits with Bartell before he told Bartell. That figured, didn't it? It really figured. All the anxiety he'd invested in preserving appearances, and now Culp had up and made his turn alone into the sunset. Happy trails.

"Buck up, son," Ike Skinner said early one evening as they walked out of Roosa's. "I don't know who shit on your parade, but believe me, it's like getting embalmed. It doesn't hurt anymore once you bleed out." That was the closest anybody came to condolences over the late partnership.

But Bartell continued to keep his own counsel and drove away, waving to Skinner as he turned north onto Flynn toward the underpass, where the street took a header under the Burlington Northern yards.

Bartell didn't make it to the underpass, though. One of the dispatch Durocs sent Collie Proell to investigate Stump Riggins. The report was that Stump was going through cars near the north-end bars, about a block from the underpass. Since Bartell was close and he knew Riggins, he jumped the call.

Stump Riggins was ninety-one years old, which made him

almost as old as the dilapidated section of town he haunted. He turned up in Rozette about a year ago, after his fourth wife died, leaving him with no family at all. So Stump sold his small ranch out near Rocky Boy and brought his money to town for a last fling. Since then he'd become a resident of the north-end drinking emporiums, mostly the Bismarck, but sometimes you could find his six-and-a-half feet of bones stacked under a big silver belly Stetson around the corner at Wally's Lucky Lady. The Stetson had a band made out of rattlesnake hide.

Other than the washing of too many years down the river, Stump Riggins had only two problems left in his life. He tended to herd around his new Bill Blass Continental like a mule team. One day after collecting on yet another traffic ticket, Judge Walter Clay threatened to toss the old man in jail if he caught him once more driving anything that didn't have hooves.

Stump's second problem was that his age, the personal habits of his new citified way of life, and the wad of bills he kept stuffed in his boots and pockets made him a very inviting target. A suicidal binge this might be, the old man told his drinking cronies, but he didn't need for some hard-case to hasten him along the road to Glory. So Stump decided to hedge that problem. For a while he kept an old sawed-off Winchester double 16 gauge hung from his left shoulder under his coat by a piece of bailer twine. Then Judge Clay nixed that, too, by impounding the shotgun for the protection of the local police.

Bartell rounded the corner of Wally's Lucky Lady and saw Stump Riggins standing next to a red CMC pickup, parked in the vacant lot beside Wally's. He hadn't seen Stump for about four months, and the word was that the old man had moved into a rest home. When he pulled over, Bartell saw right away that the years had collided like a long train with Stump Riggins. His shoulders were so stooped that he'd cut a good half a foot off his height, and that silver-belly Stetson sat low around his ears, as though his skull had shriveled. But even from a distance Bartell could see that one part of Stump Riggins hadn't changed: his large hands still looked like tools.

"Hiya, boy," Stump said as Bartell picked his way over the broken beer bottles that covered the lot.

"What's new, Stump?"

"You bring my gun back?"

"Afraid not." Even in the open air the lot was rank with urine. Bartell took another step, felt his heel slip, and looked down at the dog shit mashed under his foot. On north, across the tracks, the diesel-blackened beams of the old railroad roundhouse, in mid-demolition, were outlined against the brown hillside that rose abruptly at the edge of town.

"No gun. Figures." Stump looked at the ground and nodded. The inside of his Stetson bounced against the shelf of bone above his eyes and the rattles on the snakeskin band chattered. "Like a bunch of goddamned Communists. You a Communist?"

"No."

"Sure you are."

"What's the deal with this pickup, Stump?"

"Which pickup would that be?"

"This one." Bartell slapped his palm on the CMC's faded red hood. "The one you're leaning on."

"Oh, yeah. This here truck." Stump nodded again. "You mean this truck here."

"The very one," Bartell said.

"Gonna buy this here truck."

"What happened to your Continental?"

"Sold it." Stump let out a deep sigh and wiped his nose with the back of his hand as he looked out over the skeleton of the roundhouse. "Sold it to this Indian from over in the Mission."

"You must have some money left, then."

"Yeah. I got a hundred dollars."

"After you sold that limousine?"

"Well, see, they took most of it off me when I moved in this place. A old folks home, I guess you'd call it. Run by a bunch of Christers. Made me sign a paper, give 'em all my goddamn money. Hell, I was drunk when I did it, but I guess I did do it, so all I got left is this hundred dollars."

"At least you've got a place to stay," Bartell said. Even though it was June, the nights still had plenty of snap to them, too much snap for a ninety-year-old man to be sleeping in doorways and alleys, even if he was a cowboy. This way Stump Riggins should have enough on account at the home to buy out his days.

"Trouble is, I don't want to stay there no more," Stump said. "Hell, they won't even give you a drink. Must've been out of my goddamn mind."

"Somebody called and said they thought you were going to steal something out of this truck," Bartell said.

"Told you," Stump said, "I was gonna *buy* the goddamn thing."

"I know. Hell, I know you wouldn't go stealing out of a truck." Bartell looked inside the cab anyway. There was nothing in there to steal, unless you counted the empty Quaker State Oil can, and the fifteen years of heartbreak stained all over the ragged seat.

"That's right." Stump nodded again vehemently, then readjusted the Stetson. "Ain't no goddamn thief."

"I know that."

"Probably that goddamn Polack in the Bismarck told you that."

"They didn't say."

"Them Polacks is all notorious liars. I ain't a thief."

"I know you're not."

"Well, I did steal a woman once."

"How's that?"

"A woman. Stole a Chinese woman one time. You don't have to get excited. This was a long time ago. She's a long time dead, so nobody's complaining. I sort of married her, anyways, so it wasn't exactly like stealing."

His woman-stealing adventure had taken place back before World War I, Stump Riggins explained. In those days there was a saloon behind all the empty storefronts up and down Woody Street for two blocks south of the tracks. The bars were open round the clock, because the staggered shifts on the railroad and in the Corso Mill meant that it was always quitting time for somebody in Rozette, Montana.

"It was easy to find a decent fistfight then," Stump Riggins said. "All you had to do was poke your chin out far enough."

The Chinese woman belonged to a card mechanic who got off the train from Seattle one day and set up shop in the back room of a joint called Lord's, on the opposite end of the block from Wally's.

"He liked to deal five card," Stump said, "and he kept this Chinese gal right there at his side to help draw a crowd."

The Chinese gal sat on a stool just behind the card mechanic's left shoulder. She had muscular black hair that she kept nailed in place by an elaborate setup of combs and pins, and she always held her arms folded, her hands hidden in the billowing sleeves of a green silk dress. Everybody always figured she kept a dirk strapped to her wrist. That, along with her beauty, tended to keep most of the players distracted from the business at hand.

"Green eyes, too," Stump said. "Never seen that on a Chinese gal, you know. Must've had some white in her. Dutch, maybe, from the way she got hardheaded when her man dug in his boot for the last of their cash. Anyways, I cleaned him out, gutted him like a fish, then later on he jumped me out back in the alley. Mashed an empty bottle up side his neck." Stump Riggins shifted his weight from his right foot to his left, then cocked his head toward the ground, as though he'd just heard something.

"Figured him dead," Riggins went on, "all that goddamn blood and all." He was all set to make a run for it, when something, he couldn't remember now if it was sight or sound, but something there in the shadows behind the stack of beer barrels snared his attention and he stopped and reached for the big folding knife in his hip pocket. "It were that Chinese gal." As soon as she knew she'd been found out, the Chinese gal made a run for the street. Riggins caught her up, though, and twisted an arm behind her back. She never let out a sound.

"Wasn't nobody else around," Stump said to Bartell. "Just me and that gal and that goddamn cutthroat I'd pole-axed." So he dragged the girl back to the stable, where he'd boarded his team, along with the wagon he'd loaded up with supplies that afternoon. "Tied her up and threw her in the wagon and made tracks. She didn't have no dirk, though. I checked that right now." He was never exactly sure that the card mechanic was dead, but he wasn't about to grow any moss waiting to find out. "Took her on home up in the Shonkin, where I was in them days. Tried to let her go later on, but she wouldn't have it," he said, shaking his head hard enough to rattle the Stetson. "Then she died a couple years after that, trying to birth this baby. Christ, I got her a doctor and everything, just like you would for any woman. Died on me anyway. Baby, too. Boy. I can still—" He stopped and spit between his boots, making a small damp puddle in the dust.

Bartell felt drained. Wasn't there some way he could break himself of listening to everybody's story? What talent did he have for hearing confession? All he was supposed to do was make sure Stump Riggins wasn't thieving from cars, and here he was getting cut to the bone by the story of an old man too far gone out of time. More and more, it seemed that the story of the West boiled down to the history of old men, men like Stump Riggins.

"How about it, Stump? Why don't you let me give you a ride home?"

"I *am* home, boy." Stump laughed, as though Bartell had just made the most foolish suggestion under the sun.

"Where you staying now?"

"Over there." Stump nodded southward. "Staying with a Irishman over there."

"You eating regular?" He'd noticed that Stump's belt had run out of notches and gravity was about to get the best of the large buckle with *Montana* inlaid in copper across an oval field of silver.

"Ate just yesterday."

"Okay." Bartell told Stump Riggins to take care of himself and not go stealing out of cars or trucks, then turned and headed back toward his own car.

"You bring my gun?" Stump Riggins shouted after him.

"Didn't bring your gun. Sorry."

"I want that gun!"

"You'll have to see the judge about that." Bartell stopped and scuffed the dog shit from his boot onto the sidewalk. It was a warm evening and the dog shit stuck like simmering glue. He'd have to smell it for the rest of the shift inside the car.

"Had any goddamn hair, you'd give me my gun back."

"You don't need a gun, Stump."

Stump Riggins hitched up his jeans and walked after Bartell. "Any guts and you'd have this out with me like a man."

Bartell ignored him and got into the car. By the time he'd pulled out into the street, Riggins had reached the curb.

"You get back here, boy!"

But Bartell drove slowly off, and when he turned the corner at the boarded-up shell that had been Lord's, Stump Riggins was standing in the middle of the street, his hands poised at his sides, shouting that if Bartell would come back and face him like a man, he'd blow his goddamn brains out.

When Bartell thought about the shift later, he would think of it as one of those *And Then* kind of shifts, the kind that seems stacked up with one thing after another. Actually, he hadn't really done much. He'd gone straight from briefing to coffee with Skinner. After that he talked to Stump Riggins. Then he ran his car through the car wash on Flynn, the one where the city had a contract. His car wasn't even dry yet when the dispatcher called his number and said, *Man passed out in a car.*

Well, shit. So what? Guys pass out in their cars all the time.

The man was supposed to be behind the wheel of a white over blue Dodge Aspen. The car was parked inside a garage off the alley behind 833 Morton. Morton was on the north side, under the Flynn Street underpass, then west along the tracks, not far from the old Haig warehouse, where the bums always peeled away the corrugated tin along the crawlspace and slipped in out of the weather. Bartell figured that there were whole cities of bums under the Haig, but nobody—including Bartell—was the least bit interested in risking rat bites and disease to crawl back and roust them out. Everybody's got to be someplace, and *that* place was *not* the place for Ray Bartell. Hell, there might even be corpses under there (at least what the rats had left of them), but that was okay, too. When a guy lives that kind of life, even murder could be construed as a natural cause.

Bartell turned away from the tracks and onto Gillespie, which would cut Morton about two blocks ahead at the east end of the 800 block. The whole neighborhood was back on its heels, overgrown with unkempt hedge, tearful willows, knapweed, and automobile carcasses. All in all, it was a neighborhood not far removed, physically and emotionally, from the Haig. Time was, 800 Morton was in the heart of a solid working-class neighborhood, mostly railroaders. But that was years ago, before the great iron horse went lame.

Bartell was about to ask the Duroc to give him the complete dispatch again, just to be disagreeable, when he saw a small, young Asian woman run out of the alley in the 800 block of Morton. The woman saw his car and ran toward him. Bartell had been a cop too long to call straight out for a backup. But he also knew a pit of alligators when he was about to jump in it, so he described his situation over the radio, knowing that Culp or Proell or Skinner or somebody else would catch his drift and wander over.

The woman was Vietnamese. Bartell didn't know if she'd never learned any English, or if she was so hysterical she'd had the English scared out of her. He was out of the car by now, holding her by the shoulders. Her arms were locked at her sides, hands doubled into fists.

"What's the matter?" he asked over and over. "You speak English?" Bartell realized that he was shouting in a crude effort to make himself understood.

But the woman only screamed and babbled. Bartell shook her again and asked her what was wrong. The woman sobbed and moaned and looked back toward the alley. Then she raised her arms and opened her fists. Her palms were covered with blood.

After he had the screaming woman stashed safely behind the screen in the back seat of his car, Bartell put out an earnest call for a second car. Culp said he was almost there, and Bartell asked him to come down the alley from the west, opposite Bartell. A moment later he saw a black and white nose up to the alley and stop. Culp got out. It was strange, seeing Culp like that, coming to trouble from a different direction.

Bartell and Culp moved toward each other down the alley, both keeping well to the side, along the clusters of garbage cans and lilac hedge. Bartell heard a siren start up from across town. He walked slowly down the left side of the alley, the Morton Street side, wondering which garage went with 833. Every goddamned house had a goddamned garage and the goddamned woman wouldn't say a goddamned thing, just all that goddamned screaming and the goddamned blood on her goddamned hands. God . . . damn. A dog snarled and lunged into the chain-link fence at Bartell's back and Bartell nearly fed the son of a bitch six rounds in the snout. He glanced back at Culp and shrugged and just as he was fitting his gun back into its holster a car horn blasted out in the next garage, about thirty feet ahead, and the gun was right back out.

Culp seemed to move tighter against the hedge at his right and Bartell picked up his pace and Culp had his own gun out and just a few steps later they were at the corners of the dilapidated, unpainted garage, which was really more like a shed than a garage, as though it were built for horses and wagons and a set of double swing-out doors had been cut in the back wall to accommodate motorized vehicles.

The horn was nearly deafening, just inside the doors. Still, Bartell heard gravel crunching behind him in the alley. He snapped around and saw that Ike Skinner had just pulled in behind him. He held up his arm for Skinner to stop.

Then Bartell looked at Culp. He pointed at himself, then at the open doors and Culp nodded.

Bartell crouched at the edge of the door and took a solid two-handed grip on his gun, then looked carefully around the door at about knee height.

It was the blue over white Dodge. Bartell couldn't see inside the car, but he was able to bend even lower and look under it. There were no feet or legs showing. The garage didn't have any stacks of junk as garages often do, so it looked like a safe bet that if there was anybody inside, he was inside that blue and white car.

Bartell stood up, stepped around the door, and moved cautiously along the front fender of the car.

There was a man inside the car. He was leaning against the steering wheel. There was nobody else inside the car. Of course, *nobody else* was a slight inaccuracy, since the man inside the car wasn't exactly inside the car at all. Not any longer. The man inside the car was as dead as Ray Bartell's positive mental attitude.

"The horn!" Bartell shouted at Culp.

"What?"

"Horn!" Bartell holstered his revolver and stepped to the front of the car, but the hood was one of those dandy theft-proof outfits that could be opened only from inside.

Culp looked quizzically at the driver's door, studying for a way to get to the hood release without disturbing the scene. After a moment he carefully snaked an arm through the fully open window and popped the hood latch. Then Bartell raised the hood and pulled the wires from the horn. In the sudden quiet his ears continued to ring.

"Just for the record," Bartell said, trying to shake the ringing noise from his ears, "this is a man passed out behind the wheel of a blue and white Dodge."

"Who called?" Culp asked.

Bartell didn't know.

"What the fuck . . ." It was Skinner, standing just inside the door, blocking the light. "What're you gonna do now?"

"Where's the girl?" Bartell asked.

"Still in your car," Skinner said. "She ain't going no place. What're you gonna do now? Fuckin' gooks. Gettin' killed in our own country now. What next?"

"Shut up," Culp said.

Skinner gave him a hurt look, but he did stop jacking his jaws.

For a moment Bartell did the only thing he could. He ignored Ike Skinner. Now that his eyes were adjusted to the dusky light inside the garage, he saw plainly the dark blotches on the inside of the windshield. Those blotches turned out to be blood, which had been pumped from the man's open throat. A fly had become mired in one of the rapidly coagulating smears. Bartell could see the tag ends of the slash, despite the attitude of the man's head as he slumped over the steering wheel. There was also blood smeared on the window ledge, smears which displayed smudged finger and palm prints. Bartell figured that these had been made by the woman who'd come screaming out of the alley. He felt the back of the man's neck. It was still warm. His hair, long and oily on top, short around the ears, was sticking up on top of his head, as though somebody had held it in a fist, held the man's head back while whipping a knife across it. That would account for the blood spatters on the windshield. Bartell didn't know how many pounds per square inch the average heart pumped, but he knew it was enough for a pretty good squirt. If the dead man had struggled, he hadn't struggled for long. And he wasn't dead long, either. His body was still flexible enough to slump forward onto the horn. How had that happened? Just a quirk of balance, maybe. Maybe the woman in Bartell's car had shaken him, tipped him forward just enough for gravity to take over. Christ only knew.

"No hurry now," Culp said. The blood on the windshield seemed to have darkened in the few moments they had been there. Culp might have been talking to himself.

Bartell nodded. "Let's clear out of the garage," he said. It was still his call, his crime scene, even though he was junior to both Culp and Skinner. "Get some dicks over here. A camera. Pass it on like a dose of the clap."

"What about the girl?" Skinner asked. He punched his glasses back up on the bridge of his nose. "I looked in on her. Don't think she talks a word of American. *You fuckee, GI?* maybe. Hell, they all know how to say that."

"I thought I told you to shut up," Culp said.

"Well, they do, don't they?" Skinner said defensively. He took out his Copenhagen and shook his head. "Friend of mine told me once about this dead gook he seen over in Nam, had a tracer cookin' between his shoulder blades." Skinner wiped his fingers on his pants and fit the chew behind his lower lip with his tongue.

They were outside the garage now and Bartell noticed Culp looking past Skinner toward Bartell's car, where the caged woman waited. Bartell wondered if he would still have put the woman in the back seat, behind the screen, if she'd been white. Or even Indian. He wondered who the woman was. He reminded himself to advise the Dispatch Duroc that they'd need a translator.

After using Skinner's radio to call for detectives, the three cops spent the next few minutes doing what all broke-to-lead uniforms do at the scene of a major crime. They did nothing. The reason that they did nothing wasn't that they didn't know what to do. Hardly. They knew that the scene would be carefully photographed, measured, and sketched, jobs which any one of them—or at least Bartell and Culp— could have done with a degree of skill. They knew, too, that somebody would go through the house at 833 Morton, the house that went with the garage. They could have gone about that, too, while they waited, just as one of them could have started going door to door to all the other houses on the block, asking if anybody had seen anything suspicious, taking down names and addresses and phone numbers. Who knew, they might even have succeeded in flushing out the original complainant, who, the Duroc advised Bartell, was anonymous. She did, however, have the name of a lady in the next block who had called in to complain about a car horn disturbing her peace. Could Officer Bartell check that out please, while he was in the area? Yes, he could, thank you very much.

The three uniforms knew all about the jobs that would be done in the next few hours, and they had a good idea of how to go about those jobs. They were, after all, policemen.

What the three cops also knew was that you can do a lot of unorthodox things on the police department, some of them felonious, and get away with them, but crossing over the division of labor was not one of those things. The jobs that needed to be done were *detective* jobs. That meant that even if they proceeded with the investigative jobs at hand, the dicks would only ignore the results and do them again, because it was their job to do those jobs. And on top of that the dicks would probably complain to their captain about uniform interference, and their Captain would complain to Bud Haller, who would jerk Tobe Mitchell in by the short hairs, and Tobe Mitchell would make an omelette out of their collective testicles. No, their main job on a case like this was to dump it on the detectives, get their reports written, and get their cars rolling again in case of something *big*. Stop eating up the payroll with something as frivolous as investigating a homicide, which was a *detective job*.

After Bartell was finished with Skinner's radio, Culp went back to wait with the woman.

She sat rigid as stone in the back seat, staring straight ahead at the steel mesh screen. Her hands were laying palm up in her lap. The blood had dried to a dark flat brown. Culp opened the door. The woman didn't move. She wore a green T-shirt. Her straight black hair fell below her shoulders. Her bangs were cut straight and folded gently into her eyebrows. Culp got a whiff of the air inside the caged compartment and looked again at the woman's lap. She'd wet her pants.

"Lady? Hey, lady." Culp put his hand on her shoulder and tried to remember Vietnamese words and phrases. He'd sworn he'd never forget those words, words for things like *friend, everybody outside, don't shoot*. Stuff he was sure he'd always remember and now he needed it and he couldn't remember it at all. "You speak any English at all? Can you tell me anything about what happened here?"

The woman turned and looked at him. Mascara ran down her cheeks in dark dry smudges. She was done with crying, though.

"You understand?" Culp knelt beside the open door.

The woman's brow wrinkled and she opened her mouth and tried to form a word. Culp couldn't understand her at all, so he asked her to repeat the word several times.

"Hu-bn," the woman said finally, grabbing on to Culp's arm in desperation. "Hu-bn."

Husband.

Chapter 16

□　□　□

Who was that guy you had over on Morton? That was the first thing the other cops wanted to know, the thing they kept popping into the briefing room to ask while you were trying to manipulate one of the destroyed Olympia typewriters before your old lady called her attorney because you were two hours late getting home from work, before the shift commander got out the Vaseline to grease up your overtime slip so he could ram it where the guys upstairs believed it really belonged.

Trying to bang out a report that consisted of semi-complete sentences set down in a form that was coherent enough not to get you strangled by some defense attorney seven or eight months from now.

Nguyen Nhu. That was the dead guy's name, and he did in fact live at 833 Morton. Bartell had learned that from Culp, who checked the license plate on the Dodge through the motor vehicles computer. When the plate came back registered to Nguyen Nhu, Culp pointed down the alley, said the name to the woman, whom he had moved out from behind the cage, and she nodded her head slowly and started to cry again. Bartell typed *Nguyen Nhu* in the blank of the offense report labeled *Victim.* In the space marked *date of birth,* he typed *Unknown,* since the excavation of the crime scene hadn't preceded as deep as Nhu's wallet, where he presumably carried something with his birthday written on it. Maybe Tommy Cassidy and Sam Blieker, the first two dicks to arrive, had managed to get that information through an interpreter from Nhu's wife. Bartell didn't know. So he typed *Unknown.*

The cover sheet of an offense report has about six thousand blanks, and if you don't have this or that bit of information, it isn't enough just to leave the space empty, you have to fill it with *Unknown.* Clarity, they said. Right. Ignorance is always clear.

How'd he die? People always want to know how a guy gets clobbered, too. In the box labeled *Nature of Injury,* Bartell wrote:

Deep laceration to the throat, causing extensive loss of blood. He smiled at the sanitary, professional prose and took a sip from the can of Coke at his left. He looked at his watch. Nearly midnight. Five hours since they'd found the body.

In the column under *Severity of Injury,* he typed an *X* in the box beside *Fatal.*

Was the guy a mess? There wasn't a space on the form for that little tidbit. But that was something else most of the guys wanted to know. Especially with something high-powered, like a dismembered woman or a train wreck. In this case the answer was: No. The guy was not a mess. The car. The car was the mess.

Bartell removed the cover sheet and replaced it in the typewriter with the less cluttered form used for the narrative portion of the report, the part where he was supposed to make some kind of sense out of what had gone on.

While on routine patrol, I was dispatched to . . . blah . . . blah . . . blah . . .

Bartell couldn't get over Cassidy and Blieker. Although Blieker was a sergeant, Cassidy's supervisor, you couldn't tell it from their behavior.

"Don't mind Sam," Cassidy said to Bartell as he and Blieker got out of their gray sedan. "Sam's got the cramps today and he's having hot flashes, too." Cassidy, a natural blond, shook his head like a lion, then flicked his fingers at his hair, bouncing the perm he got once a month from some squeeze downtown. Forty bucks a pop, he told everybody. If you had to pay off in cash, he always added with a wink.

Blieker only grunted and asked the way to the stiff. He adjusted his tan suitcoat on his thick, boxy shoulders and mopped the perpetual band of perspiration from his forehead with a large white handkerchief. He consumed a frightful sigh and pasted his thinning brown hair against the sides of his head with the palms of his hands.

Bartell didn't know Blieker very well, since Blieker had been a detective during all the years that Bartell had been on the department. His impression was that Blieker was a no nonsense guy who knew his job up, down and sideways, the kind of guy who'd been around enough, seen enough, that he didn't need to worry over the jibes of any leather-clad, cathouse disco detective like Tommy Cassidy. Cassidy claimed to write books, but everybody figured it was just a scam he used to pick up girls. But people said that the Lodge—that's the Montana State

Prison at Deer Lodge—was full of guys who still believed that Sam Blieker only wanted to help them sort out their troubles. Christ, Bartell had even arrested a guy once and the asshole later complained to his attorney that he, Bartell, had violated his rights because he wouldn't let him call Sam Blieker in the middle of the night and explain why he'd thrown a guy through a glass display case full of dildos at a porn shop. Bartell figured that dirtheads like that were credentials enough for Blieker, never mind that he didn't own a polo shirt with a semi-extinct reptile over the heart, didn't possess or even covet a silk or cabretta jacket, wouldn't dream of putting his feet inside either flashy Italian shoes or cowboy boots made from the skins of dead Amazonian snakes. He didn't carry a stainless steel gun or wear a shoulder holster with enough doodads on the harness to carry everything short of a battle axe.

"We think this here's the wife," Bartell told Blieker, lowering his eyes discreetly in the direction of the woman. He had been back at the car for only a few minutes. Culp had returned to wait with Skinner at the garage.

"Stay with her, would you, Tommy?" Blieker said. "I want Ray and me to walk through this thing first. If the interpreter gets here before I get back, see what you can find out from her."

Tommy looked as though he'd just been spanked and told to go to his room. Without a word, he leaned against the fender of Bartell's car and waited.

"You sure he's dead?" Blieker asked as they headed down the alley.

Bartell laughed dryly. "Yeah. He's got this really dead look about him."

"You checked for a pulse . . ." Blieker was out of breath from the brisk walk. ". . . should always feel for a pulse, you know. . . ."

"It's not the kind of pulse you'd have to feel for," Bartell said. He went on to explain about the slashed throat. "It's more a visible kind of pulse. Trust me, Sam, this guy ain't got one."

Blieker grunted again as they pulled up beside Culp and Skinner.

"Nobody's been in or out," Culp told Blieker, indicating the garage. "House's quiet, too, far as we can tell. We just held everything for you."

Bartell cleared his throat and stuck his hands in his pockets, wondering if he'd struck a suitably matter-of-fact air for the detective. Then he felt a warm flush at the base of his throat. He pulled his hands back out and cracked his knuckles nervously.

"It was only supposed to be a man passed out in a car," Bartell said. "Then the woman came screaming out and I figured something was up."

"Complainant?" Blieker asked.

"Duroc didn't know," Bartell said, feeling almost apologetic.

Blieker nodded slowly and explained to the three uniforms how he wanted to work the crime scene. "First of all, no coroner till I'm done," he said. That was no reflection on any of the shift bosses over at the sheriff's office, who served as deputy coroners. It was just a rule of Blieker's that helped keep the traffic down. Besides, until Sam Blieker was done with a crime scene, it was nobody else's goddamn business. They would need an ambulance to haul the body to the morgue, but that came later, too. The first thing that Blieker wanted to do, before he even looked at the body, was to take a quick look through the house. He lit an unfiltered cigarette, a Chesterfield, Bartell thought, but he wasn't sure they still made Chesterfields, so he could have been wrong. As he spoke, the smoke hung over Blieker's head like ballooned captions in a comic.

"After the house," Blieker said, "we process the garage and car."

"You want me to go through the house with you?" Bartell asked. He knew he was taking a chance, offering just like that to cross the sacred barrier dividing those who solved crimes from those who merely discovered them. Blieker stared at him. Culp and Skinner stared at him. *What the hell*, Bartell thought.

"What the hell," Blieker said. "I better wait for somebody else, except they're all gone for the day. Might take an hour." He scratched his bedraggled head and attacked another cigarette, all the while staring back down the alley, where Tommy Cassidy waited next to the black and white. "Maybe you better go back to the car, Ray," Blieker said finally. "Send Tommy down here." But Bartell had only gone three or four steps when Blieker said, "Aw, fuck it. Come on back. I only bring Tommy to hold my coat." Then, to Culp and Skinner, he added: "When Ardell Wings gets here from the lab, tell him I'll want pictures and prints of the whole works, but if he starts before I get back, I'll shoot his kneecaps off."

They left Skinner posted at the garage, then took Culp through the backyard, around to the front, where he could watch the door while they went through the house. It was a small house, no more than two bedrooms, from the look of the outside. The house sat atop a squat foundation of stone, smooth tan and pink native stone, the kind you saw at the bottom of rivers. The yard was unfenced. A tall blue spruce sat in the southwest corner of the front yard, rose in a fat blue spire, with a disc of brown, bare acidic dirt underneath. There were no curtains on the windows, and nobody seemed to be home.

With the resoluteness of a somewhat-fatigued Spencer Tracy, Blieker climbed the three cement steps at the front door. By the time he got to the top, he was sucking on the last margin of his third cigarette. Bartell noticed the rivulets of sweat behind his wide ears. The threadbare cuffs of Blieker's tan slacks dragged the ground at the heels of his black brogans. Before trying the door, he didn't draw his gun, but he did tuck the flap of his jacket behind the butt, and he pulled his badge and ID from the inside pocket of his jacket.

"You looking for something special?" Bartell asked. He realized he was sweating, too.

Blieker shrugged. "Not really. But you never know what's special till later, till you needed something and were lucky enough to have it. Mostly I just want to have a quick look around, make sure nobody's here. Out of the three of you, you guys didn't watch the front . . ." Blieker let the sentence fade. He made the statement as a simple observation of fact, not an accusation, which only sharpened the rebuke. Accusations could be refuted; facts spoke for themselves. In his own mind Bartell could have blamed Culp or Skinner, since both were senior. No future in that, though. Dumping things off only meant you only learned better how to dump.

"Sorry about the slipup."

"Ah, screw it," Blieker said. "Everything's always bitched up anyways."

Bartell felt like he'd just had his hair tousled by a Dutch uncle. He didn't like the feeling.

"Your main job is to be a witness for me, okay?" Blieker banged his knuckles on the hollow core door. "What we're doing, we're just checking for people. There was just a crime of violence in the garage that goes with this house. That means there could be an officer safety problem with somebody still in the house. Or there could be other victims inside. And we can't communicate with the woman to ask her about these things, or get her permission to go inside. So I think we've got probable cause and exigent circumstances for that kind of search. Make sense?"

Bartell nodded and Blieker went on. "Now, that don't mean you don't take a good look around, you know. It's just that if we find anything other than people, we get a warrant before we take it."

"I think I get you," Bartell said, more irritably than he'd intended. He was lucky not to be back guarding a woman who couldn't even speak English. To his surprise Blieker cracked a smile.

"It's okay, chum," Blieker said. "I fucked up three, four years ago myself." Blieker smiled once more at the same time he hammered again on the door. There was still no answer.

"Maybe there was just the dead guy and his old lady," Bartell said.

Blieker nodded and took the handkerchief from his pocket and swabbed his forehead again. Using his index finger and thumb, he tried the door by gripping the stem between the knob and the door. The latch gave way, and Blieker nudged the door all the way open with his toe. Then he shouted into the house several times that he was the police, asking if anybody was home. There was no answer this time, either.

"You shout that loud, Sam, you'll wake up the guy out in the Dodge," Culp said from the street.

"I bet I could find a new line of work, I had a talent like that," Blieker said over his shoulder. He took a step inside. Somewhere deep inside the spruce, a squirrel barked and Bartell snapped his head around. "Gently, son. Gently," Blieker said. The goddamn Dutch uncle routine again.

"Right, now, we'll just make a quick pass through all the rooms," Blieker said. "Don't touch nothing, don't get a glass of water in the kitchen or take a piss when you check the John."

"You think I'm some kind of moron?" Bartell asked, unable to contain himself any longer.

"Not especially," Blieker said blandly. "Just a cop."

Blieker wandered lackadaisically into the sparsely furnished room, which smelled of something sweet. Sandalwood, Bartell thought. Maybe something they burned for their religion. They weren't like Baptists, these people, not the least little bit. The summer light fell in bright patches against the wall to Bartell's right, upon which hung the likeness of an intricate dragon airbrushed on black velvet. An ancient oil heater, connected to the flue by a rickety arm of black stovepipe, squatted like a fat mechanical Buddha against the wall at his left. How strange it must seem, this country where heat must be courted, rather than escaped or endured.

"It don't ever hurt to watch your back," Blieker said as he eyed the dragon. "Sometimes all the bodies ain't all the way dead. If you get my drift."

Bartell nodded and wandered across the room toward a door that apparently led to the kitchen. The door was on the right side of the living room. At the left end, beside the heater, a hall led to bedrooms at the back of the house. Blieker stopped next to a frayed tan couch and looked down at a stack of magazines near one end. Old editions of *Newsweek*, mostly, with a smattering of women's publications, and an issue of *Soldier of Fortune* poking out from the bottom. Other than the magazines, the room was neat as a pin, with only two other pieces of furniture, a severe-looking occasional chair against the wall between the kitchen door and the hall, and a large RCA color console TV next to the front door.

The kitchen was clean, too. No mounds of molding dishes, no pockets of garbage nestled here and there. Just the basic appliances, along with a matchwood table and five chairs. Nothing remarkable. A large pot of rice sat warming on the gas range. Blieker paused at the back door and looked out at the garage.

"More troops," he said. Wings, with his cameras and evidence gear, along with Lieutenant Frank Woodruff, Harry MacDonaugh, and Linda Westhammer, one of the half dozen women on the department. "Like flies, cops," Blieker said. "The whole mob of 'em. I had them call Woodruff. MacDonaugh and Westhammer must've heard it over the radio on their way home. Harold Hoopes, though, he ain't here." Blieker rambled on distractedly. "Harold took the day off. Something about his hemorrhoids, I heard. It's all very hush-hush."

Bartell nodded and wandered out of the kitchen, planning to check the bedrooms. Blieker followed, pausing now and again just to look around the two rooms, as though trying to divine some message that ordinary cops, the kind who wore uniforms and wrestled drunks, could not comprehend.

"Never had 'em myself," Blieker said, falling in after Bartell once again.

"What's that?"

"Hemorrhoids."

"Me neither."

"I heard once," Blieker said, "you get 'em from sitting on the throne too long while you read the paper."

"I wouldn't know."

"Must hurt, though?"

"I guess." Bartell was looking for a light switch at the head of the dark hall.

"Oh, Christ, yeah. Let some maniac loose with a knife . . . *down there?* Hurt like unto death itself, you ask me."

The hall was very dark, and it took Bartell a moment to find the light switch. Then after he switched on the light, it took a moment longer before his eyes adjusted well enough to see the boy at the end of the hall, and it was still another instant before he saw the gun in the boy's hand.

Bartell threw out his arm and batted Blieker back into the living room.

"A kid," he whispered to Blieker, who had pulled his gun almost as fast as Bartell. "Kid with a gun."

"It's the police," Blieker called down the hall. He took out a cigarette and drew on it cold. "You hear me down there, son? You understand? The police. Nothing to be scared of . . . we just wanna help you."

Christ, what would a kid like that know about help from the police? Vietnamese kid like that, you might as well tell him you were the devil himself. Same as saying you were the police. That is, if he even understood what you were saying. That was the trouble with these goddamned foreigners: you couldn't even tell them not to shoot you.

Blieker rolled his eyes and shook his head. "How old you figure he is?"

"Hell, I don't know. Thirteen, fourteen, maybe. I mean, they all look young to me . . . till they get real old." He felt guilty about saying that, like saying if you've seen one, you've seen them all. "You want to get some help in here?"

Blieker thought for a moment, then shook his head. "Next thing you know, we'll have a SWAT team and TV, the whole fucking works. I figure he's just scared, just needs some time. He knows something bad happened and he's scared." Blieker let out another deep sigh and put a match to the cigarette.

"That's gotta be it. If it was something else, he'd either of run

. . . run, or busted a cap on us while we were wandering around here with our heads where the sun never shines."

Bartell wondered what they should do next, and Blieker didn't have an answer. There figured to be a window facing the backyard, the garage, where Skinner, Woodruff, and the rest of the world would be working their way through the crime scene.

"You better go tell them," Blieker said.

"Why don't you go?" Bartell tapped his chest. "Got my vest on. Better I stay."

"You sure?"

Bartell shrugged and grinned. "Everybody knows I'm immortal." He laughed self-consciously, meaning the night George Rather should have killed him. But Blieker didn't seem to get it. "What the hell," Bartell said soberly. "I can keep him bottled up. Go on."

After a long pause Blieker said, "Okay. But you wait, understand?"

Bartell nodded.

"I mean it," Blieker whispered through the cigarette smoke. "I know what you're thinking, but don't fucking do it. Just wait."

"Come on, Sam, give me a break." Bartell managed another smile and nodded toward the front door. "You better go out and tell those guys."

After Sergeant Blieker left the house to advise the other officers about the individual with the gun, this officer determined that the safety of those officers outside the house would be improved if this officer attempted to hold the subject's attention.

Bartell almost laughed when he stopped typing and read back over that sentence. Take right hand and place securely over rectum. That was what the sentence really meant, because what he had done after Blieker left might be construed as an act of reckless abandon.

For starters all he did was look around the corner again. The hall was less than twelve feet long. The doorway on the far right side was empty. There was a second door just around the corner to his left. That door was closed, but Bartell was able to reach the knob from where he stood. He swung the door open, looked into the room as best he could, then slipped around the corner.

It was a bedroom. Bartell looked around quickly, in the closet and under the bed. Empty. Then he stood in the door and looked across the hall.

He could almost see into the far bedroom. He could see the edge of a bed, an unmade bed with blue sheets, and he could see the shadow of a lone person, which fell unmoving across the bed.

"My name's Ray," he said, keeping his voice light. "Ray Bartell. I'm a policeman." There was no answer, no sound from the other room. "You hear me? You understand what I'm saying?"

Bartell planted his left shoulder against the doorjamb and listened until his ears began to hum. His throat had gone dry. He dug into his shirt pocket and pulled out a chunk of gum. "It's your mother," he said. "At least, I think she's your mother. Real pretty woman in a green T-shirt . . . that your mom? . . . she's out in my car . . . she's fine." With his one free hand Bartell peeled the wrapper and popped the gum into his mouth. Strawberry. Sugarless strawberry, all the better for the teeth, my dear. Goddamn wives, hound you everywhere you go. First it was cigarettes, then chewing tobacco, and now he wasn't even allowed real gum. Bartell felt his pocket, then took out a second lump of gum. He looked down at the white and pink wrapper and smiled.

It was a comic book tactic, a good old Sergeant Rock-G.I. Joe number. *I can't believe this bullshit*, Bartell thought, even as he stood looking down at the gum, grinning.

"You want some gum, kid?" He hoped to Christ it really was a kid. He listened, but there was still no answer. "I'm gonna throw you this gum . . . it's like a peace offering, you know . . . something to get you to be sensible, 'cause your mother, she's out in my car and she needs you . . . you know?" He leaned out into the hall and tossed the gum toward the door, where it landed just outside the threshold.

"You can trust a guy gives you gum," Bartell said lightly. "Honest. Sugarless gum, even, good for your teeth." Jesus Christ, how many kids had been butchered after believing that line of shit?

A moment later—son of a bitch, he still couldn't believe it!—a hand reached out and took the strawberry gum, and after that, a Government Model .45 came sliding over the linoleum, sliding all the way to the baseboard across the hall and thumped to a stop.

"Why don't you come on out?" Bartell holstered his gun and squared himself to meet the kid in the hall. But he held back from taking the first step out. No need to confuse recklessness with stupidity. First the kid . . .

. . . and just seconds later the kid stepped out. He was short, about five and a half feet tall. Fourteen or fifteen years old. Shiny blue-black hair that fell straight and neat over his ears, like a helmet. The kid wore a white sweatshirt that said *Dallas Cowboys—America's Team* across the chest. The sleeves, cut off above the elbows, napped idly against the kid's skinny arms.

"What's your name?" Bartell asked as he stepped out into the hall. He still didn't know if the kid spoke English, or if he was just a sucker for sugarless gum.

The kid looked down at the .45 and Bartell reached down quickly. He scooped up the gun, dropped out the magazine and locked the slide back. Without taking his eyes off the kid, he reached down once more and retrieved the live round that had kicked out of the chamber when he locked the slide.

Bartell took several steps forward, three steps closer to a bullet, he thought once, but kept going, always glancing from the boy's hands to the open door, always listening, until the boy stepped back into the room. Bartell stepped in quickly behind him.

The boy stood beside a rumpled double mattress that lay on the floor beside the door. There were three more kids on the mattress, the oldest probably not more than ten, the youngest a toddler barely able to sit up on his own. The toddler's face wrinkled, as if he were crying. Bartell picked him up. He still didn't make a sound. None of the kids made a sound, not even when Bartell rounded them up and shepherded them out to the living room, where Blieker and Culp glared at him and shook their heads.

Bartell pulled the report from the typewriter and read it over, marking his initials where he had made corrections. Once he'd removed the kids from the house, Blieker posted him at the front door, where he spent the next hour, until he was relieved by Juju Watson and sent back to do his paperwork, the report that he was now ready to sign.

So who killed Nguyen Nhu? Bartell hadn't a clue. He finished off the Coke and tossed the can in the trash basket across the room. It was a hard throw, no touch at all, and he was surprised when the can disappeared.

Bartell didn't even know what had happened to the four kids, or to the woman, who was gone when he returned to his car. He could still smell the blood in the heat of the garage, a sharp animal smell, mixed with fecal stench that so often accompanied death.

So who killed Nguyen Nhu? Bartell sorted the pages of the report into numerical order. He signed the cover sheet in the box marked *Signature of Reporting Officer*, then added the date and time, also in the appropriate boxes. He proceeded through the narrative, signing and dating the bottom of each page. Finally, almost as an afterthought, he returned to the cover sheet and, in the box marked *Suspect*, he scribbled *Unknown*.

All Bartell knew for sure was that it was the kid's job to protect his brothers and sisters, and that he was prepared to do it with a rusty GI .45, a gun probably smuggled out of Nam by the dead man in the garage, the boy's father. He hoped that Nguyen Nhu wouldn't haunt his son because the boy had given the gun over for a lump of bubble gum—bad bubble gum to boot. Who knows, maybe the kid actually spoke English, understood that he wasn't in a war zone anymore. How then would someone explain his dead father? That was another mystery, a mystery inside a riddle inside a secret.

At the bottom of the last page of his report, Bartell read the last sentence: *Investigation turned over to detectives*. Then he looked at his watch. Quitting time. Screw it. Now he had to go home.

Chapter 17 □ □ □

The Nhu homicide passed into July with no arrests and no good suspects. And for the most part it passed from Bartell's attention, too. Uncleared homicides are a detective's ulcer, and Bartell's own life generated enough heartburn on its own. Helen had apparently come home to stay, but sometimes the whole marriage was like the night of the living dead. He had mistakenly believed that she might provide some sort of modest explanation about where she'd passed the five-day sabbatical from their marriage.

"I didn't do anything wrong," Helen said on the one occasion he'd had nerve enough to inquire.

"That's not what I asked," Bartell said.

"I know. But it's what you were thinking. I always know what you're thinking."

"You're just doing this to drive me crazy."

"Of course." There was a hint of good humor in her voice and Bartell relaxed a bit. Then she added, "I might leave again, you know. If I decide."

"Decide what?"

She shrugged. "Just decide. Who knows." She'd stopped smiling.

That was two weeks ago. She'd softened since, but he still felt like he was walking on hot coals around the house. He hoped she would stay, wanted to tell her how much he needed her to stay. Maybe she was right, though, right that staying was something she should choose for herself, not something he should press her into, which she knew he could do if she ever let him get started talking. They both deserved better than that, better than a marriage glued together by his barker's pitch about dreams coming true.

Once in a while Bartell still cornered Sam Blieker and asked how the homicide case was going. They'd interviewed people, Blieker told him. Lots of people. So far the most active theory was that Nhu had been sliced as part of some vendetta that stretched all the way back to Southeast Asia.

"Some kind of family, military, black-market bullshit," Blieker said. "Who the Christ knows? It came out sounding different from every one of those people you talked to."

In the end, the most constructive thing to result from that theory was that Blieker and Harry MacDonaugh got to make a trip to Seattle. They went to interview several people whose names had cropped up in connection with Nhu. None of the interviews panned out, but they got to eat enough salmon that MacDonaugh halfway believed they might swim up the first river they came across on the way back. They also got to see a great ball game at the Kingdome. It was the first time Blieker had ever seen major league baseball in person, and he allowed that it was just fine, even if the game was indoors, which seemed to controvert the laws of nature. Now Blieker wore a Mariners baseball cap to work. The cap went well with his wardrobe of baggy blue and brown suits.

But nobody could make a case against the killer of Nguyen Nhu.

For Bartell work went on in a fairly normal way. Babies were born and old people died and those in between continued to get in trouble. Sometimes the car felt misguided, as though out of ballast without Culp. More than once Bartell caught himself turning to ask a question, only to find an empty seat.

As time passed, though, he became more and more comfortable without Culp, so comfortable that he began to wonder if Culp had been a friend or a crutch. Bartell supposed it was possible to be both. But if that were so, it didn't say much for his character that he felt accomplished and free now that he was alone. It really stinks, he laughed to himself one day, living within the limits of your own personality.

Among the dead that summer was Stump Riggins. Some bums found his body beside a warehouse near the tracks. It was Bartell's call. A sheet of newspaper had blown over Stump's face, and red dust had drifted into two lean furrows on the leeward side of both legs. The big silver-belly Stetson was gone. They posted the body, since Stump, like a heroic old dog, had wandered off by himself to die. The causes of death were entirely natural, according to Dr. Odell Molyneaux, the sentimental and erudite pathologist. A few days later Bartell found the Stetson. Walking around underneath it was this little cockroach with an

Oklahoma drawl and a big black hound that was almost as ugly and dirty as the cockroach himself. One thing about dogs, they can at least lick themselves clean.

"Come here," Bartell said as he pulled up alongside the cockroach in the alley behind Angel's Bar.

"Me?" the cockroach said. "Me?"

"Yeah, you." Bartell didn't even bother to get out of the car.

"I ain't done nothin', bro."

"You call me bro one more time and I'm gonna get out of this car. Now get your ass over here."

The cockroach started toward the police car. The hound hung back, and the cockroach tugged at the clothesline rope tied to the bandanna around the hound's neck. The cockroach stopped about ten feet away and leaned against the dumpster.

"Where'd you get that hat?" Bartell asked. Rattlesnake hatbands weren't something you saw everyday.

"What hat you talkin' 'bout?"

"That hat. The one right there on your head."

The cockroach's eyes rolled far back in his head as he looked up at the brim. "You mean this here hat . . ." With his free hand, the hand that wasn't needed to hold the rope and keep his Thanksgiving dinner from running off, the cockroach pointed up at the silver belly. "*This* hat . . . you talkin' 'bout this here hat on my head . . ."

"Yeah," Bartell said. He was losing patience. Stump Riggins wasn't any prince, but he did deserve better than to have his corpse robbed. "That hat. The hat I'm gonna kick your ass out from under, you don't hand it over in about ten seconds."

"You can't do that."

"That hat come off a dead guy," Bartell said. "You want me to start asking you how that guy got dead?"

The cockroach's eyes narrowed as he looked at the ground.

Bartell stuck his arm out the window. "Now gimme that fuckin' hat!"

The cockroach had taken half a dozen steps toward the freight yard before the Stetson hit the ground and by the time Bartell got out of the car and retrieved it, the cockroach was out of sight.

Bartell smiled when he found the message scrawled in smeared ink around the sweatband. *This hat belongs to Stump Riggins and a curse on any son of a bitch that steals it.*

Once he had the Stetson, Bartell drove to the south end of the California Street Bridge. He walked out across the rotting wood planks, shaking the hat and listening to the rattles as he thought about curses. From near the center of the bridge he tossed that big old hat into the Holt. He watched until the hat was swallowed up by a cascade of water and moonlight about fifty yards downstream. He looked on across the way at the hulking mill, then shivered in the damp wind off the Holt and trotted back to his car.

Screw a bunch of curses.

Near the first of July Culp went back north to Lakeside and looked up Nancy. She was still working at the restaurant. Culp brought groceries at the mercantile store in Lakeside and Nancy made lunch and they rented a boat. They found a small deserted stretch of sand beach two bays south, where they ate and swam, and at dusk they went back to the motel.

Two or three days later Paul Culp ran into an old pal. He drove past Leech's and saw a bunch of motorcycle assholes taking up space on the sidewalk and in the middle of them stood Skeeziks. Skeeziks was in his forties, which made him somewhat of a *professor emeritus* among motorcycle thugs. Attaining such a dignified age also meant that Skeeziks had acquired the skill of getting along. Culp had met him half a dozen years ago, when somebody got cut inside Leech's, cut bad, judging from all the reports and from the trail of gore leading out the back door. As is the nature of such altercations, nobody, but nobody inside Leech's knew from nothing. But an hour later Culp had jumped Skeeziks a couple of blocks away from the bar.

The point was, Culp explained, that if some dipshit was cut, that was one thing. But if the asshole was going to crawl off someplace and bleed out, well, that was something else. Nobody expected Skeeziks to snitch off a brother, it's just that it made good sense to get this cut-up dude to a hospital and keep the crime level to a minimum. The brother could kill him later, under more private circumstances, if that's what needed to be done. No hurry about that.

For his trouble Culp got an address. No more. Another biker, a behemoth named Mongoose, was picked up and taken in handcuffs to St. Francis, where his life was duly saved. Mongoose refused to press any charges, as Culp had expected. He was released a couple of days later, and nobody had seen or heard from him since.

Nobody had seen or heard from Skeeziks, either, until that afternoon outside Leech's, where he leaned against maroon hardtail with nice paint and no serial numbers.

"Figured you were dead," Culp said after the other half dozen gut buckets wandered off and left Skeeziks alone. Culp got out of his car and offered Skeeziks a chew. After their previous dealings Culp figured that Skeeziks wouldn't try to kill him now for no reason.

"Maybe I was," Skeeziks said.

Maybe he was. "Nice scooter," Culp said. Culp looked at the black chopped Harley-Davidson. He was looking at the scooter, talking to Skeeziks, but his head was still up north.

"Gets me from here to there." Skeeziks reached up and retied the red bandanna that covered his head. Culp was surprised to see that he was almost bald under the bandanna.

"Seen that guy Mongoose around?" Culp asked, smiling. Flathead Lake was cold; it was nearly four hundred feet deep and fed by glaciers and it was always cold.

"Heard he took a trip. Beats the fuck out of me. You down on the lottery?"

"What lottery's that?" There were no deer in the orchard that night and near midnight they spotted the lights of a late fisherman, his boat sounding small and far on the breeze as they lay in bed, catching their breath and fighting sleep.

"One going on inside," Skeeziks said. He wasn't wearing anything from the waist up except his colors and his tattoos, both of which were state-of-the-art. "Leech got this chicken, see. Put him in a box. Box got squares on the bottom. Numbered squares. Hundred squares. Buy a square for a buck. Then he puts the chicken in the box. First square the chicken shits on, that's the winner. Hundred squares, hundred bucks. You better get down on that."

"Shit," Culp said, "makes me sick just thinkin' what you fuckers would do with the dollar I lost."

"Probably give it all to the church."

"That's close," Culp said. She was still there the next morning. Nancy. They showered and fell back into bed. By the time they awoke that afternoon, it was late enough that Culp had to race to get back to Rozette in time for work. "How much you down for?"

Skeeziks shook his head. "Nothing. Cut this deal with Leech, see. Right after it craps, I get to eat the chicken."

Life, Culp thought as he drove away, *is like that chicken, just looking for the winning number to dump on.* Like the night Helen

Bartell had come to his apartment and he was too stupid to take her to bed because he was too smart to get hung up in a bad piece of business between his friend and his friend's wife. He'd never mentioned that night to Bartell, and he knew that Helen wouldn't, either. During those long weeks before he'd looked up Nancy, Culp had thought several times about calling Helen, thought about it late at night when the drunks were loud in the alley and he couldn't sleep. That would be wrong, though. Not just because he and Bartell were friends—split up but still friends— but because when Helen went back to Bartell the next morning, Culp knew it was because she'd decided that life with Bartell was what she really wanted. Whenever Bartell grumbled about how difficult Helen was being, Culp wanted to tell him to shut up, tell him that was just Helen's way of settling accounts and sealing a bargain. A comment like that, though, might only rock the Bartell boat. If Bartell was going to punch his own holes, let him patch his own leaks. Culp had enough to do dodging chickens.

If you asked Ray Bartell today what he and Helen were fighting about on the night that everything turned to shit, he couldn't tell you. Not for sure, anyhow. Not the specifics, the nitty and the gritty. It is enough to recall that he was dozing on the couch, his head full of cobwebs, when the phone rang. It was nearly two a.m. He knew that much because there was a clock on the wall above the phone in the hallway. Helen had clocks every goddamn place. Maybe that's what they'd fought about that night, the fucking clocks. Or something equally stupid, something that had to do with *Helen's Way*, which was what the battles invariably came down to. All the rest was just tactics.

Anyhow, it was a Duroc on the other end of the phone, and she told him he was requested to meet Captain Bud Haller at the east door of the Drexel School. The east door. That was where they had the command post.

Command post?

That's right. The command post. For the hostage situation that had developed at 841 Morton. What was Bartell's ETA? Captain Haller wanted to know.

Bartell told her he'd be there in ten to fifteen minutes, then rang off. He heard a second click, which meant that Helen had been on the phone in the bedroom upstairs. Bartell stretched his back. He thought about making some instant coffee, but there wasn't time. He went upstairs and dressed in the dark. Fumbling with his clothes, he told himself that he didn't want to turn on a light and disturb Helen. But the truth was, he was sneaking off like a martyr. Know the truth, the Bible said, and the truth shall set you free. If that was the case, then freedom sucked. Bartell turned on the small lamp on his dresser.

"Will you be all right?"

He stopped tucking in his shirt and looked across the room. Helen was sitting up in bed.

"You heard?"

"Only the part about hostages." She pulled the sheet up under her chin.

"All I have to do is talk to the guy," Bartell said. He'd explained to her before how negotiating works, and from what he'd told her about other jobs, she knew the kind of things that went on. Once, though, when he was on nights, he'd gotten called into a job and hadn't been able to phone her to say he'd be late getting home in the morning. Helen had found out about the incident when she heard it on the car radio while driving to work. Since then she liked reassurance.

"I know, but . . ." She stopped talking and Bartell sat down and put on his shoes. When he finished, he unlocked the small drawer on his dresser, where he kept the short-barreled Smith and Wesson revolver and extra set of cuffs.

"It'll be okay," he said airily, fitting the cuffs behind his belt after he'd slipped into the shoulder holster. He walked to the bed and kissed Helen lightly.

He turned to leave, but she caught his arm. "I don't like you going off like this . . . not after we've been this way."

"You mean the fights."

Helen nodded.

"Then I guess we'll have to stop."

"Stop fighting, you mean."

"Sure. What'd you think I meant?"

"Nothing. I just—"

"I didn't mean that," he cut her off. "I just meant—"

"You better go," Helen said. She let go of his arm and slid back down into the bed. Bartell looked at her for a moment and then left. Drexel School. The east door. They had specified the *east* door. That meant that the east door was out of the line of fire.

Two blocks east of Drexel School Bartell doused the lights on his pickup. He downshifted into third, then depressed the clutch a second time and coasted to a stop against the curb. There were three black and whites and two unmarked units parked nearby, like circled wagons. All of the police cars were empty. Bartell wondered where they'd set up the perimeter. The house was about two blocks west of the school. He remembered that much from finding Nguyen Nhu in the same block.

Bartell looked out across the playground, through the skeletons of swing sets and jungle gyms, which cast frail shadows in the moonlight across the asphalt. July heat lingered even through the mountain night. Sheet lightning played on the horizon to the west and a dry wind tore fitfully through the child-weary locust trees around the playground. Bartell started for the school, where Blieker waited for him on the steps.

"Nice night," Bartell said, yawning.

"Nice night for assholes," Blieker amended.

"Who you got for negotiators?" Between the police department and sheriff's office, Rozette had a six-member negotiating team. But it was always tough, especially in the summer, to turn out all six.

"Besides you, there's just Woodruff, and Joey Yarno from over at the county," Blieker said. "I'm doing your intelligence because they couldn't find Harold Hoopes. I don't know where the other two are, either."

Blieker dusted cigarette ashes from the front of his baggy brown plaid sport shirt, the old-fashioned kind with a square tail, which he wore outside his pants to cover his gun and cuffs. Tonight was the first time Bartell had ever seen Blieker without a coat and tie. Things must be down and dirty.

Blieker pushed the blue Dodgers cap back on his head and said, "Frank thought I'd be good for the intelligence workup. I know the asshole inside."

The asshole inside, Blieker went on, was this guy named Richard Thacker, a wacko son of a bitch they'd looked at last week, trying to make him for the Nhu killing.

"Thacker's got a woman in his house with him," Blieker said. "He lives at 841. That's right next door to the Nhu house."

"How'd you connect him with the homicide?"

"He's got a Vietnam hang-up."

"A vet?"

"No, his brother. We're trying to pin that down now. But some neighbors clued us that he'd got this hang-up, and it seemed real strange that he'd move in right next to those people."

"He do it?"

"We talked to him. He said he didn't. There isn't any evidence that points one way or another."

Bartell nodded and took another look around before going inside. It was a real heartbreaker of a summer night, the moon hooked on a fragment of stratus. The kind of night made for long drives through the country with girls and the top down. A regular Babylonian night, the stars thick as flies on a corpse. Just turn up that jungle music and let her rip.

"Anybody talked to Thacker yet?" Bartell asked. "How'd the call go down?"

"Let's get with Woodruff first," Blieker said. "I tell you all that now, he'll just tell you again in half a minute."

Together they climbed the cement treads into the school. A darkened hall stretched ahead, warmed by light from an office perhaps fifteen feet ahead. Drexel was an old school, the kind with thick plaster walls, tall ceilings and creaky wooden floors, the kind of school where learning was serious business, a way out of the neighborhood. In the late-night stillness, you could almost hear the children complain. As they approached the office Bartell heard Frank Woodruff's voice. Inside he saw that Woodruff was talking with Bud Haller.

". . . so there's no need to take him out," Woodruff was saying. "Not yet. Not even close."

Haller nodded and looked up at Bartell. "Hiya, Hollywood," Haller said, scowling.

Bartell winced at the memory of the Quentin Davies escapade.

Haller sucked a tooth and rubbed his chins with the back of his hand. "You ready to work some miracles? This lieutenant has been filling me in on how you guys will set up."

"There's no containment problem," Woodruff said to the room in general. "Arnold Slayton and his SWAT guys have a solid inner perimeter, and Uniform Patrol has the outer perimeter covered. You're going to do the talking tonight, Ray. All you've got to do is talk the son of a bitch out. Any problems with that?"

Bartell shook his head. "What's he want?"

"Well, that's the rub," Woodruff said. "We don't know."

The evening's activities had started about an hour ago, when Thacker took up beating on a woman downtown at Angel's. An Asian woman, it turned out. When Thacker started breaking up the capital improvements inside the bar, the bartender took it upon himself to protect his employer's investment—to say nothing of his own safety—by calling the cops. But when the cops swung through the front and back doors of Angel's, they learned that Thacker had just left, taking the woman with him at gunpoint.

"The bartender knows Thacker," Woodruff said. "Knew where he lives. Four officers went to 841. There was only one light on inside the house, but they could see him moving around, see the woman, too. They watched the place for a while. Then two guys went to the front door and just knocked. Figured, what the hell, what'd they have to lose. Thacker answered with four rounds through the door. That was when everybody decided to play this thing a little closer to the vest."

"Anybody talk to him at all?"

Woodruff shook his head. "We've been waiting to get set up."

"Any more shots?"

"The house has been quiet."

"So we're starting from scratch."

Woodruff nodded again and proceeded to roll up his sleeves, despite the clammy air inside the office. Haller bummed a smoke from Blieker. The way it worked out was that Bartell would ring up Thacker on the telephone, make deals, keep him calm, whatever it took to get everybody through the night in one piece. Besides Bartell on the phone and Blieker doing background, Yarno would assist Bartell, while Woodruff kept Haller and the rest of the world off everybody's backs. Tactics belonged to Bartell, Woodruff, and Yarno. Haller had the final call on strategy.

"Not that it matters," Bartell said, "but how come I'm talking?"

"Yarno's technically outside the department. And I talked to Thacker before, about the homicide. You seemed the best choice. Any problems with that?"

"You mean like a hangover from last winter?"

"The shooting. Yeah. I guess that's what I mean. Anything else, too. You got problems, let's hear them now."

"No problems," Bartell said. Woodruff appeared to take his word.

Bartell stood beside the desk for a moment, thinking. He was excited, yet strangely detached from the incident a couple of blocks away. Who the fuck was this Richard Thacker, anyhow? And what the fuck did he want, snatching a woman like that? A nut, obviously. What did he look like? Was he short? Tall? Fat? Did he have bad skin and sour breath? Was he drunk? Probably. He'd been at Angel's, hadn't he? How did his voice sound? Where was he from? What did he like to do with his free time? Besides snatch women, that is? What did Thacker *want?* What would Bartell *say* to this *asshole* when he picked up the *phone?*

"Does he have a phone?" Bartell asked. The job was a lot harder when they had to deliver a portable phone, too.

Woodruff smiled. "I've verified the number and everything through the phone company, along with letting them know what we're doing here. Yarno's taking care of the warrants to record and search."

"Where's Yarno now?"

"He's in a classroom downstairs," Woodruff said, rising and walking around the desk. "He's talking to the bartender from Angel's who turns out to be a fairly good friend of Thacker. Soon as Yarno gets some groundwork—just a few more minutes now— we'll try to phone."

They would use the phones in the principal's office, which was through the door just to Bartell's left. Just Yarno and Bartell. And Thacker. And the tape recorder that Woodruff now carried into the inner office. He also carried two yellow legal pads and a fistful of ballpoint pens, which he had taken from the small duffel beside the secretary's desk. Haller remained seated on the left side of the desk. At his elbow two walkie-talkies sputtered intermittently. Haller seemed to ignore them as he hunched forward in his chair and waited.

"Sam," Woodruff said, "while we're waiting, why don't you tell Ray the Richard Thacker story."

Blieker grunted and examined a small clay figure he'd picked up from the desk. The figure resembled a whale. A pink whale.

"You said you looked at him for the Nhu killing," Bartell said. "Before you talked to him, how good a suspect was he?"

Blieker grunted again. "Well, if by that question you mean, did Thacker have the opportunity, the inclination, the requisite personality, and skills to cut a man's throat, even more specifi- cally a Vietnamese man's throat, if that's what you're asking me, then I'd have to answer yes to all of the above." Blieker paused for dramatic effect, setting the whale carefully back on the desk. "He was good enough it broke my heart to walk away from him. On the other hand there was so little evidence—really no evidence at all—it would've broken my heart to keep him. Some days you're just doomed to get your heart busted."

But Blieker and Woodruff had still liked Thacker well enough to do some considerable digging. Richard Thacker was from Idaho. He'd grown up poor, along with his brother Wilfred, outside Bonners Ferry. Richard Thacker was thirty-five years old. Wilfred would have been thirty-six, except that Wilfred Thacker was dead, killed one night in the northern highlands when Charlie turned a Claymore back on him. That in was 1967. Richard Thacker was in Vancouver in 1967, mucking out bars, doing odd jobs, smoking dope, whatever draft resisters did when they got north of the border. He'd come back to the States shortly after the amnesty a few years ago. Of course, there was no amnesty in Bonners Ferry, Idaho. Worse yet, there was no amnesty inside Richard Thacker's head. So Thacker ended up on the skids in Rozette, Montana, where he'd managed to squeeze by between a rock and a hard place for the last two years.

The only thing about Thacker in local records was a misdemeanor assault arrest about a year ago, which, it turned out, was the result of Thacker's mental problems. Thacker had punched out his psychiatrist, who returned the favor by having him arrested, hoping to force Thacker to accept some responsibility. Blieker was at a loss to understand why the police hadn't had any contact with Thacker before now. Perhaps, Blieker speculated, he had spent the last two years winding himself tight enough for this very moment.

"You must've talked to his shrink," Bartell said. "Would he tell you anything?"

"About what you'd expect. Told us Thacker hates Vietnamese. Guilt. Feels like he ran out on his big brother. Can of worms. You get the picture."

The picture indeed. While Thacker might not have killed Nhu, the homicide might nonetheless have opened for him a world of possibilities.

"The shrink tell you any more?"

"Said Thacker's become obsessed with military stuff. Kind of a transference, I guess. Likes guns. Wears surplus clothes. Shit like that. I think he's genuinely afraid of Thacker. He opened the door a lot wider than therapists usually do, considering we obviously don't have a release from the client in question. We got a call in to the shrink now, trying to get him down here."

"What was Thacker like when you talked to him?"

"Weird," Blieker said.

"Very, very weird," Woodruff added. A moment later Joey

Yarno stepped into the office and Woodruff said it was time to go to work.

Joey Yarno's brown Stetson was keeping the glare off his infinite forehead. A pipe protruded from his mustache, which meant that somewhere behind all that brush was a mouth. Yarno nodded at Woodruff and handed Blieker a sheet of yellow legal paper.

"That's a list of names, phone numbers, and addresses," Yarno said. "People the bartender says can maybe give you a line on Thacker."

"And?"

"And hang on to your ass," Yarno said, rifling through his notes.

Bud Haller slumped against the wall below a cluster of diplomas and certificates.

The bartender's name was Dale Roemer and he'd known Thacker for over a year, long enough to understand that distance was the only vaccine to protect you from guys like Richard Thacker and his peculiar strain of psychosis. Like the distance between here and Mars. Maybe Jupiter. Thacker spent a lot of time in Angel's, where he invariably sat by himself at a table in the back, near the rest rooms. At about closing time, though, when most of the clientele were in their cups and past talking, Thacker would come out of his corner and talk. Talk about the past, about his brother and the war and all the things—the people—his brother did in the war. At the start, it had all sounded normal enough to Dale Roemer, just garden-variety grief, the kind everybody packs into a joint like Angel's. The thing about Thacker, though, was that he didn't drink.

"'Clean as baby's breath,'" Yarno said, quoting Dale Roemer. "Does lots of physical stuff, running, stuff like that to stay in shape."

"Drugs?" Woodruff asked.

"Roemer doesn't think so—"

"Jesus Christ, sounds like he doesn't need any," Haller interrupted.

Yarno stared at him a moment, then went on: "Says he's just crazy, that's all, just plain fucking *crazy*. Over this thing with his brother. And the thing was, see, that for a long time, Roemer thought Thacker was raving about his own life in the war, and then he realized one night that Thacker was talking about his dead brother, about what had happened to Wilfred over there, and then after a while Thacker himself forgets he's talking about Wilfred and it's all just one big fucked-up mess inside his brain."

Bartell sat down behind the principal's desk and began laying out pencils and paper in neat, compulsive patterns. "This bartender say why Thacker lives next door to the Nhu family, since he's all in a knot about the Vietnamese?"

"Sure." Yarno even laughed, an uncharacteristic break in his professional demeanor. "Because he's crazy. Said he moved in there on purpose. Got a real charge out of infiltrating a bunch of gooks."

Bud Haller looked like he needed to have his colon irrigated.

"Told Roemer about three months ago he'd moved in next to a tribe of slopes. That's what he called them. 'Tribe of slopes.' Said he was going to rescue his brother."

Bud Haller looked like his colon was *being* irrigated.

"Did Roemer know the inside of the house?" Woodruff asked.

"No."

"Weapons?"

"He had a handgun tonight at the bar. Roemer thinks a .357 wheel gun," Yarno said. "And some kind of assault rifle at the house. An AR-15, maybe an HK. Thacker never showed it to Roemer, but Roemer said he told him about it."

"And the woman?" Bartell asked. "Any line on the woman he grabbed?"

"Julie Chin," Yarno said. "Early twenties. Chinese, but born in the States. She's not a regular at Angel's, and Roemer doesn't know her, but he made some calls. He doesn't think Thacker knows her. She's just Asian, and that made her part of his trip."

Bartell scribbled a few notes on the legal pad. Blieker and Yarno had told him everything about Thacker except the key, the magic phrase that would either unscramble his lunatic brain. Or light his fuse. Maybe Julie Chin was already dead. Maybe Thacker was dead, too. In that case, none of this was necessary. But how would they find out? If Thacker and Chin were dead, who would pick up the phone inside 841 Morton and tell him? The *what-ifs* were starting to snowball. Bartell looked up at Yarno. "You ready?"

Yarno pulled off his hat and dragged a chair over beside Bartell. "No bald jokes," Yarno said. The mustache squirmed; he may have smiled. Then he busied himself with the cassette recorder and monitoring device that attached to the phone.

"Agreed," Bartell said. And to Woodruff: "Anytime you're ready."

Woodruff ushered Bud Haller out of the principal's office, giving Bartell and Yarno some breathing space, then stepped back in. Bartell noticed the gray saucers under Woodruff's eyes. A sandy cowlick wobbled on the crown of his head. At least a guy like Yarno didn't have any trouble with cowlicks. Bartell started to say something, but restrained himself, remembering the deal he'd just struck with Joey.

"We'll call in just a minute," Woodruff said. "After we time it out with Arnold." For the last forty minutes, in addition to commanding SWAT, Arnold Slayton had supervised a team of patrolmen in the evacuation of all the houses in Thacker's line of fire. So far the operation had come off smoothly. Nobody wanted to set off a shooting spree by ringing Thacker's telephone.

"Know what we're going to say?" Woodruff asked.

"Tell him to knock this shit off," Bartell said.

Woodruff nodded thoughtfully. "Then what'll you say after he tells you to go screw yourself?"

Bartell shrugged. "Air strike, maybe. Poison gas. The Devil. Whatever it takes." Fortunately air strikes and poison gas were strictly against policy. But the Devil . . . that was a real gray area.

Joey Yarno buffed his head with the palm of his hand. "What the hell. I'll even let you make bald jokes."

Bartell took out a toothpick and gouged it between a couple of molars. "You think of anything else, Joe?"

"Just weird," Yarno said with a completely straight face. "Weird enough to write your mother about."

"Terrific," Bartell said, exchanging glances with Woodruff. "Weird. Fucking terrific." He took off his watch and set it on the desk beside the legal pad. It was nearly two-thirty. "Can you find us some coffee, Frank? Lots of it. And maybe some doughnuts to soak up the coffee. And some Maalox to keep it all down. Can you do that?"

Woodruff said he'd do what he could. Bartell thanked him. His eyes felt hollow and dry as spent brass. His belly was busier than an anthill.

Chapter 18

□　□　□

Finally, it was time. When Bartell looked back down at his watch, the LCD numerals read 2:43, but it seemed like hours since Woodruff had left the two of them, Bartell and Yarno, alone to collect themselves. Yarno had spent time doodling on his legal pad, small hashed figures resembling gnomes.

Bartell wondered if Culp was outside. Of course he was. Culp was SWAT, a forward observer. He would be out there, holed up somewhere in the dark, waiting, along with the rest of Slayton's people, for Bartell to succeed or fail.

"Let's try it," Woodruff said, stepping suddenly into the office. He handed Bartell a slip of paper. A phone number.

Bartell nodded and adjusted the headset and glanced at Yarno, then dialed. Yarno switched on the cassette recorder. After nearly a dozen rings a man answered.

Yeah?
Hello, is this Richard Thacker? Who the fuck're you?
My name's Ray Bartell. I'm a police officer. Is this Richard Thacker?
Don't know no fuckin' Thacker. . . . What the fuck you want?
Listen, you're in a tough spot, Richard . . . I think we'd better—
Fuck you—

Yarno switched off the recorder and Bartell pushed the microphone away from his mouth.

"Goddamn, I hate it when they just hang up," Bartell said. "Son of a bitch."

"It's a little early to be getting frustrated," Yarno said. He sounded more than a little cautionary.

"I'm okay," Bartell said, waving him off. "Just butterflies." He took several deep breaths. "Let's try him again."

Yarno activated the recorder while Bartell dialed again.

Before you hang up, Richard, I want you to write down this number, okay? Write this down . . . it's 555-8503. That's the number you can—

How come you keep fuckin' botherin' me? Fuckin' asshole.

Just write the number down, Richard. That's the number where you can get me . . . Ray Bartell.

Why the hell would I wanna talk to you?

Well, to start with, there's that woman you—

You some kinda pervert? Pervert asshole calling up guys in the middle of the—

You grabbed that woman, Richard, then you—

Pervert asshole, that's you all right.

You fired a bunch of shots at some cops, Richard. I think you're in a bad spot. I think you better let me help you.

I don't deal with no pervert assholes!

Bartell looked at Yarno.

"Nobody said it'd be easy," Yarno said. "So you're a pervert asshole."

"How did he find out?" Bartell said.

"It could be worse," Yarno said. "You could be a bald pervert asshole."

"Or a bald pervert asshole with a mustache," Bartell said.

"Exactly." Yarno got up and went into the outer office, where Woodruff and Haller waited. A moment later he came back, closing the door behind him. "Your captain says to keep calling, until either the guy quits answering, or you think there might be some danger to the girl if we don't ease off. You got any problems with that?"

"No. Could you hear anything in the background? Anything to give us a fix on what's going on?"

Yarno shook his head.

Bartell looked at his watch: 2:51.

Hello?

Julie?

Yes?

My name is Ray Bartell. I'm a police officer.

Yes?

Are you hurt?

No.

Are you able to talk freely?

No . . . he's . . . he keeps talking about his brother.

What about his brother?

His brother, Freddie. He said he wants his brother Freddie . . . he says he'll kill me if they don't turn his brother, Freddie, loose . . .

Did he tell you where his brother is?

He said . . . he just says I know . . . you know . . . he says he'll trade me for his brother.

Can I talk to Richard? Will he talk to me?

He says no.

Did he write down the number I gave him?

No . . . I don't see it . . . I don't think he did.

It's 555-8503. You got that? 555 . . . 85 . . . 03. That's how you can get me if you need anything . . . while I'm setting this up about his brother. Okay?

Okay.

Can you answer some questions for me? Just yes or no answers?

I'll try.

Does he still have the gun?

Yes.

Is there more than one gun?

Yes.

What room of the house are you in?

I think—

Julie? Hello? Julie?

"Wonderful." Bartell leaned his chair back on two legs and rubbed his temples with his fingertips. His hands were cool and dry, almost bloodless.

"I'll tell Frank," Yarno said, standing.

"You might as well bring him and Haller in. This is going to take some doing. I'd say we have a serious problem, considering we're negotiating the release of a dead man."

The saucers under Woodruff's eyes looked even darker. Bartell wouldn't have wanted Woodruff's job for anything. The care and feeding of captains wasn't the kind of thing you'd wish on your worst enemy. Not that there was any specific problem with Haller. But who wanted to be the acolyte for a man who might have to decide soon that it was time to kill another human being? And then there was the press. Sooner or later reporters would be baying outside the door, and they were Woodruff's job, too. Bartell only had to deal with a madman.

"Do you think he'll shoot the girl?" Bud Haller asked. Long strands of gray hair kept slipping from the top of his head. He slapped them back with his blunt hand. "That's the bottom line as far as I can see. Will he hurt the girl. . ."

"All I can tell you," Bartell said, "is he hasn't hurt her yet. And if he's going to hurt her, we can't stop him."

"Son of a bitch is crazy," Haller said. "Swap for a fuckin' dead man."

"But that's something he wants," Bartell said. "That's the key right now. That's the transaction he wants to make—"

"—and it doesn't matter now whether we can or can't actually do it," Yarno said. "The important thing is that Thacker *believes* we can. You've got to be very careful about that, Ray."

"Exactly," Bartell agreed. Dealing with lunatics didn't bother him as much as it used to, not since he'd learned that lunatics are the most logical people in the world. Some people can be difficult because they *want* two plus two to equal five. But for a lunatic, two plus two *always* equals five. With a lunatic, you only have to learn if you're counting apples or oranges, and then make sure you stick with the right commodity. "You found Thacker's shrink yet?"

"He'll be here anytime," Woodruff said. "Dr. Markham. Arthur Markham."

During the next several minutes the four men considered their options. If Thacker did not do booze or drugs, then there was no danger that misapplied chemistry would send him over the edge. The downside was that he probably wouldn't improve with age, since there were no mind-altering substances from whose grip he might be released: they were dealing with the authentic Richard Thacker.

Using one of the walkie-talkies, Bud Haller checked with Arnold Slayton and reaffirmed that the houses adjacent to Thacker's had been successfully evacuated. At least until morning, when people started to move around, the job was secure.

"My people say no lights, no movement inside the house," Slayton said. "We're on hold."

"Check specifically the Nhu house, number 833," Woodruff said.

Slayton reported that the evacuation team had been unable to get any response from the Nhu house, either by phone or in person.

Woodruff pursed his lips. "I don't like that at all," he said to the men inside the school. "In fact, I think it sucks. But I don't know what we can do except negotiate for the brother, eat up some time. Ray?"

"Suits me. I'd feel better talking to the shrink first, though. It's only about ten minutes since the last call. He has our number. I think we can afford to wait."

"I agree," Yarno said. "Let him cool out for a while. Now that we know there's something he wants, I think it's a safe bet he'll call before doing anything wild."

"I want some idea," Bartell said, "of how tough he'll hang on to this thing with Freddie. I don't want to get halfway into this thing, then have him go lucid on us and think we're jerking him around."

Woodruff excused himself to go outside and watch for Dr. Markham. Bud Haller tried to bum a cigarette from Bartell and Yarno. Since neither of them smoked, he had to settle for a handful of vitamin capsules from the plastic fly box he carried in his jacket pocket.

"In the old days," Haller said, swallowing the pills dry, "we'd have kicked in the door and mashed the prick and thrown his ass in jail and that would've been the end of it. If he was still alive. Now we're *responsible*. Responsible to innocent bystanders that this maggot might kill because we didn't get them out of the way first. Responsible to the hostage and all the hostage's relatives, clear back to the Old Country. We're even responsible to the jerkass criminal himself for what we might do hurting him on account of the shit *he* started. Sometimes I don't know how I stand it." Haller looked up self-consciously at Bartell. He smiled apologetically. "Sorry. I guess it just galls me taking this kind of shit from a prick like that." He jabbed his thumb in the general direction of 841 Morton.

"Nobody's hurt yet," Bartell said. He settled back in his chair and laced his fingers behind his head. "That's the only way to figure it."

"Oh, I know that," Haller said. "Don't misunderstand. I know this is a better way. It's just a more difficult way."

Bartell knew what Haller meant. Patience is a hard road for most cops. By necessity policemen think in terms of distinct actions that lead to the resolution of conflict. Strip away the psycho-sociological bullshit, and that meant acting just like Haller had said: you tell people to knock it off, and if they don't, you bust them. Neat and to the point. You aren't paid to take shit, you're paid to take charge. So how do you reconcile that attitude with the situation at hand, with waiting for some shithead to call you on the phone and tell you what he's going to do if you don't kiss his ass? If he could just keep Thacker from getting excited—

The telephone jarred Bartell back to life. It was 3:06.

Bartell.

You guys got my brother yet? No, we—

Whadya think, I'm just fuckin' 'round here or somethin'—

Just hang on a minute, okay—

You think I won't dust the gook bitch?

—okay, Richard? Just take it easy . . . we're trying.

Yeah, my ass.

Just keep in mind we're doing what we can, Richard—

Shit.

—and something else. I want you to think about something else while we're working on our end.

What's that?

The trade. Think about that. Look, you've got that girl in there, and I assume you want to trade her straight across for your brother. That right?

Fuckin' A . . .

Then I want you to figure a way to do that. A way so the girl's safe, so your brother's safe, you're safe. I want you to think us out a way we can do this trade so nobody gets hurt.

You just send my brother in the house . . . what's so fuckin' hard about that?

I know it sounds easy. But I don't think my boss'll go for it. I mean, look at it from his standpoint. He's got to know the girl will be okay before he just hands your brother over. He's got to. Would you send the girl out without getting something from us?

Hey, that's bullshit, man!

You're right. So you've got to come up with a plan—

That ain't my—

You're the only one who can do it, Richard. You're the only one with enough control of this thing.

You better fuckin'—

You think about this thing. I'll get back to you.

Bartell broke the connection and grinned at Yarno. "I just wanted him to know he was talking to somebody," Bartell said.

"Who knows?" Yarno said. "He might even help us figure out this goddamn mess."

"Goddamn right," Bartell said. "He started it. It's only fair." That was the tough part of negotiations, the part that most people didn't understand. Most people figured that negotiating was something you did because you were afraid to deal with the situation, take charge like a real cop. But to Bartell's way of thinking, it would be easier to mount a charge, then heap the dead and injured at the feet of the criminal. When you listen to horrible threats, though, and ignore them, shove them right back in the guy's lap, when you have to decide what you, all by yourself, will put on the line next, well, there's nothing especially evasive about that. Bartell remembered the night George Rather was killed, the way the gun had risen in Rather's hand and he had believed Rather was going to lay the gun on the hood of the car and Culp saw it different and the only man who could say for sure was the man who was dead in the snow. Rule Number One is that you don't second guess. And Rule Number Two is that you always break Rule Number One. So weeks from now, when Richard Thacker was in jail or the nuthouse or underground, after all the reports were written, all the briefs filed, no matter what happened, everybody would still wonder if Bartell did the right thing. Years from now Rozette cops who hadn't even been hired yet would listen to the story and decide for themselves if tonight Ray Bartell and his partners were full of shit.

Chapter 19 □ □ □

Culp felt good about the place he'd set up across the street. He was at the corner of a house, with the shrubs providing concealment and a concrete foundation providing cover. Never mistake concealment for cover. He smiled at the way TV cops always leaned across the roofs of their cars, like the windows could stop a bullet. Mushroom it out real nice on the way through, that's what a window will really do, so the bullet *really* rips you up.

Never mistake concealment for cover.

Jungle was concealment. A fucking bunker was mother-fucking cover.

Culp wanted a cigarette. He adjusted his ears inside the radio headset and rechecked the safety on the AR-15. He always used to want a cigarette when he was hunkered down like this, waiting for the craziness to start. He could never have one, of course, but he always had a smoke to look forward to and now he'd quit like some kind of dumb shit, worrying about cancer. Never worried about cancer back then. Cancer. Fuckin' joke.

Lead cancer. That's what you got in those days.

Cigarette. Real cigarette, like a Winston or a hump, not the junk that passed for smoke today.

I'd walk a mile for a Camel.

Where'd you hear that?

Grapevine, man, motherfuckin' grapevine.

Status.

It was Arnold Slayton, making a routine check on each member of the team.

Culp listened as everybody reported, first the snipers, Bright in front, Richardson at the rear of the Thacker house. LaFontaine and Butch Durrant, the rear assault and arrest team, checked in then, followed by Porky Petrovitch and Culp in front. Porky had a shotgun paired with Culp's AR-15. Any assault or arrest initiated from the front of the house was theirs. On assaults Arnold

Slayton, the team leader, went along. For an arrest the third man was normally Slayton. Or, if the asshole inside would surrender only to the guy he'd been dealing with, then the negotiator was the third man.

"We're still on hold," Slayton said. "The negotiator has made contact. Any movement?"

"All dark in the back," Durrant said.

"I get periodic movement inside the room to my left," Culp said. That was the only room with lights on. Culp couldn't see who was doing what, because of the curtains. "Looks like two people."

"I get the same," said Bright, the front sniper, who was in the attic window of the house that gave Culp cover. Porky Petrovitch was along the porch of the house to Culp's right.

"Who's negotiating?" Richardson asked.

"Bartell."

Wasn't that wonderful? Put a guy with something to prove in a pressure cooker like that. Totally and completely wonderful.

Culp closed his eyes for a few seconds and took a deep breath and tried to relax, tried to stop *staring* at the house across the street, tried to settle into the scenery and *connect* with things, tried to *absorb* what was going on and not just *see* it because if you fuckin' waited to *see*, you were fuckin' dead, because this shit went down too goddamn fast and the next thing you knew, everybody was running around screaming and there was all kinds of fucking smoke and noise and nobody knew what was going on until they started stacking up the fucking dead and by then there wasn't nothing left you could do except listen to the goddamn grapevine and smoke a fucking cigarette.

Culp opened his eyes and shook his head and looked around, as though he were looking at the Thacker house for the first time. Christ, he'd taken a detour back in country. If Slayton knew what kind of an edge he was on, he'd pull him off the line in less time than it took to say *Adios, chum.*

There was still just the one light on in the Thacker house, and two shadows occasionally moved in front of the window with the light. The house was the third from the west on the block, next door to the one where they'd found that gook with his throat cut and Bartell brought out the kid with the .45. Crazy kid, thinking he was still protecting his family. Kid not even fifteen years old, about the same age as the kids Culp might have left behind in Vietnam, if he left any. No way of knowing about that.

Beyond a description of the man and woman inside and his immediate job of securing the area, Culp knew very little about the incident. He knew that the house belonged to a wacko named Thacker, and that for some reason this idiot Thacker had snatched a woman named Julie Chin and was holding her inside the house. As of now nobody had been hurt. The point of arrest was the street in front of the house, which meant that any planned arrest belonged to Culp, Porky Petrovitch, and either Slayton or Bartell. An entry would initiate from the rear, since the alley was darker and provided more cover, and there were no lights on in the back of the house. There were black-and-whites at each end of the block, diverting the sparse traffic.

It was a warm night and Culp wished he could pull off his camo fatigue shirt and body armor. He knew better than that, though, knew that without the shirt, he'd be a bright target that not even jungle could conceal. Without the vest, he'd be a fool. He looked up at the sky; the moon was just right, full enough to give some visibility, yet not too bright. He rubbed the sweat from his eyes and leaned his cheek against the cool cement foundation of the house. So hard to find a cool place. The cement felt good on his cheek. Cool. He settled lower into the ground and foliage.

Lots of times guys wanted a joint instead of a cigarette, but not Culp, at least not when they were on an operation. He'd almost beat a kid to death for that one night, one night after they'd taken some bad shit and he was checking the perimeter after the squad settled in and he found this fuckin' rookie asshole sucking on a hash pipe and by the time the other guys pulled them apart, the kid was unconscious. The next morning the kid's face was swollen and all he could manage to say was some shit about bringing charges. Before they got back, though, the son of a bitch got knocked off, so fuck him.

Fuck 'em all.

Culp looked down at the AR-15 and smiled, remembering the time he'd taken an oath never to carry a rifle again with the safety on. Different circumstances now, though. Now you've got to be a lot more deliberate about who you kill. Like with that guy at the mill last winter. Can you imagine it? They'd talked about pulling him off SWAT after that, like he'd done something new. Like not letting you back in a car once you'd learned how to drive, that's what it was.

He looked at the AR-15 and rechecked the safety again. He remembered when he was a kid, just before he went in the army, he'd read a story in *Guns and Ammo* about this hot new weapon, the M-16, that the U.S. military was switching to. Over the years he'd become, you might say, intimately acquainted with the M-16 and its civilian counterpart, the AR-15. Now the weapon was practically an antique, with everybody going to 9mm HKs, Ingrams, and Uzis.

Kills just as dead, though, he thought, tightening his grip on the rifle.

He took another deep breath and tried to connect up with the house across the street. He still wanted a cigarette. And he wanted something he couldn't name, too, wanted it bad. When all this was over, he was going to have to talk to somebody. Maybe he'd drive back north to the Flathead and look up Nancy. Maybe she was the one who could help.

At 3:30 Dr. Markham arrived and the cops nearly ate him alive. Joey Yarno said later that he was disappointed Markham didn't have a Viennese accent, but that was okay, since he managed to turn out in a Harris Tweed jacket in the middle of July. Markham's stock shot higher when he loaded his pipe with a Dunhill mixture and torched it off with an S.T. Dupont lighter. If Joey had seen by then the Mercedes 300TD that Markham had left hitched at the curb, he might have forgotten the hostage job altogether and headed straight for the nearest couch.

Bartell wasn't so easily swayed. "Will this asshole kill somebody?" he asked after Markham had been briefed by Woodruff.

"Asshole?" Markham unfurled his eyebrows, then struck them in a contemplative scowl.

"A figure of speech." Bartell's face ached with nonchalance. He dug a used toothpick from his pocket, flicked a fleck of lint from one end and stuck it between his teeth. "I just want to know if he's nuts enough to kill the girl because we can't turn over his dead brother. I think that's a pertinent question here."

"*Nuts*, you say." Markham nursed his pipe. "That's such a . . . euphemistic . . . layman's term."

"All right, what term would you suggest?" Bartell didn't care if Markham *did* have a Rolex.

"Would you accept *crazy*?" Markham said, his round face suddenly beaming like the man in the moon. "I mean, we're talking crackers here. The Prince of Fantasy Island."

Bartell suppressed an urge to demand to see Markham's diploma. Hell, it was probably from some clinic in Bombay.

"Maybe, Dr.—" Woodruff started.

"I know." Dr. Markham held up a manicured hand like a cop halting traffic. "I know I'm being a little lighthearted. Believe me, that's only a touch of self-therapy. I know exactly what's at stake here. I'll do everything I can to help."

Civilians. Despite Markham's explanation, Bartell still felt snippy. The newspapers weren't going to crucify Markham if Julie Chin ended up with fourteen bullet holes. Markham wasn't going to be dragged through the public muck, through internal investigations, police commission hearings, and civil suits that could stretch into the next century. Bartell glanced at Woodruff, who looked sincere, and stopped himself from telling Markham to go to his room. Instead, he wrenched out a smile and told the shrink they were glad to have any help he could give them.

"Of course, there are certain confidences . . ." Markham ventured.

"Of course," Bartell said acidly. He wasn't sure why he was being so antagonistic. Maybe it was Helen. Or more exactly, Helen's acceptance of that whole herd of snake-oil salesmen like Markham who said your world would be okay if you just kept the right tape playing, explored your potential, chanted the right rationale around the fire at midnight, and stuck your pin in the proper doll.

"Certainly." Dr. Markham smiled, an I've-seen-your-type-before smile.

Bartell parried with his eyes. "Some specific items concern us at the moment."

"Anything at all."

"If it involves a confidence . . ."

"Please, I'm only too happy."

Woodruff cleared his throat and rustled through the papers in his yellow legal pad. The first thing he wanted to know was how strongly Thacker would stick to the delusion about his brother. The last thing they needed was to base an entire strategy upon a foundation of madness that could collapse into sanity at any time.

"Can we trust him not to realize his brother's dead?" Woodruff asked.

"Richie and I have had perhaps twenty hours of conversation." Dr. Markham said. "I know that twenty hours isn't a long time, but when you spend it over several months, it's actually quite a bit. Please understand that I *can't* tell you any of the things

Richie told me. What I can tell you, though is that he never expressed any sort of belief that his brother was still alive. Do you understand what I mean?"

"Negative evidence," Woodruff said. "At least in my world, that's what you're talking about. The absence of x tends to prove the existence of y."

"Exactly," Markham said.

"But what does *this* negative evidence prove?" Bartell asked. He glanced at the telephone out of the corner of his eye, hoping that it would not ring for a few moments, dreading that it would never ring again. "I mean, there are any number of meanings we could attach to what you've just told us."

"That's right." Markham rapped his pipe on the rim of a wastebasket, then dropped the pipe into the side pocket of his jacket. "In this instance, I would say there are two possible meanings. The first is that Richie's belief that his brother is still alive is extremely vital, that it's possible he hasn't expressed it until now because it's the core of all his problems."

"What exactly are his problems?" Joey Yarno interrupted. "In clinical terms, I mean."

"Acute manic depressive, I'd say. With flashes of paranoia. I'm sorry, but I'm a little uncomfortable with that kind of vocabulary, even though I know it's necessary. But the mind isn't like the body, you can't say a person has appendicitis or needs his tonsils removed. So you see, I was only half kidding when I described him as crazy. Sometimes with laymen—and I don't mean that in a derogatory way—the use of clinical terms can set up expectations of behavior that are dangerously misleading."

"And what's the other possibility?" Bartell said. "With the delusion, I mean."

"Well, obviously it's just the opposite. The delusion his brother is alive could be something completely new—he never spoke of it with me because at the time of our conversations it didn't exist."

Bartell looked at the toothpick, which he'd chewed into a soggy fan. He dropped the sliver onto the floor and took another from his pocket. He was starting to get anxious and he looked at the telephone again.

"Somebody ask Slayton what's happening outside," Bartell said.

"Nothing's happening," Haller said. He'd been standing just

outside the door, listening to Markham. "We've got to come up with something here."

"Why?" Woodruff said. "We're at a stalemate. You know what stalemate is, Bud? It's that state of things when nobody's getting hurt. Nothing wrong with that."

"You still haven't told us if we can trust the delusion." Bartell said to Markham. He was sweating heavily now and the harness of his shoulder holster had begun to chafe.

"Maybe you should give him a call," Woodruff said. "Just to touch base again."

"No," Bartell said emphatically, ignoring his own need to do something. "If everything's quiet, let's just let him cook."

Woodruff nodded and shifted his eyes to Markham, as though inviting him to offer up a miracle.

"I don't think you should rely on manipulation of the delusion to get you through this," Markham said.

"Is this an objection to lying?" Yarno asked. "For moral or therapeutic reasons?"

Markham laughed and reached again for his pipe. "Hardly. We all tell lies all the time. For all kinds of reasons. If it weren't for certain necessary lies, we'd all be savages. Look at it this way . . ." In a manner that struck Bartell as completely theatrical, Markham busied himself with his smoking accoutrements. ". . . Richie's a manic-depressive. That means that sometimes he's really hyped up, like now, and other times he's completely dulled out. Now, it takes a lot of energy to stay hyped, and it takes a lot of energy to maintain a delusion to the degree that you'll kill an innocent person over it. That energy is like a mountain and sooner or later he's going to crest that mountain and head down the other side and only God knows how steep the fall will be. If he's held the delusion of his brother very deeply, then he may not have the energy to keep it on the surface until you work him through this thing. Or, if the delusion is a recent phenomenon, then he may lack the energy to keep it intact. Either way, in my opinion, once he takes a plunge, you run the risk that he'll just get too tired to keep on believing his brother's alive."

"But we want him tired," Bartell said. "We want him too tired to keep this up . . . too tired to kill anybody."

"I understand completely," said Markham, gnawing at a haunch of pipe smoke. "And that's a very good approach. The problem is that if he gets too tired to hold up the delusion, then sees that you've played him for a fool—and I think there's a good chance that's how he'll see it—then you could get him all hyped again . . . and then he's going to be madder than a pack of wild dogs at *you*. So where does that leave you?"

"Shithoused," Bartell said.

"Exactly."

Bartell nodded slowly and considered the possibilities. The last thing he wanted was to get into a pissing match with Thacker over a man who's been dust in Southeast Asia for fifteen years. Not with a woman's life at stake, no thank you, sir.

"Then you'd pop his cherry," Bartell said.

Markham smiled. "Have you ever considered analysis, Mr. Bartell?"

Bartell let the question pass. "What's he going to do when I challenge him on his brother?"

"Oh, he'll probably get suicidal," Markham said. "That was the reason for my initial contact with him. Suicidal impulses."

"Will he actually *try* to kill himself?"

"There's every chance of it."

"How?"

"Why, with a gun, of course."

After some brief discussion they thanked Dr. Markham and turned him over to Sam Blieker. In the bunker, as Bartell had come to think of the principal's office, he and Yarno and Woodruff and Haller played mental football with strategy and tactics. Bartell was pleased when Haller held firm that there would be no SWAT assault unless somebody could prove to him that there was an immediate and irrefutable threat to Julie Chin. Haller and Woodruff then went back into the outer office.

"I feel like I'm in trouble," Joey Yarno said. "In the principal's office, I mean. I went to this school. Me and my best friend, a kid named Erickson."

"I went to a little school in Lehman City," Bartell said. "Least, that's where I went when we weren't moving around. It was almost like a country school."

Yarno rubbed his bald head slowly, them fumbled with his own pipe. He didn't drag down enough paycheck to smoke anything blended by Dunhill. Yarno sat hunched forward, his elbows on his knees. He seemed to be talking to the floor between his feet as he rocked from heel to toe and back.

"Erickson and me, we got in lots of trouble, like I said. Then we went on to high school, grew apart. Funny, I could never tell whether he got worse or I got better. Anyhow, one night he stuck up a little mom and pop grocery store up on the high line. Him and a couple of other guys."

Yarno's eyes glazed over as he remembered. Bartell felt good in his company. A car pulled up outside and its lights flashed momentarily in Bartell's eyes, nearly causing him to sneeze.

"Crazy part," Yarno went on, "was they could've got away clean. Erickson and the other two were outside and everything was cool, I guess . . . then *my friend* went back inside and took those two old people in the storeroom and just dumped them. Took a .357 and blew their heads off. Over two hundred bucks he'd already successfully stolen. Now he spends all his time on appeals. I understand the noose has turned him into a not-half-bad attorney."

Bartell stared at the silent telephone apparatus. How long would Thacker wait to call? Woodruff had talked to the phone company, and any call Thacker made would automatically come to Bartell. So Thacker wasn't trying to call anybody . . . maybe Bartell should call in . . . so *goddamned* hard to do nothing.

Yarno seemed remote, withdrawn down a tunnel of years to some lost winter afternoon, when he'd sat in this same office with The Man and his friend, the future murderer, and been scolded for some inconsequential prank.

"When I was eighteen or nineteen," Bartell said, "I was riding around one night with this bunch of guys in Missoula." He didn't know any of the guys very well. They were cruising around in a big Buick that belonged to somebody's mother and it was in August or September, Bartell couldn't remember for sure, but it was warm and they had all the windows down and the radio going full blast, drinking beer and looking for girls, when they went past this hitchhiker and somebody said, *Let's pick him up.*

"So we picked him up. Put him in the back between me and this other guy, and he says he wants to go to Great Falls. Right? So we start driving around, going every direction but toward Great Falls and the guy's getting nervous. After about twenty minutes all he wants is out of that car, and one of the guys in front says, 'Why don't we just take this guy out and kill him?' About ten minutes later the guy shit his pants and we kicked him out because he stunk up the car."

Yarno laughed sympathetically and kicked his cowboy boots up onto the principal's desk. "Just the bat of an eye between an interesting experience and accountability for a homicide. Just the bat of a fuckin' eye."

Bartell laughed, too, then belched and rubbed a hand over his stomach. "I feel like Mount St. Helens."

"Me too."

"We should just tell Haller to snipe this son of a bitch, you know?" Bartell waved toward the phone as though it were Thacker's proxy.

"Yeah. If it wasn't for the girl . . ."

"And some poor bastard someplace that was Richie Thacker's pal."

"You're nothing but a bleeding heart," Yarno said.

"Sue me then, asshole."

"Fuck you."

Bartell laughed again and propped his own feet on the desk, and then nearly fell out of his chair when the phone rang.

Bar—

What is this shit?

What do you—

You listen to me, son of a bitch . . . I look out—

Settle down, Richie—

You give me this line of bullshit that you're gonna help, gonna help like you said, and you say—

Richie!

—so I look outside and there's nothing but fu . . . fucking cops!

I know.

Like I was some kinda jerkoff.

Settle—

Lyin' assho . . . hole!

Richie!

What!

Calm down.

I am calm!

Trust me, Richie, you're not calm . . . you're not calm at all.

'Kay . . . okay . . . I'm calm. The girl's calm. Everybody's calm R . . . R . . . what the fuck's your name?

Ray.

Yeah, Ray, I'm squared away, you know, and then I look outside and I take a look and there's cops all over the goddamn place, you know, fuckin' cops and when I—

You're gettin' wound up again, Richie.

Yeah . . . yeah . . . I know, Ray, man, I know it . . . I'm sorry . . . But fuck!

Listen to me, Richie. You took that girl at gunpoint—

Yeah.

You shot at the cops.

Yeah!

You say you're gonna kill the girl . . . Julie Chin, that's her name.

Yer goddamn right!

I know, um, I believe you . . . we all believe you . . . that's what all the cops means, you know? It means you got our attention.

Gonna kill my ass, that's what you're gonna—

No.

You fuck, you lie—

No . . . that's not why I'm here, Richie.

I see that goddamn shit on TV . . . you think I'm some kinda fool . . . some kinda . . . get me out there and—

It's not like that at all, Richie . . . it's because of the neighbors . . . you know? . . . 'cause we don't want some dumbass to wander into this thing and fuck it up.

There was a long pause. Bartell could hear the muffled voices of Thacker and the girl. He looked out the window and saw people standing beside a white van that had just pulled up; Quentin Davies directed Conrad Stark as Stark assembled his camera and a bank of lights.

You still with me, Richie?

Yeah.

You getting along?

Um, fuck—I . . . yeah. I guess so.

You want anything?

Need my fuckin' brother, like I told you a hundred times . . . you said—

I know—

You. . .

Yeah. I know. And we tried to find him . . . that's why I didn't get back to you before.

You better fuckin' find him . . . you better fuckin' do more than try.

We tried the best we could . . . we ran him through the computer.

Bartell looked at Joey Yarno, who glanced away so that he would not laugh. *We ran him through the computer.* What a stroke of genius. Run him through the fucking computer and you've done everything humanly possible.

We ran him through the computer, Richie . . . the big one in Washington, D.C. The one that has everything in it.
You're lyin'!
Everything, Richie! You know which one I'm talking about . . . the one where they keep a file on everybody.
Don't tell me that fuckin shit . . . how you gonna—
Because it's a big deal, that's how. You think people in D.C. ain't gonna get out of bed when somebody's life's at stake?

Bartell swallowed and got ready to call the biggest gamble he'd ever taken; with several lives on the line, he'd told an obvious lie to set up the truth.

He's dead, Richie.
No!
I'm sorry.
It ain't fuckin' true—we was, I . . .
He was killed in Vietnam . . . I guess maybe you've been away from home and didn't know.

Bartell rolled his eyes at Yarno, whose fingers were poised over the controls of the tape recorder. The headset was quiet for a moment, and then Bartell heard Thacker and the girl talking again. He couldn't make out the conversation. Yarno was scowling, straining to hear, but the sounds were blurred, as though a hand were partially clamped over the mouthpiece of Richie Thacker's phone.

Richie?

Bartell heard Thacker's receiver clatter against something hard, the table, or the floor and then he could hear Thacker screaming at the girl. He heard Thacker screaming and he glanced at Yarno, whose face was tied in a knot, and then he heard a burst of five, maybe six gunshots.

Ri—

Hear that, asshole? You know what that was, huh? You shit-for-brains, you figure out what that was?

You hurt anybody in there, Richie?

You'd like that, huh, shit-for-brains . . . like it for me—

You better tell me Richie, 'cause—

Sure, you like it if I dust the crack so's you can bust on in here and do my ass.

Lemme talk to Julie.

Shit.

Lemme talk to the girl, Richie.

There was no answer for several long seconds, during which Bartell shut off his transmitter and called to Woodruff. He remembered later that the conversation had gone five ways at once between himself, Woodruff, Yarno, Haller, and Arnold Slayton, who kept jacking his jaws over the SWAT radio, which Haller clutched to the side of his face like a security blanket. Bartell didn't believe he'd hurt the girl, but he couldn't prove it and it wouldn't be long, with shots fired, before Slayton would be leaning hard on Haller for a green light. But the girl wasn't hurt, he didn't know how he knew, he just knew. When he told Haller they couldn't pop Thacker without making him show them the girl's body first, Haller looked at him like he'd just escaped from someplace far away. "I think he's getting more rational," Bartell said, and Haller screamed, "Rational? Rational? Jesus Christ, we're talking about somebody whose capacity for reason is about as well developed as a duck's. You bigshot hostage negotiators have certain standards you apply to manner of death, or would it be enough that the girl was just plain ordinary dead?"

How's come . . . you can't prove he's dead, you can't prove nothin'.

Tell me about the shots, Richie. You gotta tell me what you were shooting.

There ain't no way I can . . . is there? Huh? No fuckin' way.

Richie—

We was always gonna go to California, you know, was gonna cut a record, 'cause he was a singer, he was good, you know, and I used to could play piano, learned myself playing on a old upright come outta the movie theater in Bonners Ferry, and there was him and me and these three other dudes, played the bars up north, got pretty good and Freddie and me was gonna make this record, see, in San Francisco . . . ah, fuck.

Once again, Bartell heard the receiver clatter as Thacker set it down. And to his great relief he heard the girl talking, asking Thacker to let her go. He quickly switched off his transmitter and called out to Woodruff and Haller that the girl was alive. Haller was in the middle of asking Bartell, Woodruff, and Yarno for still another plan of attack when Thacker came back on the line.

I'm sendin' out the girl.

Chapter 20

Culp believed to the bottom of his gut that he was ready for anything, but after the volley of shots from inside the house, he wasn't anywhere near ready to see Julie Chin come ripping out the front door, then turn left and hot-foot it for the black-and-white at the end of the block.

"Friendly-friendly-friendly!" Culp hissed over and over on the radio, hoping that if nothing else, he'd at least tie up the radio so that nobody could send or receive a kill order.

"We've got her," Arnold Slayton said. He was stationed at the car to which Julie Chin had run. "We've got her, she's okay. Everybody hold your positions."

Culp tried to settle himself; he really wanted a cigarette now.

The house looked even more quiet than before, with no movement at all behind the curtain. Culp heard a bird squawk and looked at his watch. Nearly 4:30 a.m. First light in another half an hour. His eyes felt suddenly grainy and, crazy as it was, after trying to get cool, now he caught a chill. It was the dawn. Always the tiredest, coldest part of the day, that half hour just before first light. Culp rearranged his legs to keep them from getting numb, then looked at his watch again.

4:31.

Richie, have you thought about just coming out?

Hey, fuck you guys, you know, man?

What's your problem with that, Richie? I mean, I know you're scared, but look, you really ain't done nothing too bad tonight. Nobody's hurt. The girl's safe. There's nothin' here we can't work out.

You just wanna kill me, man, I know how that works. You don't give a fuck about me, just some more body count.

Richie, you tellin'—

Just like my goddamn brother—

You're tellin' me you're afraid if you come out you're afraid somebody out here's gonna shoot you?

Hey, fuck, man, don't jack me around, there's fuckin' cops all over out there. What kinda dumb fuck you think I am?

You ain't no kinda dumb fuck, Richie. You think I don't know that? You're just a guy—

I'm tellin' you, don't fuck with me, that's what I'm tellin' you, you got that, Bartell?

Sure . . . sure, I got that Richie. But look, tell me this, tell me this, Richie, what can I do that'll make you feel safe enough to come out?

Sun's comin' up, Bartell.

What?

Said the sun's comin' up. You goin' deaf . . . ?

I got the earpiece on this headset screwed around in my ear . . . I couldn't hear what you said.

Said the sun's comin' up. What's so goddamn hard to hear about that?

I told you, it's the—

Me and my brother, you know, we used to get up this time of day and head out fishing.

What kind of fishing?

Usually trout . . . sometimes bass or pike.

I like fishin' in rivers . . . I never catch many fish, though.

My fuckin' brother, Jesus Christ, he was so good he could catch fish out of a pothole in the middle of the goddamn road, he was that good.

Comin' out, Richie, you know, it's just like goin' fishin' . . . 'cause it's first light and you're tired, but it's a whole new day and all you gotta do is step out the door and there it is, just a few steps and you're on your way.

I didn't mean to hurt nobody, Ray, you know—

I know.

—and it's just like I get all bottled up and something's gotta let go, you know—

Yeah.

—when I done somethin' wrong, like I done back then, runnin' away like I guess I did, but you gotta understand . . .

What's that? What do I have to understand?

Just how hard it was all them years ago, when I left, went to Canada. Hard to know what was the right thing to do.

It was hard as hell.

And it keeps getting harder to remember how it was back then. But I believed what I did, I wasn't scared.

No.

Never scared. I'll prove that to you all right now.

You don't have to prove nothing.

You're fuckin' right.

I know. Why don't you just come on out? We can sit down—

They ain't gonna let me get away with this . . . they ain't never gonna let me loose from here.

Why not?

Cause they know what I done, all them cops . . . they ain't gonna let me walk away from what I done. First Canada, now this . . . everybody out there waiting for me. They ain't gonna let me live—

That's bullshit—

I'd kill myself, I had the guts.

You're not gonna do that.

I just wanted him back, you know—

Sure, I know—

Don't wanna hurt nobody—

I know—

But I woulda! You better goddamn believe I woulda taken off that little bitch if I thought it'd get me my brother back . . . I mean—

You don't have to explain.

—mean, I thought when I did it it'd work, you know, man, but shit, man, I guess I was . . . it just gets all confused, you know, man?

If I was there, would you feel better, Richie?

What do you mean?

I mean, if I was down there at the house talkin' to you and when you came out, I'd be right there with you, would you feel safe then? Would you come out like that?

Yeah . . . yeah, I could do that.

Okay, then, Richie, okay, now, I want you to listen to me real careful. . . . You listenin'?

I'm listenin', man.

Okay, now, I want you to wait inside till you hear me calling to you from outside. Don't come out till you hear me. You got that?

Yeah.

Now, when I get down there, I'm gonna tell you leave all your guns inside, then come out the front door with your hands high over your head, and the palms of your hands open. You got that?

I got that man, yeah, fuck yeah, I got it.

Great. . . great. . . now, after you come outside, I'll be tellin' you to walk all the way across the yard and to the street. Now, there may be some car lights pointing toward you, I don't know, but that'll just be so everybody can see everything and nobody gets nervous. That okay?

Sure, yeah.

Okay . . . now, when you get to the street, I'll be walking up to you. You'll know it's me because I'll be talkin' to you, and because I'm wearing an orange windbreaker. And there'll be two other officers walking up to you with me. You got any problems with that?

Just fuckin' get down here, Bartell. Can you please to Christ just get down here and get this over with?

Okay, Richie, I'm coming right now . . . I'm gonna give the phone now to a friend of mine named Joe Yarno. That okay? He can keep you filled in till I get down there. Okay?

Yeah, fuck, that's fine, just get going.

Bartell pulled off his headset and glanced at Joey Yarno, who was listening on a headset of his own.

"Richie, this is Joe . . . "

Bartell stepped quickly into the outer office, where Woodruff and Haller had been monitoring the conversation. Woodruff handed him a walkie-talkie and a set of keys to an unmarked car and waved him on. Bartell ran down the hall and outside, taking the front steps four at a time and landed in the pool of light from Quentin Davies's mobile camera setup.

"—and this is Officer Ray Bartell now." Davies nearly stuck his microphone down Bartell's throat.

Bartell elbowed him aside. "Not now."

"A minute, just a minute here, our viewers have a right to know."

"Fuck your viewers." Bartell jumped in a gray sedan and as he powered into the corner at the end of the block and turned toward 841 Morton, he heard Davies and Stark shouting at each other and a moment later he saw the headlights of their van in his rearview mirror.

Culp was lying on the ground, watching the house through the bushes, when he got word from Arnold Slayton to expect Bartell at his position in a few moments. The asshole was coming out, Slayton told them all, but of course he didn't call the asshole an asshole over the radio, because lots of innocent bystanders listened in on their scanners and the chief would be having him for lunch if he'd called an asshole an asshole over the radio.

The birds were getting louder and Culp couldn't keep his teeth from chattering in the predawn chill. Luckily, both sides of the street were clear of cars for at least one house on either side of his position and the suspect house across the way. Good field of fire, but no cover, Culp thought, planning ahead to when he, Porky Petrovitch, and Bartell would have to approach Thacker. The houses sat near the street, and the street was narrow, which meant that once Thacker made it to the street, he wouldn't be much more than a dozen steps from the arrest team, who wouldn't reveal themselves until he was spread-eagled on his belly on the cold hard ground.

Culp heard a car engine wind out and approach from the east. That figured to be Bartell on his way down to put a wrap on this little drama. God willing, Bartell was still in one piece, psychologically speaking. Then he heard someone walking toward him down the alley. Finally there was a rustling in the grass behind him and he turned and looked up at Bartell.

"You get the word?" Bartell asked.

Culp nodded, turning back to his view of Thacker's house. "He on the level?"

"Close as I can tell, yeah, he is." Bartell took a moment to catch his breath and study the front of the house. He stood just to the left of Culp's legs and leaned against the side of the house. By bending forward at the waist, he was able to see just around the edge of the wall. There was one light on inside the house. Bartell saw no movement inside. He leaned back and knelt beside Culp, so the two could whisper.

"I told him out the front door, hands all the way over his head, palms open, then walk slowly to the street."

"Fine," Culp said. His teeth had stopped chattering and he felt warmer now that he'd stopped sweating under all his clothes and gear. He looked over the AR-15 and got a sight picture on the front door. "He got a porch light?"

"I don't know."

"See if somebody can find out . . . have him turn it on."

"I guaranteed him safety."

"What kind of pricks do you think we are?"

"You know better than that," Bartell snapped.

"Just get him to turn on that goddamn light, if he's got one."

Bartell pulled the walkie-talkie from his hip pocket and asked Woodruff to relay the request to Yarno.

"He may want to see me before he'll come out," Bartell whispered to Culp.

"You expose yourself now," Culp said, "you're fuckin' crazier than I think you are."

The porch light came on.

"Tell him I'm here," Bartell said into the radio. Soon after that, he saw the front door open and heard Thacker shout his name from inside.

"Richie! You hear me in there, Richie?"

"I hear you, Bartell."

"You ready, Richie?"

"They're gonna shoot me, ain't they?"

"Just do it like I said, Richie."

"You sure that's you, Bartell?"

"It's me, Richie." Bartell stood up and stepped to his left so that his upper body was exposed above the bush. "It's just like I told you, Richie. I haven't lied to you yet, have I?" Bartell could hear Culp whispering into the SWAT radio. He could feel Culp tighten up at his feet, heard the safety click off on the AR-15. "Come on, Richie! It's okay!"

Then the doorway filled and Richie Thacker stepped out onto the stoop, hands high, as though grasping the quarter moon like a trapeze.

"That's it, Richie, now come on ahead slowly to the street . . . terrific . . . you're doing great."

Thacker stopped about three feet from the curb.

"Have him turn a three-sixty," Culp said, still maintaining his position on the ground and speaking intermittently into his headset.

"Richie, first I want you to turn a complete circle for me, okay?"

Thacker began slowly to turn. He looked nothing like Bartell had expected from his voice. He looked too young and his hair was black and straight instead of curly and blond and he had a paunch and slight shoulders, not that raw, hard-as-nails look the bartender had described, the look you heard in his voice.

"That's fine, Richie, now I want you to slowly get down on your knees . . . that's it, right, keep your hands up . . . fine . . . now you can let your arms down and put your hands on the ground way in front of you . . . that's it . . . now go ahead and lay all the way down on the ground. Good. Now spread your feet apart, and keep your hands all the way out from your body."

"He's ready," Culp said, standing. "Here we go."

For an instant the night sat on the edge of its seat and then Culp and Bartell stepped around the bush and across the yard and toward the street. Bartell looked to his right and saw Porky Petrovitch advancing with them. Porky carried a shotgun at his shoulder, held it level on the prone Thacker, while Culp covered him in the same manner with the AR.

They reached the curb and then very deliberately stepped down off the curb and across the asphalt. Then they reached the far curb and Culp and Petrovitch stepped up onto the grass while Bartell, between them, waited in the street.

"I'm here with you, Richie, just like I promised. Everything going okay?"

Thacker turned his head and looked ahead at Bartell, then rested his chin on the ground and closed his eyes.

"Now listen to me, Richie, we're almost done . . . here's what's gonna happen . . ."

Nobody was ready for the shots, and later Bartell would remember how strange it was that he could hear at the same time both the explosions from the gun and the smack of the bullets slamming into Thacker's body. He couldn't tell by the sound where the shots had come from, but the four quick flashes of light on the porch to his right caught his eye and before he even focused on the figure there, he knew it was Nguyen Nhu's son and he knew the boy had stayed behind, hidden out to protect the family, just as he'd done the day that summer when his father was murdered.

It was all so fast it broke your heart.

"*Ban!*" Culp screamed, lunging across Thacker's body as Petrovich brought the shotgun around.

"*Tôi muǒn bân!*" Culp reached ahead and batted the shotgun down just as Petrovitch fired, filling the air with flame and noise and dirt and then the boy fired again, knocking Culp to the ground. Before either Bartell or Petrovitch could return fire, Bartell heard the rifle shot from behind him, felt the faint blast as the round sped above his head, and then the boy was down, too.

Holding his shotgun at the ready, Petrovitch crept up to the boy, whose head was blown half away.

"Clear," Petrovitch said, kicking the boy's .45 out of reach just incase.

"Ah, shit," Culp said and began to choke. The round had caught him under his left arm, just above the body armor as he'd reached ahead toward the shotgun. "I just knew it was that fuckin' kid."

"What was that you said to him?" Bartell asked. He started to lift Culp's head and shoulders onto his lap, but when Culp groaned and started choking blood again, he let him lay back on the grass. The grass was heavy with dew and soon Bartell's legs were soaked as he knelt beside Culp and he began to shiver. "That word, what was it?"

"*Ban.* Means *friend. Tôi muŏn bân. I want to make friends.* I thought I forgot all that."

By now there were cops and lights everywhere, but for Bartell the night remained dark and still and he could hear the birds making an awful racket as the sun came up.

"That kid . . . he okay?" Culp closed his eyes and listened. He could hear the sounds of things growing in the ground and he smiled, then nearly panicked when his lips stuck together and he lost his breath for a moment. "He okay?"

"He's fine."

"You're a lying bastard." Culp started to open his eyes but held off. "I know that, you know, because I can hear him. Hear him screaming and moaning, same as they all moaned and screamed, not wanting to be gone." Culp decided he wouldn't open his eyes again. It always scared him, the way the dead look with their eyes open, and he didn't want to look like that.

"Nancy, she never even knew who I was." Culp heard his chest gurgle and it sounded the same as those things he'd heard earlier, the things growing in the ground. "She was right about the mountains and the snow."

Bartell didn't know what the fuck he was talking about.

The street was chaos, cops running in all directions and shouting and at the same time it was completely calm and precise inside Bartell's mind and he stood up and looked down at Culp and Culp didn't look hurt at all, except that he was dead—you just knew it from the stillness about him—and Bartell was afraid to look away from him because to look away would be to let him go.

Somebody was calling his name and he looked up without thinking and saw Quentin Davies running toward him from the west end of the block. The tails of Davies's bush jacket flared as he ran and Conrad Stark humped along under his camera in Davies's stellar wake.

Bartell looked back down at Culp and saw a flat, unfamiliar face and then he walked toward Davies and they were less than twenty feet from Culp when Davies pulled up and started to say something and Bartell mashed him in the nose and Davies fell from his feet behind a spray of blood.

Davies started to get up and Bartell put his foot in his chest.

"Get up before I'm gone," Bartell said, "and I'll kill you."

Epilogue

Bartell dropped his pack and dug out the water bottle from one of the side pockets. His knees ached and he felt the start of a blister on his left heel. He hadn't made the climb up Bride's for several years, years that had taken their toll. He wasn't sure how much the pack weighed, but it weighed plenty. Tent. Enough food for four days, though he only expected to be out for three. Winter weight bag, because at this altitude the nights were cold in late September. And water. He carried three bottles, since he might find the country dry until he got down to the lakes.

Below, the alders were just beginning to turn and in a month the mountainsides would be lit with larch trees flaring like matches. The air smelled of dust, even at this altitude. It had been a long fire season, with slurry bombers droning in and out of the airport day after day. A campfire was out of the question. Just lighting the small pack stove made Bartell nervous. Earlier, he'd seen a thunderhead rising above Yellow Pine, which was the next drainage west of Bride's. The storm looked dry, but lightning kept snapping off the hillsides. He hoped the storm played itself out before moving into Burnt Milk or Bride's.

He'd been hiking since early morning, when Helen dropped him off at the trail head, and now it was midafternoon and he hoped to be well down into Burnt Milk by evening. If everything went according to plan, he'd call Helen from the Bittercreek camp in three days and she would drive in to pick him up. He'd asked Helen and Jess to come along, but Jess told him it was uncool and Helen cited her long-standing aversion to heavy loads, climbing, and sweat. Bartell wondered if the true aversion was to him. He didn't think so. He hoped not. Things had been better, but you never knew for sure. Sometimes disputes simply fade. Sometimes a lack of energy is mistaken for forgiveness. She told him about the night with Culp, the night before she came home. She told him this after Culp was dead. She said nothing happened. Bartell believed her. He believed her because it made sense that there was no need to say anything if something really had happened. He also believed her because he wanted to trust her. That part was more difficult. And he believed her because even if something had happened, and even if Culp were still alive, it wouldn't matter. She'd come home and so far she'd stayed and he felt good about that and that was enough.

Bartell drank again and made a fist with his right hand. The bones had healed well and the cast had been off for about a week. He hadn't liked doing office work around the station for almost two months, but chances were they would have pulled him off the street after the shooting even if he hadn't broken his hand on Quentin Davies's face. He'd heard that Davies's nose wasn't doing too well. Too bad. They should've put a cast on his head to match the one on Bartell's hand. According to Bud Haller, Davies had wanted to file forty different kinds of criminal and civil complaints.

"He'd of done it, too," Haller said. "Except his station manager took a look at the whole thing with you and Culp from the start all the way up to the night Culp died. Told Quentin if he so much as looked under *Lawyer* in the Yellow Pages, he'd kill him himself. I'm supposed to officially reprimand you: Don't punch Quentin Davies no more."

The shooting of the Nhu boy was ruled justifiable. That didn't do much for Bright, the sniper who'd killed him. Within a month Bright had resigned from the department and moved with his family to some little town in eastern Washington, where his wife had people.

They found what was left of the Nhu family huddled in the basement of the house, where they'd gone after failing to understand what the evacuation meant. Or maybe the kid knew more about Richie Thacker than he'd let on. There had been a lot of death that dawn in 800 Morton, but the mystery of who killed Nguyen Nhu remained alive and well. Sam Blieker, though, was satisfied that Richard Thacker was their man and had told Bartell he planned to let the case just fade away.

Bartell took a last sip of water and closed his eyes. He remembered how the Burnt Milk had looked on all those nights when he'd imagined it before he slept, and when he opened his eyes the country looked just as he knew it would, the folds of green and brown descending to the three lakes like beads on a rosary, a country men had sought for generations and found when the stars lined up just right and wind pointed your face just the right way.

Our Father, he thought and zipped the water back into the pack and stood up and shouldered the pack. The pack was still heavy. It would lighten as he ate the food, but he would grow more tired and so the pack would always be heavy.

Culp's two sons had sat with their grandfather at the funeral. They both looked like Culp, like he must have looked twenty-five years ago when the old man sitting next to them still had all his fingers and let his son drive the old Buick along Bittercreek while he fished his way home.

Bartell fastened the hip belt on the pack and snugged it down.

They had the funeral in the evening, because of the huge crowd and the heat. Cop funerals are a civic affair and there must have been seven or eight hundred people there, with cops from all over Montana, Washington, and Idaho, cops from as far away as Seattle. So many people they had the service in the Civic Arena, which was fine, since Culp hadn't set foot in a church since the time he and Bartell arrested a burglar inside one nearly three years ago.

Bartell bounced on his heels several times, testing the load, then adjusted the pack straps.

They listened to some preacher Culp never knew give a sermon about cops being an arm of God and then all the cops lined up between the door and the hearse and they all saluted when they carried Culp out—Bartell was a pallbearer—and then they hauled him away. From the cemetery, you could see the red and blue overheads on all those police cars stretching miles through the dusk clear back into town.

Bartell had never seen anything like those lights, a hazy red and blue line reaching as far as you could see and everybody doling out honor.

Bartell made a last adjustment to his gear and struck out for the lakes down in Burnt Milk. The thin alpine soil and dry bunch grass gave way easily under his boots. He turned along the base of a granite cliff and started to laugh as he headed for the trees.

Those stupid flashing lights, all that *respect*. Culp hated goddamn shit like that. Always did, always would.

"Let's ride," Bartell said.